The Cocaine Diaries

GUCCI'S STORY

REESE

I'm gonna keep it hot with the dedications. I made a promise that each one of my books would touch on a different subject that effects people. If you find yourself lost and repeating the same crazy shit repeatedly, well then, this book is for you. We all deal with our ups and downs. For this book, I wanted to write it for all the girls living fast paced lifestyles. If you need to be fucked up to do something, then it ain't for you. Someone told me this a long time ago, a free high is your worst high. Stripping is a fast-paced lifestyle, and it's easy to get caught up in the money, drugs, liquor, and attention. To Jodie, Tommy, K-Smoke, and everyone who is locked up, remember they can't hold you forever.

Contents

Acknowledgments

To my father, Jason, who first introduced me to reading. We used to share countless conversations where you would talk shit about urban fiction. Please come visit me soon in my dreams so we can have another one. To my Husband who has helped me turn this from a vision to a reality, I love and appreciate you. To my children who inspire me to want to do better, I love you more than words can explain. Thank you to everyone who has chosen to come down this rabbit hole into this crazy mind of mine. I appreciate you.

Special Acknowledgement: To my editor, thank you for the countless conversations and helping me turn my ideas into this work of art. Cyn, I appreciate you, girl!

Prologue
GUCCI

"Where are we going, Snow?" I asked excitedly. Today was special. It was only me and my daddy in the car. I loved when it was just us because I got to ride shotgun. My daddy's name was Snow, and everyone called him that, even me. I placed my hands on my lap and waited for him to answer. He didn't answer me right away. He was too busy looking in the mirror thang that hung in between us.

"Snow!" I whined again. I shouldn't have done that, but I couldn't help it. I was too excited. A police car was behind us, and I knew my daddy had to focus. I hated the police. They were always messing with my daddy. The car drove past slowly, and a white officer looked at us real hard before he sped off and turned his lights on. Show off!

"What's the most important thing in the world baby girl? You get it right, and I'm a get you a new pair of sneakers." Snow looked over at me and winked. I had to concentrate to make sure I got this right. I was only seven, but I loved to get new things. My mamma and auntie taught me that. I tapped my finger on my forehead and repeated the lesson my father taught me since I was old enough to talk.

"Money is everything in this world. Without it, people will not respect you. Money brings the power to do whatever you want. Loyalty is something that money can't buy and is earned through time." I held my head high and repeated each line like it was my favorite rap song. When my daddy laughed, I knew I got it right. I smiled at him and imagined my new pair of sneakers.

Snow nodded his head as the light turned red in front of us. With one hand on the steering wheel, he leaned over and kissed me on the forehead. "Bet my baby won't be no stupid bitch when she grows up."

"Nope!" I said, and we both laughed. Snow was raw like that. I loved how he always talked to me like I was a grown up.

I sat back in my seat and looked out the mirror to make sure the police weren't following us. I didn't do that good of a job because I fell asleep.

My eyes opened, and the first thing I saw was a big blue sign with white letters that said *Welcome To South Carolina*. This was my first time leaving North Carolina. "Snow, why it ain't no cars on the road?"

"This the country, baby." That's all he said. If this was all it had to offer, then I hated the country. It smelled different down here, and there was nothing but rows of farms.

"Gucci, you can't tell no one what you see or hear today," Snow warned.

"Not even Mama?"

"Especially not your mama. This is our secret."

I nodded my head and sat up a little straighter. This was important business wherever we were going. Out of all the people in the world, he could have trusted with his secret, he chose me. I might be seven, but I wasn't like them other kids at my house. All they wanted to do was play with dolls and little kid toys. Not me! I loved playing with guns. My daddy took me to the gun range every time he went.

While we rode down the highway, I made sure to look back in the mirror to make sure no one was following us. I bopped my head to 50 Cent's "Get Rich Or Die trying" that was blasting through the car's speakers.

I wasn't like the other girls who were my age. I never questioned Snow or my mama, Prada. My Mama was the flyest woman in the world, even prettier than those singers I saw on TV. I loved my mama, but it was no secret Snow was the parent I wanted to be like when I grew up.

My eyes closed again, and the next time I opened them, the sun went down. I could read very well for my age, so I knew we were in a city named Hilton Head, and it was in the state of South Carolina.

Snow drove down a dead-end street and stopped in front of a pale pink house. I was surprised to see an older woman sweeping the porch this late at night. The woman's long gray loc's were pulled halfway up in a bun and the rest of her long locs hung down her back. She had smooth dark skin that was

3

the color of a Hershey bar. Her face looked old, and her body looked young. I didn't know if I should call the woman pretty or ugly. In my opinion, she was both. She had big pretty eyes and high cheek bones. When she smiled at us, I could tell the front of her teeth were rotting. Then I noticed a black cat sitting in between her legs, and it was watching us.

"Snow, I've been expecting you, and look at little Gucci," the woman sang out, walking toward the car.

Snow frowned at the woman. I wondered how the woman knew my name. Something started calling me toward the house. I wondered did my daddy hear it. When I tried to ask him, I couldn't. No matter how hard I tried, my mouth wouldn't move. My finger pressed the car lock button. I pushed the door open and jumped out of the car. My daddy called my name, but it sounded so far away. Normally, I would listen to him, but I couldn't. The only thing on my mind was getting to the woman.

Snow ran toward me and grabbed my arm tightly.

"Don't be upset. The child couldn't help it," the old woman said.

How did she move so fast? She was just on the porch. All I did was blink my eyes, and now she was standing in front of us.

"I never told anyone I was coming here. When my partna told me about you, I didn't have a daughter at the time, so how you know her name?" Snow asked, looking down at the woman.

The old woman swung her gray locs and let out a low chuckle, causing the little lines in the corner of her eyes to go up and down.

"I know everything. Now, are you ready? You didn't ride all this way to shoot the breeze with an old woman," she responded calmly.

"Yeah," Snow replied as he followed the woman up the creaky wooden stairs.

I didn't want to go inside the woman's house. She scared me, but I didn't want to leave Snow alone and something bad happen. Plus, if I acted up, he would never take me with him again. I slowly followed behind him. Snow reached back for my hand, and he held it tightly as we entered the house. Large sculls that were stained with a faint tint of red hung from the ceiling. The house smelled like an old wet cathedral mixed with mint. I knew better than to say anything. I wrapped my arms around Snow's leg and hugged him tightly. Who was this old woman? Why did she have skulls hanging in her living room, and why was the cat following them like he was listening?

"Don't mind him. He's my late husband. He's nosy!" The old lady swatted the cat with a broom and continued to scream at it. "Yo ass betta be lucky I ain't put you on my skull wall with the rest of them niggas. Keep testing me, Leroy, and you will be joining them," the old lady fussed at the cat.

My mouth dropped open, and I remembered I had to use the bathroom. I was so scared to leave my daddy that I wet my panties. I knew I was gonna get a whooping when I get home. Mama told me not to mess up my pretty dress. Normally, I felt protected when I was with Snow, but today, I didn't. I don't think his gun could do anything if the woman decided to turn us both into cats. The woman looked away, and now it was my chance to warn him.

"Daddy!" I whispered. I never called Snow daddy, but I needed to get his attention.

"Hold up, Gucci." He was so focused on watching the old woman he didn't notice that I called him Daddy. That hurt my feelings. Snow always made sure I was okay, but this lady made him forget about me. Stupid old lady, she couldn't read my mind. Things like that only happened in movies. I was gonna test her and see if she did it again.

"Go ahead. Don't be scared!" the woman said as she stopped at a clear table lined with crystals and shells. Snow looked back and forth between us.

I folded my arms across my chest and whispered inside my head. If she can read minds, then she should know what I was thinking. *I wanna be rich and feared.*

"Interesting request for a little girl. If your father has enough money, I think I could pull that off. Rich and feared. That's a first." The old woman shook her head. "Forgive me. I'm Madame Boudet." Madame Boudet hummed something under her breath, and then she grabbed a stack of tarot cards. "These are my favorite Tarot deck. You are a very important little girl, so we'll use these."

"Why are they special?" I asked, peering up at the cards.

"They were passed down from my grandmother. She was a popular voodoo priestess in New Orleans."

"That's what you wanted, lil mama? Tell me you were thinking that before I give this old bird my money?" Snow interrupted our conversation.

"Yes, Snow, give it to her! How did she know what I was thinking? I made sure not to think of anything she could guess," I rambled. I was so excited, I forgot that I ruined my dress. Madame Boudet intrigued me. When I grew up, I want to learn how to read people's minds.

The woman winked at me. "Snow, sit here." I followed Snow to the old worn leather chair and stood next to him. "You're not the first hustler who has graced my door looking for power and wealth." She paused to shuffle the cards before she continued to speak, "Children are innocent. Your daughter is wise beyond her age. She's special... destined for greatness. When the time comes, and you have no one by your side, she will be the only person you can depend on. Guard her with your life. But she will bring you great shame, and when she does, you must remember this day. Don't judge her. Guide her to reclaim her natural destiny. If you don't, your bloodline will be cursed."

The hairs on my arms stood straight up. I watched her place the deck of cards down in front of Snow.

"Now, for this to work, you must sacrifice something. Baron Samedi, the God of Death, requests this to answer your prayers. He wants your daughter's soul temporarily. I must warn you; he will give you unlimited wealth and power. There will come a time when he comes to you when you least expect. He's a trickster and will try to get you to make his hold on the girl permanent in trade for you having all the riches this world can offer. You must refuse and remember the girl is destined for greatness. She must go through hell. It will be your job to help her escape once your debt is paid. The choice is yours."

7

Chapter One

Present Day

"Nigga, back up! I ain't trying to hear nothing you got to say," I screamed at the older man who had been following me for the last twenty minutes. I first noticed him when I walked past the food court. When he approached me, I ignored him, hoping he would go away. I wasn't in the mood to deal with anyone's bullshit. All I wanted to do was come to the mall grab what I needed to beat my face and go home to prepare for my mother's funeral.

I walked faster towards the mall exit. The man shoved his dingy white air force one into the revolving door. I tried to push the door, but his fat ass was not trying to move. I was insulted that this nigga would even approach me, let alone believe I would ever fuck with someone of his status. I could tell all I needed to know about a man by three things, his hair, watch and shoes.

"Sweetheart, why you tripping? Damn, let a nigga get to know you!"

Through the glass door, I watched his eyes travel up and down my body. I gagged when the smell of beer and black and milds hit me full force.

"Nigga, back the fuck up off me!" I screamed, losing my patience. A couple of people that were strolling past us stopped and stared. Running my hands through my curly hair, I attempted to ease past him. This nigga wasn't letting up and continued to block me from exiting the mall.

"Bitch, who the fuck you barking at?" he shouted. His face twisted up as his eyes bulged out his head. This shit was new for me. Normally I had security with me anywhere I went, but that was before...

My mother's murder changed me forever. My mind wouldn't let me erase those memories. I remember hearing gun shots outside our mansion. Six Haitians jumped out the back of a truck and began shooting with their automatic weapons. I sat motionless, as each member of my family fell one by one. The last word my mother said to me was run. I questioned if I could have done anything to save her life. The moment I witnessed a bullet pierce through her chest, I went into survival mode. Instead of firing my gun I ran and grabbed my cousin Dior. She fought me all the way to the panic room my father had installed for situations like this. She wanted to stand alongside our mothers and fight. In the back of my mind, I wondered if she blamed me for their deaths.

Tears formed in the corner of my eyes. I'd never been the

emotional type but, for the past three days, I'd done nothing but cry.

Biting my bottom lip, I debated if I could reach for my baby nine before this crazy nigga lashed out. Humbleness was something I was not used to. My entire life I lived somewhat sheltered. Not saying I was one of those rich-ass kids, who had no idea how to carry themselves in the streets, but my father, Snow, ran the state of North Carolina, and it was an unspoken law that I wasn't to be fucked with. Fuck it. I had two choices. Allow this fuck nigga to get whatever he planned off or protect myself the way I'd been taught my entire life.

Enough was enough. Since he wasn't trying to respect what I was saying, I had no choice but to show him who he was fucking with. I reached inside my Gucci purse, and with one smooth motion, slid the safety off my baby nine. Once my hand squeezed the cold steel handle, I spun around and buried it into the side of his stomach.

"Nigga, back the fuck up! You can play with me if you want, but I ain't got shit to lose."

His eyes widened and he stumbled back. The people that stopped to watch our interaction mouths dropped. I guess they never expected me to be strapped.

Like the bitch he was, he backed out of my way, allowing me to exit the mall. Grabbing my bag tightly with one hand, I kept the gun pointed at him as I backed out of the mall. I didn't trust anyone at this point, so I continued walking backward until I put enough distance between us.

By the time I got to my Range Rover, a present my father bought me for my seventeenth birthday, I was a mess. The tears falling from my eyes were coming from a place of frustration. Now that my father was locked up, my mother and her twin sister were dead, and my Uncle Dro was on the run, it felt like I was on a never-ending rollercoaster.

I hit the alarm on my car, threw my bags in the backseat, and peeled out of the parking lot. The clock on the dashboard flashed eleven forty-five. I had less than an hour to get back to the north side, take a shower, do my makeup, and get dressed. Today was my mother and aunt's funeral, and I was not ready, mentally or physically. My grandmother had full control of planning the funeral since my father was incarcerated. My mother hated her, and she was the last person my mother would have chosen to plan her funeral, but it was what it was.

The last couple of days, I spent hours on the phone with the county jail, trying to see if my father would be able to attend the funeral. I got nowhere with them, so it was up in the air if he would be coming today.

My father shouldn't even be sitting inside the county jail. His case was weak. The DA had no solid evidence, but none of that stopped the judge from giving him a million-dollar cash bond. He could have posted that easily, but his lawyer advised once he did that, it would open a new can of worms. Tax evasion. My father had several businesses in Greensboro. A barbershop, a hair boutique, and a couple of laundromats. None of those businesses could produce the paperwork to support him posting a million-dollar bond, so he was forced to sit.

As I raced through the city, I tried to calm myself. The way I was moving, my mother would have been disappointed. Prada

Snow was the epitome of a bad bitch. No one could ever say they saw her with her hair a mess, face not beat to the gods, dripping in a thousand-dollar outfit, but that materialistic shit wasn't what made her the queen of the south. It was the way she carried herself. My mama was active in these streets. She helped my father climb his way up from a corner boy to eventually the biggest drug dealer this state had ever seen.

"Fuck!" I screamed at the roadblock in front of me. German shepherds were sniffing the trunks of several cars they pulled over. The police had the drivers and passengers of the vehicle face down with their hands cuffed behind their back. Every car that attempted to drive down Gate City Boulevard was getting pulled. I needed to get to the highway, and this detour was going to add fifteen minutes onto my trip. Making a sharp right turn, I hit the back blocks until I was able to hop on the highway.

There was no way I was stepping foot inside my mother's funeral looking crazy. I wouldn't be going through this if the feds hadn't seized our mansion along with all contents that were inside. The caseworker from Social Services allowed me and my cousin Dior, to take three bags full of clothes. That was a joke since we had a closet the size of most people's bedrooms. I was in a state of shock that day, so the things I grabbed weren't anything I could wear to a funeral. I overslept this morning and didn't have time to run to Charlotte like I originally planned.

I still wasn't used to living with my grandmother Ma. At

Ma's, I shared a room with my cousin Dior. Instead of her waking me up she allowed me to oversleep. When I got up, I rushed to get dressed. I couldn't find anything. Our room was the smallest in the house. I was unorganized since I wasn't used to sharing a room with anyone. A part of me refused to unpack anything. When I sat down to do my makeup, I realized I left my makeup at my old house. I was in and out of Sephora so much they tried to offer me a job. I denied the offer because at the time, I didn't have to work. Unlike most seventeen-year old's, my parents were rich, so I never entertained doing makeup professionally. The crazy part was, hands down, I was one of the coldest bitches to do makeup in my city. I only blessed my family member's faces, and that was only when I was in the mood.

All I had to do when I got to Ma's was jump in the shower, do a light beat, and I would be ready to go. Hopefully, Dior didn't fuck with the outfit I had laid out on the queen-sized bed we were forced to share. I never had to share a room with anyone a day in my life, and I didn't think I would ever get used to it. Our parents were siblings who chose to live together in a big ass mansion off Gate City. Our old bedrooms were the size of most bitches' apartments, so imagine my frustration.

I looked back at the brown Honda Civic through the rearview mirror. Each time I switched a lane, the car would wait a few seconds before moving over. It could be my paranoia, but with everything going on with my family, I couldn't help but feel like a walking lick. I called my Aunt Fendi through the car's Bluetooth. Fendi was my mother's youngest sister, who was three years older than me. Tapping my pink stiletto nails against the wheel, I waited for her to answer.

"Girl, why you ain't tell me you left?" Fendi's raspy voice filled my car.

"I needed some makeup and didn't feel like waiting for no one. Listen, I got into it with this nigga at the mall, and I feel like he might be following me."

"What nigga? Girl, how the hell you get in some shit that quick?" I heard Ma in the background talking shit. I immediately disconnected the call. I don't know what type of shit Fendi was on. She knew I hated to be on speakerphone unaware. She also knew I didn't fuck with Ma like that, so there was no point in her having me on speaker. Since the first night we moved into Ma's house, she'd been on some bullshit. When the cops found out Dior and I were under the age of eighteen, they immediately contacted social services. The caseworker refused to hand us over to Fendi, even though she was of legal age. Fendi had no income and was now also homeless due to our home being seized. Ma was the only member of our family who had not been involved in the Federal drug raid. No one asked her to come take custody of us. If all she was gonna do was complain and talk shit about my father being broke, she could have left us where we were at. That bitch wasn't fooling anyone. The only reason she stepped up was because she thought she would gain access to my father's stash. Joke was on her. Whoever was responsible for the hit emptied the safes inside our house, along with the safes my father had at other locations.

I let out a sigh of relief when the Honda took the exit

behind me. I was too young to be this stressed. I wouldn't be surprised if a bitch had gray hairs by the time, I turned eighteen. I was more mature than a lot of women twice my age because of the shit I'd seen in my life. My daddy always talked to me like I was an adult and put me on game from a young age. I may only be seventeen, but I was damn sure ahead of my years. I needed to call my father's lawyer and check on his case. He'd been sitting for two weeks, and I needed him home, but first, I had to get through this day. This was gonna be the hardest day of my life. Not only did I have to bury my mother, but we also had to bury my aunt, Dior's mother, Chanel. My mother and aunt were going out the same way they came into this world together. Money was tight, so Ma decided to have a double funeral. I was cool with that. I didn't think I would be able to handle attending two funerals.

When I pulled up to Ma's white ranch-style house, cars were lined up in the driveway and on the lawn. I passed the house and drove a couple of houses down until I found a parking space. Damn, they could have made sure I had somewhere to park. It was my mother's funeral. Ma knew my mother and Aunt Chanel didn't fuck with none of these people. People I never knew or saw when my mother was alive were now all of a sudden concerned. I wasn't stupid. My parents were hood celebrities, and people were either around to be nosey or hope they could somehow come up on some money.

I opened the gate, and the smell of barbecue filled the air. I walked past my cousin Troy, who was grilling in the yard. He didn't speak and neither did I. There was a group of men sitting on the porch drinking beers. They didn't look like they were dressed for a funeral.

"How you doing?" one of them yelled out to me.

"Fine," I said, squeezing past them. I hated living at Ma's. I would think she would tell her customers she was burying her daughters and she was closed for the day. My grandmother ran one of the most popular liquor houses in the city. The liquor stores closed early as hell in Greensboro, and Covid had most of the clubs shutting down early. Ma was not the only liquor house in the city, but she's the most popular spot right now. Now that I was forced to live with her, I could see why my mother didn't fuck with her ass.

I walked in the house, and Ma started her bullshit. "I hope you ain't have no one follow you to my house!"

I had to stop myself from telling her to mind her fucking business. Instead, I took the higher road and said "No."

Shit, she was not my mother, and I don't know these people she had sitting inside the living room to be explaining myself. Without saying another word, I walked out of the living room and toward the back of the house.

I walked inside the bedroom and dropped my bags. Dior was sitting in the middle of the bed looking like a hot mess. Her weave was tangled, and her eyes were bloodshot. Dior was unraveling. She wasn't eating or bathing and spent most of her time in bed.

"Dior, get up and fix your hair!"

Dior didn't respond. She continued to stare straight ahead like she didn't hear a word I just said. Dior was emotional as fuck and with the mental state she was in right now, I didn't want to come off too hard on her. Dior also lost her mother, and everyone grieved differently, but at this point, neither of us could afford to shut down.

I walked over to our dresser, grabbed a brush and started working my way through her tangles. Brushing Dior's hair reminded me of when my mama used to do my hair. She made it a point to brush my hair every night, no matter how old I got. The memories were too much for me to stomach. My eyes filled with tears. I was scared that if I allowed one to fall they wouldn't stop.

"I can't do this shit. If you wanna show up to our mother's funeral looking a mess, that's on you," I said, dropping the brush next to her.

Dior was a beast when it came to hair. I was counting on her to fix my hair. I grabbed the Sephora bag off the bed and walked over to the full-length mirror I bought from Walmart the other day. Back home, I had a led makeup mirror I used to apply my makeup. I couldn't afford to replace it, so this bullshit would have to do.

I applied the Fenty foundation and looked at Dior through the mirror. She was rocking back and forth with tears falling down her face, and her eyes were blank. What she needed right now was comfort and to hear that everything was gonna be okay. Unfortunately, we had no one to provide us with that comfort. Not only did we lose our mothers, but we lost our sense of security

"How are you able to go on like everything is okay?" Dior asked. Her voice was softer than normal, and If I wasn't actively trying not to get lost in my thoughts, I might not have heard her. Anything was better than dealing with the thought of my father not coming home. No one mentioned anything directly to me, but I overheard conversations. The feds were attempting to prosecute him with running a criminal empire. The streets called it Kingpin status. All I know was the minimum sentence was twenty years and the maximum was life in prison. Somehow watching her break down made me feel better inside. Dior was my baby, so I didn't mean on a spiteful or weird vibe, but her breaking down let me know I was not alone. Someone else felt my pain and wasn't carrying on with life like everything was okay.

"The only reason I'm not crying is because I know mama and Auntie Chanel wouldn't have wanted that for us. Our parents prided themselves on being the coldest, strongest, and most feared individuals in this city. Dior, people are waiting for us to break. Our parents have a list of enemies, some we are unaware of. All we have right now is each other and the lessons they taught us. Now, get the fuck up and fix your hair so you can do something to mine, and I can do your makeup."

I guess my little speech did something for her because Dior jumped off the bed and began plugging in her flat irons. While she fixed the blonde 360 wig she had on, I continued to beat my face.

Today wasn't about us. It was about representing our parents, and I would never allow my father, who was dealing with enough bullshit, to worry about me. Dior's father was my Uncle Dro, my daddy's baby brother, and he was on the run, or at least that's what we are telling ourselves. No one had heard from him since our mother's death and my father's incarceration. I didn't want to believe my Uncle Dro was dead. The men that stormed our mansion were still somewhere plotting. Who was going to stop them from finishing what they started? My Uncle Bishop was the only form of protection we had. But he's only one person. He refused to discuss business with anyone other than my cousin Kash. So, he wasn't much help. Uncle Bishop warned me to be careful of what I said to my father since the jail phones were tapped.

Kash was a few months younger than my Aunt Fendi. When she first got in the drug game our relationship changed. She didn't want to kick it with us as much, everything was always about business with her. Yea she might have been twenty, but she didn't act like it. We never saw her kicking it with no niggas, and she didn't party. If you wanted to find Kash you had to go on the block.

Twenty minutes later, Dior and I walked out of the room, and nobody would be able to tell she had a breakdown. We both decided to wear our mother's favorite designers to the funeral. I had a white tweed Prada suit on that my mother brought back from her trip to Paris. Dior had a white Channel outfit on that had her looking like an angel. Dior wasn't as curvy as me, but today, I could see her hourglass shape that she normally kept hidden with sweats and hoodies.

Ma had an obsession with designer shit and made sure to name all three of her daughters after a designer. Our mothers followed the same ghetto ass tradition when they had their children. That was how I got my name Gucci. My daddy said with the last name Snow, I didn't need a middle name. He was right about that. I was the only bitch named Gucci in my city and the last name Snow was powerful in this state.

Everyone was downstairs in Ma's living room. Fendi sat on the couch and her face was lifeless. Her doe eyes were crimson, and her face was dull. She had on this badass white dress with some four-inch white red bottoms.

My cousin Kash was tomboyishly attractive. People often compared her to Bernice Burgos. She wasn't quite as thick as her, but she had the same deep mahogany skin tone. Kash had on a pair of tight white slacks with a purple silk shirt and a pair of shoes that matched her shirt.

Ma, of course, had to showcase the new BBL she got in Miami. The dress she wore was a bit much for a funeral. She probably wore that shit because she knew every get-money nigga in the state was gonna be at the funeral to show respect for my mother and aunt.

The limo was quiet as we rode through the streets to the church where the funeral was being held. I looked over at Uncle Bishop, who was rocking back and forth with his 4-five in his lap. Ma tried to get him to put the gun up, but he had to remind her who we were and that the Haitians were still out for blood. I hoped he was wrong, and we would be able to bury our mothers without some haters trying to shoot up their funeral to get some clout in the streets. Uncle Bishop made sure there was heavy security. He was the type of nigga who was always gonna make sure he protected his family, no matter who he paid for the service.

"Damn, this shit is crazy! Do y'all see all those foreign cars?" Fendi turned her head to look out the limo's window. Yeah, there was nothing but Range's, Tesla's, BMW's, and about every type of foreign car I could imagine, lined up in the parking lot next to and across the street from the church.

Fendi's comment was uncalled for at this very moment. The fact that she was more concerned about who was at the funeral than if me and Dior were okay did not sit right with me.

Fendi had always been selfish as fuck, and I blamed my mother for that shit. Before I was born, Fendi was my mother's baby. She used to always say that Ma was incapable of being a mother, so she stepped up. Fendi was introduced to the finer things in life the moment my mother and Aunt came up in the drug world. Pictures of the three of them dressed in designer clothes sitting front row at various concerts and paper view fight nights lined our house. If anyone in this car should have been as distraught as us, it should be Fendi. Instead, she was sitting across from me checking her makeup and fingering through her platinum blonde blunt-cut bob.

When the car stopped, I grabbed my white oversized Chanel frames out of my bag and slid them on my face. As we walked toward Saint Lucia's Cathedral, my mind was still trying to process that this would be the last time I ever saw my mother's beautiful face.

I scanned the crowd of people lingering in front of the church. I raised my head higher and made sure to switch my hips to remind them who the fuck I was. It felt like everyone was waiting to see my family break. Some of the people I passed had looks of sympathy on their faces, but the majority of the people looked happy at the thought of us no longer being the most powerful family in Greensboro.

When I walked inside the church I heard the sound of laughter. Three bitches sat in the aisle on live with their camera' s directed towards the caskets. "Y'all got to put them cell phones up." I stopped walking and stood in front of them.

I had no idea who they were but recording a funeral was disrespectful in my opinion.

"Excuse me. It's a free country and we could do what the fuck we want." The light skin girl said pointing her phone towards me. My family stopped walking and Uncle Bishop walked back towards where I was.

"Who the fuck you think you talking to?" he asked walking toward the girl. Everyone in the church turned to look back at us. I crossed my arms and waited for her to talk that shit to him, but that never happened. One of the ushers came over and removed the girls. It was a damn shame that we had to announce that no cellphones were allowed inside the church.

Dior gripped my hand as we continued walking towards the white caskets. My family wasn't religious. This was my first-time stepping foot inside a church. The smell of mothballs, cheap perfume, and dry air hit me. I would think they could have splurged on some plugins with the amount of money they charged us to have the service.

An usher opened the double doors and allowed us to enter the main section of the church. The floor seats were filled, along with the balcony seats they had above us, and people were forced to stand.

"Oh, they look cute!" a woman whispered as we passed by.

What you expected, I thought to myself. My eyes landed on the white caskets lined with gold. My heart raced and tears formed in my eyes. My mother and Aunt Chanel looked like two Angels dressed in their custom-made Alexander Wang Gowns. Whoever did their makeup and hair did a good job. Ma asked me and Dior if we wanted to do it, but that would have been too much for us to handle, so we declined.

"You good?" Kash whispered into my ear as we approached the casket. I was lost in my thoughts and didn't notice she was now holding my hand. My feet froze mid-step, and I was seconds from breaking down. My mind was playing tricks on me, and I halfway expected my mother and aunt to stand up and tell us this was a bad dream.

"I don't know if I can do this shit," I said. I tried not to cry, but I couldn't help it. I broke down in front of my mother's casket. I couldn't see who was trying to help me up through the tears.

"Mama!" I screamed. I gasped for air. My chest tightened, and I imagined my life without her.

"Y'all, go sit down. I got her," my Uncle Bishop kneeled and wrapped his arms around me. I buried my face in his chest and he squeezed me in his arms. "I got y'all!"

No other words needed to be spoken. I felt an instant burst of relief and allowed him to help me up and walk me to my seat.

I was numb the entire service and tried my best to hold it together. Dior broke down when they closed her mother's casket. I placed a kiss on my mother and aunt's coffin and turned to walk out of the church. We still had to attend the burial, and Ma was having a repass afterward. I needed a moment to catch my thoughts before we left the church.

"Where you going?" Uncle Bishop grabbed my arm and excused himself from the light skinned man he was talking to.

"I got to go smoke before we leave." The funeral director walked past us and shook her head. I ignored her and continued looking in my purse for a lighter. My parents were aware that I smoked. I could care less about what other people thought.

"Nah, hold up. Let me send someone outside with you."

There was no point in me trying to argue with him. I waited for him to speak with two of his workers, and they escorted me out of the church.

The wind was blowing so hard we had to walk toward the side of the building for me to light my cigarette. While I struggled to get it lit, one of my uncle's workers yelled out, "What's good, Sosa?"

I heard the name Sosa before but had no idea what he looked like. He wasn't on social media like every normal person in the world. His name would often come up when I went to the nail salon for a pedicure. They'd discuss how fine he was, how much money he was getting and he took care of all his bitches. I looked up toward the church to see if the rumors were true. Damn, this nigga was fine as hell. He had smooth dark skin and his shoulder-length locs were styled in rope twists. I appreciated that he had a suit on. Most of the niggas who came to show respect were in their normal street attire. As he walked down the steps of the church, his double-breasted suit jacket swung open, giving me a glimpse of the gun he had tucked on his waist.

I turned my attention back to my lighter.

"Not shit. I came to pay my respects. Why y'all got her out here like that?"

I didn't have to turn around to know it was Sosa talking. His deep voice held authority.

"Excuse me? I'm grown. They can't let me do a mother-fucking thing," I lied. He didn't need to know that I wasn't legally an adult. My lighter finally flickered and came to life. I rushed to light my cigarette before the wind blew it out. Once I got it lit, I took a deep pull and looked up at him.

Sosa's face was as solid as a piece of stone. He started barking orders to the workers, unfazed by my attitude. "It's a war out here. Y'all niggas know that it should be one at her front, one at her back, and call two more niggas to take her side."

Sosa's words caused the soldiers to pull out their cell-phones and demand more workers come outside. This nigga didn't look that much older than me. He had a baby face, but his eyes were dark as hell. I held my breath and watched him walk toward me. He had that big dick energy that women loved. When he got close to me, I could smell a light scent of weed on his suit. "My condolences. Your family is good people. Make sure you are always aware of your surroundings. These streets are wicked, ma."

Sosa licked his thick lips before he walked off and left the scent of his Tom Ford Cologne lingering in the air.

Chapter Two
SOSA

T oday had been a crazy day. A nigga normally didn't do funerals, but I had to show my respect to the Snow Family. Snow was my first connect when I jumped off the porch with this hustling shit. He was not one of them plugs who was all for self, and I appreciated that about him.

I just finished rolling a fat ass blunt, filled with some sticky Gelato, I got from my connect in Cali when my phone rang. Bishop's name flashed across my iPhone twelve screen. "Yo!"

"Good looks on earlier. My little niggas told me you put them up on game about my niece."

"You already know. I saw them niggas wasn't on point, so I stepped in. That ain't about nothing."

"Nah, that's about everything! When you get some free time, we need to chop it up. We all have a problem with mice, and we need to discuss the best method of extermination." Bishop was speaking in code. With everything going on in the

Snow camp, I didn't blame him. The feds probably had all of them niggas phones tapped. The streets were crazy right now. In less than six months, every get-money nigga in the city was either dead or facing an indictment.

"I got you. My ears are to the streets as we speak. This situation needs to get handled ASAP."

"Bet, I'm a let you go. We gonna link soon." I disconnected the call and replayed Bishop's conversation in my head. I lit my blunt, adjusted my seat, and stared at my trap that sat in the middle of Ray Warren Projects.

There weren't too many people out, and I preferred it that way. I had several trap houses throughout the city of Greensboro, but this particular location I used for cooking work. I had another apartment in a duplex not far from here that I used to distribute work. I had a team of bitches who cooked the work that majored in chemistry at Bennett College. They were from out of town and trying to make some extra bread. My system was flawless. It allowed everyone associated with me to eat and avoid dealing with any fuck shit in the streets. All I sold was cocaine and Za, even though I'd been tempted to fuck with the boy. That shit was the new wave now that the pill poppers had graduated to a stronger high, but the football numbers they were giving out for that shit forced me to stay in my lane.

I was a private nigga, and I surrounded myself with individuals who had the same goals as me. Get money and stay out the fucking way. These other niggas did too much, always trying to show the next motherfucker how they were moving. That was why I avoided social media. Nobody would find any pictures of me on there unless I was being posted by whoever ran that stupid ass Greensboro Tea page. Whoever was running that page was playing with fire. As soon as I figured out who they were, I got a hollow point with their name on it. Niggas got caught up in indictments over stunting on the Gram. I'd be dammed if I got caught up because the next motherfucker wanted to use my name for some likes.

Niggas been moving crazy lately. Every other week there was another home invasion on the news. To the average eye, you would think they were hitting residential locations randomly. If they were in the streets, then they knew what it was. Nothing but trap houses, stash spots, and nigga's residential homes had been targeted. Thankfully, none of my spots had been hit, but I was not arrogant enough to know it was only a matter of time before one of these fuck niggas tried to catch me slipping. That was why I stayed with my strap ready. Fuck a safety.

Niggas used to laugh at how militant I moved in the streets when I first started hustling. I ain't trust no one and was always on point, so I advanced quickly in the dope game. I ain't playing no games. Let me think a nigga was flaw, and I was pushing their shit back.

I was twenty-three and ain't been knocked, shot, or robbed. I didn't fuck around. I got my money and kept it pushing.

My phone vibrated inside the cup holder, and Jada's name flashed across my screen. Jayda was a slide that I only fucked on occasion. In the six months I've known her I think I might of took her out once or twice. Jada's mouth was good for one thing, and she wasn't in my presence, so I hit decline. The weed was so good, it had me in a zone, and I wasn't in the mood to talk. Jada was the type of bitch that would blow my shit up until the battery died. Before I could put the phone back down, it stopped ringing and there was a long ass text message that popped up.

Nigga, this ain't about why you been ignoring me. This nigga Nas is in the liquor house talking shit about you. I ain't trying to stand here typing and shit. You know them niggas know I fuck with you. Call my phone and mute yours. I'm close enough to where you can hear it for yourself.

I got halfway through the first message and stopped reading. I hit her name on my iPhone and waited for her to answer. The phone connected, and it sounded like it was in her pocket. I turned my music down, but all I could hear was Jada's drunk ass screaming "Pooh Shiesty, you my dog but, Pooh, you know I'm really sheisty!" A lyric from the rapper Pooh Shiesty's song "Back In Blood". I brought the phone closer to my ear and tried to hear what was going on. The music was so loud, it sounded like she was in the club, and her stupid ass screaming wasn't helping the situation. "Oh, shit. My bad, hold up bae," Jada yelled into the phone.

Before I could respond, I heard "Excuse me." I waited for Jada to get somewhere where she could hear me. I wasn't about to play with her ass today. My finger was about to hit the end call button when I heard, "Fuck that nigga, Sosa. His bitch ass thinks he's invincible. Raise the bounty to one hundred fifty. Y'all niggas ain't moving fast enough!" Nas' deep voice came through so clear, Jada had to be standing next to him. She was trippin, for real. It ain't no secret that we were fuckin, and if that nigga fucked her up, I ain't running in there on some captain save a hoe shit. "That nigga to fuckin low key! We've been watching his spot on Benbow for damn near a month " Nas continued running his mouth like a bitch.

"Bro, keep that shit low it's too many ears," another voice said. Whoever was talking had more sense than his leader. The liquor house was the last place a nigga wanted to discuss any form of business. Too many drunk and nosy motherfuckers in one place. Everyone's looking for their next come up. I swear this virus got the whole city fucked up.

"Bitch, fuck you looking at?" another voice spat.

"You! I've been trying to get past y'all to get to the bar."

"My bad, sweetheart. What you drinking?" Nas asked, sounding faded. He had always been a tender dick nigga, so I was not surprised he was trying to push up on Jada.

That was all I needed to hear. On my mama, that nigga was dying tonight.

I banged on Jada, sent a group message to my hittas, and told them to meet me at the daycare center I owned. I acquired the center a few years ago when the nigga who owned it couldn't keep up on his monthly payments. My mother talked me into it, and that was the first business I purchased. To the single mothers who I hooked up with free childcare, the daycare was heaven-sent. Only certain members of my team knew what was up with the location. If someone Googled Sunshine Daycare, all they would see were five-star reviews. The daycare was advertised as being open twenty-four hours, but I made sure all the kids were picked up by nine in the evening. The daycare was the perfect coverup for the weight we had stashed inside. No one ever suspected anything foul was going on when they saw my team go in and out of the location.

Since that nigga, Nas, wanted to be on that fuck shit, I was gonna show him how to do it. After I murked his bitch ass, I was gonna make his baby mama Juju suck my dick while I stood on his grave. When I first met Juju, she lied and said she was single. I didn't find out the truth until three months later. That nigga was about to lose his life over a bitch who didn't want him. The few times we were in the telly, that nigga would blow her phone up, trying to act tough. His bitch would laugh and ignore his ass, drink my seeds, then wanna lay up and pillow talk about his stupid ass. Juju wasn't anything more than something to stick my dick in. I had to laugh. That little nigga was bugged out. The bitch's pussy was not even worth the trouble.

Twenty minutes later, I pulled up to my daycare and drove around back to the parking lot. The daycare used to be a residential home. Thankfully, the nigga who sold it to me installed the parking lot on the extra acres of land.

Good, these niggas are here.

When I called a 911 meeting, everyone stopped what they were doing, so I was not surprised they beat me here. I passed my nigga's cars and pulled in the parking spot that read *owner*. Niggas knew not to park in my spot.

When I got out of the car, my foot sank in the damp grass that was still wet from the rain. I made sure to avoid getting dirt on my new sneakers. My phone rang.

"Yeah!" I answered, not bothering to look down at the screen.

"Sosa, I wanna see you! I know you're mad that I fucked your car up, but this should make up for it. I risked my life for you, bae. You think Elle is the only bitch that you got who will ride for you, zaddy?" Jada whined into the phone.

"What liquor house you at?" I asked, getting to the point. Wasn't shit Jada could do or say to make me fuck with her. She killed that shit when she busted the windows out of my Range and lied and told her brothers I beat her ass. Jada's mother Monique was good peoples and did a lot for the community. Every year, she would throw back to school drives to help provide school supplies to low-income mothers. If it wasn't for me fucking with her mother, I would have killed her ass.

"Ma's. You about to come get me?" she asked excitedly.

"Hell no. Kill that shit! Did you not hear that nigga say he got a bounty on my head? You think I'm worried about getting my dick wet?"

"I hear you!" Just that quick, her voice switched from calm to aggravated. Her ass was bipolar as fuck, so I wasn't concerned with her sudden mood change. She stopped talking and the phone went silent. I had better things to do than listen to her drunk ass breathe. "Watch that nigga, Jada. If he leaves, hit my phone." I disconnected the call and dialed my mother, who didn't answer. After the third call, I gave up on her answering and continued toward the back of the house. I forgot my keys because I wasn't planning to go to the daycare. I banged on the screen door and continued to text my mother. She was gonna be mad as fuck, but I needed her to get out of town until shit died down. A few seconds later, she called me back.

"What, boy? I know your ass better have a good reason for disturbing my beauty sleep," my mother snapped. Her smooth voice instantly calmed me, and I shook my head at her theatrics.

"I need you and Bonnie to go out of town for a minute. I'm a send Lance to your crib to drop off some bread. Go ahead and book y'all a flight and an Airbnb. I need y'all gone ASAP." Out of all the niggas who worked for me, Lance was the only one I trusted to run errands for my mother. Lance was an older cat that used to work for my pops back in the day. My mother was comfortable with him, so shit worked out perfectly.

"Sosa, what the fuck you got going on? You know what? Don't answer that shit! Bonnie, get yo ass up!" she screamed to my fifteen-year-old sister. I could hear movement in her background. It sounded like she was in the bed when I called.

"Call one of your homegirls and take them with you," I added that in so she wouldn't bitch about me inconveniencing her.

"Yeah, I'm a call Roe and see if she wanna come. She can bring Alexis and keep Bonnie company. How long this time?" she asked. This wasn't nothing new. Any time I had issues in the streets, I got my mother and sister up out the city. With the shit I had going on, I needed to know they weren't accessible. That was the main reason I didn't have kids or a girl. Niggas loved to go to what they thought was your weakest link.

"Give me a couple of weeks. A month tops. Lance is on his way to you now."

"Little nigga, don't be rushing me. I know what the fuck I'm doing. Shit, yo daddy was the king of this shit. Stay safe, son. I love you."

I knew from the sound of her voice, she was worried for a nigga. I ain't need her stressing over what I had going on. The way I moved, the only person who should be worried was that nigga Nas' mama. By sunup, she would be picking out black dresses and suits for her pussy ass son. The only reason I was making my mother leave was that I still didn't know who was behind these stick-ups.

"I love you, too. I got to go. Hit me when y'all about to get on the plane."

I was so caught up talking to my mama, I didn't notice Elle opened the door. Elle was the only bitch on my team who was allowed to come to the daycare. I allowed her to get away with a lot of shit that I wouldn't tolerate from my other workers. I fucked with Elle hard. Even though she wasn't my girl, she was the closest I'd ever been to having one.

"What's good, dimples?" Elle rolled her eyes and continued to stand in the entryway of the daycare. I winked at her and told my mama I would call her back.

Elle was different from any female I had ever met. Shorty wasn't in it for the money. I know she genuinely fucked with me. With her, it was more than a nut. Don't get me wrong shorty was fine as fuck. My eyes traveled up her slim frame. The gray tights she had on were so tight I could see her fat pussy print. The cool night air had her nipples hard, and the barbell's print was exposed through her thin white tee shirt.

"Don't hang up with yo bitch for me." Elle opened the screen door with a scowl on her face. She twisted her lip up and placed her hand on her hip, blocking me from entering the building. We had been rocking for about two years, and you couldn't tell Elle she wasn't my girl. Part of it was my fault. When she started acting crazy, I never checked her. I wasn't about to argue with her retarded ass. Instead, I hit redial on my phone.

"Make sure you keep that same energy when she answers." The phone was ringing, and I swore Elle looked like she was seconds away from losing it. Her eyes weren't the normal light brown color. They were dark and glowing like she was possessed.

"You a disrespectful ass nigga for real! Nigga, you think I'm fuckin stupid? Every time I fuck you *unprotected* you putting my life at risk," she said, emphasizing unprotected.

"Who the fuck you think you talking to? I'm not that lame-ass nigga you lay up with every night," I gritted through my teeth. We weren't about to do this back-and-forth shit tonight. Elle had a whole nigga she was fuckin and lived with, but was always questioning who I stuck my dick in.

"That lame nigga got more goin' for him than you do! He has a fuckin degree, a career, and he's not scared to love a woman," Elle spat.

I had to laugh at her stupid ass. She was sitting here running that nigga's resume off like it was supposed to hurt my feelings, when we both knew if I was to say I wanted to wife her, she would leave that nigga in a heartbeat.

"All that sounds good. You might wanna stop sliding on my dick and stop playin with yo future, love."

"Boy, why the fuck do you keep calling me? I can't do shit

with you blowing up my line," my mother's voice interrupted the intense stare-down we were having. Elle's mouth dropped, and she had this dumb ass look on her face.

"My bad, ma. Elle told me—"

"Don't do that, Sosa!" Elle pleaded.

"I ain't got time for y'all shit. Bye!" my mother snapped, disconnecting the call. Elle was the first and only woman to ever meet my mother. That shit wasn't planned it just happened. My mother and me were out celebrating her birthday when we ran into Elle at the nail salon. I wasn't trying to be all weird, so I introduced them. They started talking and my mother invited Elle to join us at Ruth Chris. My mother fucked with Elle somewhat, but she was quick to let me know she didn't think she was the woman for me. It was no secret Elle had a nigga, yet everyone in the city knew she was my bitch.

I knew Elle's ass felt stupid as fuck when she heard my mother answer the phone. I wasn't even mad at her for acting jealous. She was a female, so that was in her nature. What I didn't like was she knew we were meeting because a nigga was trying to put a hit on me, and she was worried about this stupid shit. That had me questioning if she was capable of being a member of my team. If she kept fucking with me, I was going to demote her from managing my traps and she could assist with running the daycare.

"Who you got cleaning this shit? It's dirty as fuck! Don't fuck up the floor. I just got finished mopping! You're welcome, nigga" Elle stepped to the side to let me in.

A nigga was already pissed off before I arrived, and Elle

added to my frustration. I purposely stepped on the slightly damp floor like I didn't hear what she just said. The reception area was clean and tidy, except for a blue mop bucket filled with that purple Fabuloso Elle was obsessed with. I walked around the room making sure everything looked correct. I peeked my head inside the kitchen. The counters were clear except for the baby bottles in the rack drying. I made a mental note to have a staff meeting to go over cleanliness.

"Trifling ass nigga!" Elle mumbled under her breath. I turned around and watched her slide the latch in the bolt lock we had on the door. Once she was finished, she turned around and walked back toward the bucket that was placed by the door of the kitchen where I was standing. Her spiteful ass purposely knocked her foot into it and the dirty mop water splashed on my shoes. The purple water landed on my white retro Jay's that took me months to find.

I shook my head. This bitch was pushing her luck. She knew I didn't play when it came to my sneakers.

"What's good with you?"

Elle rolled her eyes and tried to walk past me. When she bent over to grab the bucket, I grabbed her arm and pulled her close to me. She looked down at my hand like it had shit on it and tried to push me off her.

"Ask that bitch you took to New York!" she snapped. Elle had the nerve to look me up and down like I owed her an explanation. This was the shit I didn't like and made me regret fucking someone who hustled for me.

Now wasn't the time for me to address her attitude. I let her arm go and ran my hands through my locs. I ain't have time to be going back and forth with her like she was my bitch. Out of all the bitches I fucked with, Elle was the one who had been around the longest. We met a couple of years back through one of my homeboys, who vouched for her. Her mother wasn't about shit, and she needed to make some bread, so I allowed her to start working in one of my cook-up spots.

"Everyone downstairs?" I asked.

"Yeah. We've been here. How you gonna call a meeting and be late?" Elle snapped, crossing her arms.

"You know why I called this meeting, right?"

"Yeah," she replied, rolling her light brown eyes.

"Aight, act like it. Now is not the time for you to be in your feelings," I snapped.

Elle needed me to check her from time to time. She lived in this delusional ass world thinking shit was sweet. Instead of having an attitude, she could have asked if I was okay. I brushed past her and headed toward the basement. The door was cracked, and I could hear the sound of guns loading.

My niggas were sitting around the conference table. No one was laughing or smiling. Instead, my niggas were preparing for war. They had semi-automatics, revolvers, and a pile of ammunition in the middle of the table.

"What's good, Sosa!" my right-hand, Scrap, yelled out. He never looked up and continued to load the desert eagle in his hand.

"That shit gonna jam on you, nigga." I said walking up on him.

Scrap shook his head and continued fuckin with his gun.

For as long as I known that nigga, all he used was the same Desert Eagle, no matter who we were at war with.

"Fuck you, nigga. My bitch ain't never jammed up on me."

We locked eyes and I had to laugh. That nigga was stupid as hell. We both know that rusty ass gun done jammed plenty of times in the middle of shootouts.

I pulled out a chair and reached for the Uzi with the extended clip. I could tell it was a new gun. My gun connect did his thing. I'd been wanting one of these

"This Nas situation is lightweight, but whoever is knockin niggas off is a problem. If your head ain't in the game, then that's a problem. We beefing with the unknown right now. All we know is they taking down entire crews, and they don't give a fuck if women or kids get hit. Y'all niggas need to make sure anyone you give a fuck about is situated." I looked each of them in the eyes so they could see I wasn't playing. The niggas that were in this room were shooters and about that action. What I needed them to be aware of were their families.

They nodded their heads at me, but I wasn't convinced they understood how serious this was. Times like this, I regretted my decision to become a leader. Any nigga could bark out orders, but it took a different type of man to lead. These niggas in this room were lost before I pulled them in and taught them how to properly conduct themselves in the streets.

Everyone pulled their phones out, except for my nigga, Dee. This nigga was busy cleaning his pistol, and out of everyone at the table, his family situation was the most problematic. He stayed in and out of child support court, with his baby mother Reesha. Normally, I would take that as a sign of disrespect.

When I gave an order, niggas listened. Dee had come to me multiple times about his trifling ass baby mama, though.

"Dee come upstairs and holla at me." What I was about to discuss was not for everyone else's ears. If he decided to open up to niggas about his situation, that was on him, but I was gonna make sure I protected what he told me in confidence.

Dee and I walked out the room and up to my office on the first floor. I didn't need anyone overhearing our conversation. Dee leaned against the wall and pulled his red fitted cap over his eyes. Since he started working for me, that lil nigga had come up on a car, crib, and wasn't out here splurging recklessly like some of my other young niggas. He only brought the necessities and made sure he stayed fly. That nigga was fresh as hell in a pair of Gucci Joggers with the matching slides and socks.

"What's good, boss?" Dee asked, looking up at me.

Clearing my throat, I tried to get my thoughts together before speaking. "My nigga, you already know I don't like getting in y'all business, but as your leader, it's on me to make sure you moving correctly. Whatever you got goin on with your baby mom, don't allow that to make a careless move that will come back to haunt you. We about to go to war with them north side niggas, and I ain't tryin to take no casualties, ya feel me?"

Dee let out a deep breath and looked into my eyes, something I appreciated. When a man held eye contact, it showed he was serious. Dee was one of the coldest niggas I'd ever met, yet the man stood before me humble, and his eyes glistened with tears. "I love my little girl beyond this life. I never thought I was capable of that shit my nigga. Ain't no one ever shown me no love. That bitch Reesha is trying to take that love from me. The bitch had the nerve to tell me if I fuck her she would drop my child support case. I'm tired of running back and forth to the courthouse so this bitch can get more money or try to stop me from being a father."

I could feel the passion, anger, and pain in his voice. I didn't see a young get-money nigga at this moment. I saw a young black man that was lost and tired of fighting a losing battle. Now, did I understand what he was going through? Hell no. I never planned on allowing a bitch to put me in a situation where she could have my freedom snatched or dictate my relationship with my child. His baby mama is a headache. One I've had the displeasure of meeting a few times. The bitch would pop up at our traps causing scenes and shit. I heard about her crazy ass from our workers, but that particular day, I was in the house when she came. I had to let her ass know all that stalking shit was dead. She tried to go back and forth with me until I pulled my strap out.

"My nigga, I feel you on what you sayin, but you not gonna be able to live with yourself if something happens to that little girl. Fuck it. Send her and the baby on a vacation."

From the look on Dee's face, he wasn't feeling spending any bread on his baby mom.

"Man, fuck all that. It ain't about that bitch. It's about your seed. A money-hungry bitch ain't gonna turn down a free trip, and a chance to stunt on the Gram." I paused and checked my phone to see if Jada had hit me back. I didn't have any missed calls. That was either because her ass was too busy turning up or that nigga was still partying.

"Aight, Sosa. Let me call this girl, and I'll be back inside. I'm about to take out all my frustration on them niggas. Fuck nigga got me about to waste my bread on this bird ass bitch! Yeah, them niggas gonna feel me tonight.," he mumbled under his breath.

I nodded my head and walked back down to the basement. Now that everyone had their families in order, we could get down to business.

Forty-five minutes later, we were six cars deep on our way to Ma's liquor house. I hadn't been to her shit in months and was surprised the law hadn't shut her shit down. It'd been so many shootouts inside her crib, it don't make no sense. Jada was my only connection inside that house, so I had no choice but to pull my phone out and call her. After several seconds, she answered sounding out of breath.

"Hey, babe! My bad. Me and my homegirls were dancing. I ain't hear you calling."

I laughed because Jada knows damn well, she doesn't talk to me like that. Jada loved to appear like she was more important than she was. She was lucky I needed her ass, or I would have been banged on her.

"Step away from whoever you are around."

"Aight, hold up. There's mad niggas in here." She said. I exited the highway and took the back streets toward Ma's crib. She was the only crazy motherfucker who would have all these niggas know where she rested her head at. I was surprised Bishop ain't been shut this shit down. If niggas couldn't get to him, they would have no issue locating his mama.

Ma's house was located in the cut. One thing I'd always

hated about her liquor house was there was one way in and one way out since she lived on a dead end.

Looking down at my A watch, the clock read one in the morning. That was the time when Ma's started jumping. All the clubs were about to close, and if people wanted to drink, they were gonna have to find a liquor house.

"What's up?" she asked once she got to a quieter location.

"That nigga still inside?" I asked, getting straight to the point. The closer we got to Ma's house, the more cars I saw lined up on the street. A couple of cars were circling the block, trying to find parking, that was how thick it was.

"Yeah, and that nigga is so fuckin extra. He done blew through a couple of bands on some stripper bitches and swear he the plug."

"Aight, bet!" I disconnected the call. This was about to be the easiest hit I ever pulled. The nigga, Nas was too flashy. I wasn't about to run inside Ma's crib out of respect for my nigga Bishop. Nah, I was gonna make his bitch ass come outside to me. I dialed my little niggas line, who was positioned outside Nas's baby mama's crib.

"Spray that shit up," I said as soon as he answered. People might think I was wrong for involving his bitch, but how I see it, it was her fault I was in this situation.

Chapter Three
KASH

" **K**   ash, what's good with the shipments? A nigga is dry
as hell. You know I fucks with y'all, but if Snow
being locked up is gonna affect business, let a nigga
know now. We all got families to feed, ma!" Rico stood in the
middle of the warehouse asking questions I didn't have the
answer to. Rico was one of my father's workers. He wasn't no
one important but I guess because my father wasn't here he
was testing me.

I made sure to maintain a straight face. My workers were
hungry and ready to jump ship. Rico continued brushing his
waves as he waited for my response with a smug expression on
his face. I looked down at my Apple watch and shook my head.
My father was late for our distribution meeting that we held
religiously on the first and the fifteenth of each month, and
that wasn't like him.

"Rico, ain't shit changing. Snow's incarceration is a minor
setback." I kept it brief when I answered his question. Who the

fuck did he think he was questioning shit, anyway? As a worker, he' was not privileged to certain information. Shit, I wasn't even telling my cousins what I knew about business. Snow's case was looking bad. The connect refused to do business with anyone other than him and his brother, Dro, who also happened to be Dior's father.

"Nah, ma. The fact that we've been sitting here for the past three hours instead of bleeding the block tells me it is."

"Rico you're right, young blood. This sounds like a personal problem. The shit is simple. We need to be hitting these streets before we lose control," Prime's old ass yelled out from across the table. If looks could kill he'd be dead. I expected this from the young niggas, but I was surprised to see Prime entertaining Rico. This nigga had been down with our family since before I was born. The workers began to mumble amongst themselves, and everyone was looking toward me for answers.

I wasn't prepared for this shit when I walked inside the meeting. I thought I was gonna get my work and bounce. My father hit me up last minute and told me there was a problem with this month's shipment and to wait for him to get to the meeting to explain. Lately, my father had been moving real secretive. He didn't want to involve me in all the family's problems, but what he needed to understand was I was grown, and I knew the lifestyle I signed up for. Times like this, I wanted to say fuck it, get my own work and branch out on my own. I knew for a fact I had some real niggas behind me, and I didn't need my father holding my hand as I navigated my way through the drug game.

"Kash hit me up when y'all get straight. Rico is right. We've all tried being patient with y'all, but time is money," one of the workers interrupted my thoughts. He stood up, pulled his fitted down, and dapped everyone up at the table before walking out the room.

I let out a deep breath and looked around the room, disgusted with the men. Instead of us trying to figure out our next move they were focused on the wrong shit. The Haitian army we had on our heads operated militant. I wasn't about to beg these niggas to stay down with the team. Men automatically assumed because I had a pussy, they could treat me any type of way. If my father was running this meeting, these niggas wouldn't have dared to question him. I stood up from my seat and ran my hand through my curly bob. Without trying, I had all their attention as I slowly walked toward the center of the room. Each one of these niggas had begged to fuck me over the years, and I was proud to say no one in this room knew how my pussy felt. Today showed me I was correct in my decision. Only a real nigga would ever be able to say they experienced me.

"Y'all niggas been working for my family for years, and we appreciate each one of you. I'm not gonna sit here and beat y'all head in with no bullshit. Y'all know that's not my style," I paused and looked each one of the ten lieutenants in the eyes before I continued speaking. "We're in the middle of a war, the feds are handing out indictments, and—" A message popped up on my watch that took my breath away and interrupted my speech. "Y'all, give me a second."

I walked out of the room not waiting for a response. Once I got into the hallway, I had to lean against the cold wall to reread the text. I had to bite back a scream as the words flashed across the screen.

Unknown: *Shut down the meeting ASAP. the Jake's ran down on yo pops. I got my ears to the street. When I figure out what's going on, I'll hit you.*

I blinked three times and reread the message, hoping Bag would text back and tell me this was a joke. I wanted to call him back so bad to see what the fuck was up, but I couldn't. Bag was one of Snow's top lieutenants, and he also fucked with my Aunt Fendi. I knew Bag before Fendi did, but we never been close enough where I would explain the nature of me and Bags relationship. I had never fucked Bag. We just vibed and used that to our advantage to keep each other up on game. When living this life, I needed a couple of people in my corner. I had no idea how he knew my father got knocked, but I was thankful he gave me the heads up.

When I walked back into the room, the first thing I noticed was Rico whispering to the nigga sitting next to him. "This why a woman can't handle being in a position of authority."

Rico's voice was so low, I almost didn't hear him. He was so caught up in his conversation, he must not have realized I walked back into the room. His lip was turned up in a smirk, but when our eyes connected, it quickly disappeared.

"Speak up, nigga! You got something to say to me, here I am." Now wasn't the time for me to play games with none of these niggas. The text message I just received had me questioning everyone. Outside of Rico being an arrogant bastard, I never had reason to question him, but something about him was not sitting right in my spirit.

"Shorty must be on her period!" Rico said, looking me up and down.

"Kash, I just got word from our connect downtown them people are heading our way," Black interrupted. Black was my father's right hand, so I trusted what he said.

"I guess we won't be getting our work," Rico said. He stood up, and the other members of our team followed him out of the room. I didn't have the strength to argue with his black ass. I needed answers to what was going on with my father.

Chapter Four
GUCCI

I should have followed Kash and Dior when they took it down early last night. Instead, I kept partying, knowing I had to be downtown for court the next morning. My mother's death weighed heavily on my mind. I hadn't slept in days. Every time I closed my eyes, I saw her lifeless body. The liquor helped me temporarily escape. Now we were late and had no time to find parking. As a result, we had to park in the expensive ass parking deck. That's more money that we didn't have wasted. Fendi and I walked out of the garage together. As we got closer to the courthouse, I could see a line forming.

By the time we made it to the courthouse the line had doubled. I swore I had been standing in the same spot for the last thirty minutes. The one thing I hated more than anything was standing in lines. I was used to receiving the VIP treatment wherever I went, so I was spoiled. A bitch was already hot that I had to wake up at nine in the morning. Then, to make shit worse, the line was long as hell and barely moving.

"Any updates on Uncle Bishop?" I asked Fendi as we continued to stand in the line. My Uncle Bishop got knocked yesterday. Any hopes of us getting out of this situation relied on my father getting released. They had a special task force that was targeting drug dealers, and boy, they were not playing. Looking at this line, it felt like every criminal in the city had court today.

"Nah. Most likely they have him in interrogation. Kash has been trying to locate him since last night."

That was the last thing I needed to hear. Uncle Bishop was the only person left who was holding us down. First, I had to deal with the death of my mother and my father's incarceration, and now, my only safety net was gone. No one had heard from Uncle Dro since everything went down, and I was just bracing myself for the day we get a phone call that he was dead.

"This shit is fucking bad. I feel like one of these hoes put a root on our family."

"The only way that shit works is if you believe in it!" Fendi tilted her head in my direction and went right back to typing on her iPhone. She had the nerve to have an attitude like it wasn't her fault we were late.

"Girl, I told you we were going to be late," I said.

"So, what. They probably haven't even started calling the docket yet. Besides court never starts on time. Don't lie and act like you ain't have fun last night either." Fendi laughed.

I cut my eyes at her and continued walking towards the courthouse. She was right I did have fun last night. The day started of stressful, my Uncle Bishop got knocked earlier that afternoon. After we found out he didn't have a bond it felt like my father's situation all over again. We were bored sitting in Fendi's bedroom. After two weeks of living at Ma's, we decided to go downstairs and chill. I couldn't even lie, that shit was lit. Normally liquor houses weren't my thing, but my nerves were so damn bad, one drink led to another.

I looked up at the line that still hadn't moved. If money wasn't an issue, I would have paid someone to cut in front of them. When I woke up this morning, I was tempted to throw on my Yeezy slides and keep it moving. Instead, I decided to rock my brand-new Prada peep-toe stilettos, which I was now regretting. My pinky toe was throbbing. All I wanted to do was get inside so I could sit down. Ma told me I was crazy to wear heels to go down to the courthouse, and I was regretting not listening to her. This was my first time stepping foot inside the courthouse, so I wasn't prepared for the massive line. Appearance was everything in this city, and I couldn't afford for anyone to see me looking crazy. That was why I made sure my thirty inch jet black weave was flat ironed to perfection, and I made sure to beat my face, even tho we were running late.

Inside this glass building, these crackers were holding a king, and what they didn't understand was the streets needed Snow. Now that Uncle Bishop was locked up, I had no idea what we were going to do for money. Kash was stressed out because she had no idea where she was gonna get work from to continue hustling.

I lit my cigarette and inhaled deeply, hoping the nicotine would help calm my nerves. Smoking cigarettes was a new habit I recently picked up. Today's court date was to see if the judge would reduce my father's bond. In the past, I took for granted all the small things my family did to make sure I was secure. When I pulled up to the gas station the other day, instead of filling my tank up, I was forced to put twenty dollars in. Times like this, I wished I had a nigga to depend on. Life would have been so much easier. The only way I'd been able to remain sane was to tell myself that my daddy was about to post bail, and I could get back to living the way a bitch was used to.

"What are you thinking about? I told you to chill. I texted Kash, and she said they ain't started yet." Fendi was in denial about how fucked up our lives were. Instead of her trying to come up with a plan if shit didn't go the way we expected, she had been too busy turning up at Ma's. A bitch loved to party, but I couldn't get with that shit knowing my pockets were hurting.

"Fendi, can you please stop talking to me! I have a hangover."

"Girl, smoking them cigarettes is a bad look. I don't know why you picked up that habit." She frowned and looked down at the cigarette in my hand.

"Coming from the bitch who smokes Black and Milds." I rolled my eyes and continued to smoke my cigarette. Fendi loved to try to put the next bitch down to make herself look better. That shit might work with Dior and Kash, but she knew I had no problem correcting her ass. My attitude was on ten, and the way I was feeling, anyone could get it.

The sound of the two girls standing in front of us giggling caused me to look in their direction. I tried to remember where I knew the girl with the stiff ass weave from. Then it hit me. She was one of the girls Fendi and me had gotten into it with from Smith Homes, a project on the South Side. This bitch had to be a bird brain. The way we beat her and her homegirl's ass last summer, I would think she would have learned her lesson. From the stupid ass look on their faces, I knew they recognized us, but I didn't give a fuck. Today was not the day to test me.

"Fuck y'all hoes looking at?" Fendi barked at the pair of friends. The tall light skinned girl pulled her sweatpants up like she was about to do something. I could kill Fendi for having us beefing with these broke bitches in the first place.

"Girl, bye ain't nobody paying y'all broke asses no attention. You might want to pipe down. From what I heard, y'all naked in these streets."

"These hoes ain't that tough without they people, are they?" The short dark skin girl looked us up and down with her lip twisted up.

"Who the fuck y'all broke hoes think you talking to?" I said, throwing my cigarette down. I made sure I was on point in case one of them tried to run up on me. They must have thought because we had heels on, they could get that disrespectful shit off.

"I thought a broke bitch who lives in a liquor house said something!" The light skinned one said and busted out laughing.

"Fuck these hoes, Dinata. They ain't nobody." The dark skinned one said, pulling her friend back into the line.

My blood was boiling as I watched them turn around and talk shit under their breath. They were nobody important, let's be serious. What did I look like arguing with bitches who still rocked K-Swiss? I didn't give a fuck if Ari recently had them shits on. They were wack back in the day, and they were still wack now. What had me in my feelings was these bitches knew my business. I was a private person. Before I moved into Ma's house, no one could say anything about me. Now, it seemed like my name was in every broke bitch's mouth.

"Damn, I can't stand these bitches always in the next motherfuckers business!" I spat, loud enough for both of them to hear me. They ain't say shit back, but I still was tight that they had the nerve to approach me.

"I swear I can't wait for your father to come home! I'm a fuck around and go to jail fucking with these stupid ass bitches," Fendi mumbled under her breath.

Thankfully, the line started to move. The last thing I wanted was to have to stand near these bitches too much longer. I was liable to smack the shit out of one of them and end up in the county along with my father. My father's lawyer told us to start preparing for the judge to lower the bail. He had submitted a bond reduction motion. Several prominent members of the community had provided character witness statements to the lawyer. Instead of entertaining those two dirty bitches, I started calling bondsmen in case the judge dropped his bail to a reasonable amount.

The first thing I was gonna do when my father was released was make him cop me a new whip so I could stunt on all these hoes. If everything went as planned, I'd be back inside my mansion in my king-sized bed wrapped in my silk sheets before the night was over.

After waiting for what felt like hours, the line started to

move, and we now had ten people in front of us. A tall white sheriff stood outside the front door directing people inside. It was hot as hell outside, and his face was turning various shades of red as he barked out orders to the crowd of people waiting in line.

"Remove any belts, electronics, jackets and place them inside the bucket!" He handed each of us a gray bucket when we approached the door. I grabbed the bucket and dropped my cell phone and purse inside it. Then, I had to wait for the line to start moving so we could enter the inside of the courthouse. By the time I went through the search process, my shirt was drenched with sweat. I stood to the side and waited for Fendi. Her shoes made the metal detectors go off, so she had to be searched with the wand before she could enter.

Fendi grabbed her items from the bucket and switched in her three-inch Christian Louboutin cheetah booties to where I was standing. I watched her walk toward me and had to admire my aunt. Fendi reminded me of the rapper Dream Doll. They both shared similar features. People always questioned if she was fully black, due to her exotic features. Men stopped to stare as she walked by. I couldn't blame them. The tight ripped black jeans she had on accented her slim-thick figure to perfection. When she got to me, she adjuster her Birkin bag on her shoulder, grabbed my hand, and pulled me toward the elevator. While we waited for the elevator, she pulled me in for a quick hug. "Girl, fix your face. You know your father is probably stressed out. The last thing he needs to think is you out here stressing."

I nodded my head and tried to mentally prepare for what

was going to happen in this courtroom. She was right. My father needed to have a clear mind today. We could worry about everything else once he touched down.

Once the elevator landed on our floor, it took no time for us to arrive where the bail hearing was being held. It was a short walk from the elevator to the courtroom. People were lined up in the hallway talking to various lawyers. One lawyer stood out in the sea of cheap suits. His gray suit was tailored made, and he walked through the hallway like he owned the courthouse. I could tell from the way his gray suit fit him it was designer. Out of habit, my eyes dropped to his black Gucci shoes that I recognized from the last time I was inside the store. Jason was in his early thirties, which was young for a lawyer, but according to my grandmother, he was a beast.

"I'm about to go talk to the lawyer," I whispered to Fendi. She nodded her head and continued toward the courtroom. I had to hurry up if I was going to catch him before he disappeared inside the courtroom. My heels and the slippery ass tile were making it hard for me to speed up.

"Jason, can I talk to you before you start?" I yelled out, catching him before he reached the courtroom doors. I was sure he already knew how important it was that my father was released, but it wouldn't hurt for me to remind him.

He turned around and his eyes flashed when he recognized who was calling him. Jason smiled, and his cold blue eyes traveled up and down my body as I walked toward him. I ignored his lustful stares. I knew I had that effect on men. I learned not to pay attention to it. If he wanted some of this chocolate, we could make that happen. I wouldn't mind having a handsome young white lawyer Sugar daddy.

"What's up, Gucci? How you doing? I see you still look good."

"Of course. Nothing will ever change that. What are the chances my father is leaving today?" I asked, getting straight to the point.

Jason extended his hand toward me. I grasped it and when I tried to pull my hand back, he pulled me into an empty room. I didn't expect this to take long, so I remained standing instead of sitting in one of the chairs that sat around a small table. These men didn't give a fuck that I was seventeen. All they saw was my pretty face, fat ass, and slim waist.

"I'm going to do everything in my power to make sure Snow is released on bail at least, but then again, the prosecutor keeps rescheduling the hearings due to not being able to locate a witness."

"So, if the witness doesn't show up, he's good?"

"I didn't say that, but if the witness is not present and the prosecutor tries to reschedule the court date, I'm going to fight it. I let it go as long as I'm willing. Either your father will be released on bail, or I will request a speedy trial. Don't worry. I got this."

We exited the room and he walked toward the lawyer's entrance while I walked toward the door that everyone else used. Up until I spoke to the lawyer, I was feeling optimistic. The last thing I was trying to hear was my father might not be released today.

Sighing, I walked into the crowded courtroom and scanned

through the bodies, trying to locate my cousins and Aunt. That didn't take long. The way my bitches were killing everyone in this courtroom, it was not hard to spot them. A girl was in front of me trying to get her toddler to behave, which gave me a moment to observe my family. Kash had her long hair pulled back in a bun, and her chocolate skin was flawless. The diamond hoop earrings she wore shined across the room. She didn't bother to get dressed up, but she still looked cute in her Amiri sweat suit. Dior sat next to her with her arms crossed like she had an attitude. I wasn't up when she left this morning, but from where I was standing, she looked cute. She had two long feed-in braids that stopped at her waist, and she had her school uniform on. The fact that Dior could still focus on school at a time like this was crazy to me. The only thing on my mind was my father and how I was gonna get some money if he wasn't released.

I walked through the courtroom like I owned it. If they were gonna talk about me, I hoped they added how good I looked today.

"Hey, Gucci!" this girl who used to fuck with my Uncle Bishop yelled out from one of the rows. I looked over at her, gave her a half-smile, and continued to walk toward the front of the courtroom. Once I reached the aisle, I waited for Fendi to scoot over so I could sit down.

"See, I told you they ain't start yet. These motherfuckers never on time," Fendi whispered in my ear as soon as my ass hit the seat.

"Quiet in the courtroom!" the bailiff yelled, looking in our direction being extra as fuck. Everyone was talking in the courtroom, but he decided to focus his attention on us. If he wanted a reaction, I wasn't gonna give him one. This was why I didn't fuck with pigs. They hid who they were behind their badges. If this was the streets, his ass wouldn't have dared to speak to us that way.

The sound of laughter filled the courtroom, and we all turned around to see what was so funny.

"This bitch!" Kash looked back at the aisle. Unlike everyone else in the room, her face remained straight.

"Is that bitch wearing a Dashiki? Who the fuck is that Kash?" Fendi's loud ass yelled, causing the people in the row behind us to bust out laughing.

"That's the fuckin prosecutor and don't let them cheap ass shoes and black lives matter shit fool you. That bitch is one of the worst prosecutors to have on your case. From what I heard, her husband was a narc and got killed during an undercover drug bust. That bitch hates drug dealers. This shit is personal to her."

Out of the corner of my eyes, I watched the bitch who was trying to take my father's freedom. She was a hot ass mess. Her shoes were leaning to the side. Instead of a suit, she had the nerve to have on a yellow dashiki.

"All rise. The honorable Judge Clarkson of the Third District Of North Carolina," the Bailiff yelled out. An older white judge who resembled Colonel Sanders walked into the room. This shit reminded me of modern-day slavery. The way the judge looked at us like we were animals in a zoo made my blood boil.

The prosecutor started calling defendants one by one. Out of ten cases, the judge had only granted bail to one man.

"Fifteen-minute recess!" the judge yelled out and banged his gavel.

"This is some bullshit. His ass ain't even been up there a good two hours, and he's already talking about a recess," Fendi said under her breath. She was right. At the rate the judge was moving. I wasn't even sure if he was gonna be able to see everyone on the docket.

"I can't take any more bad news y'all," I whispered, rocking back and forth.

"Come take a walk with me. I need to smoke," Kash said, standing up.

"I ain't going through that security check again. Y'all can have that," Fendi stretched her arms and laid her head on Dior's shoulder. Dior made no attempts to get up from her seat, so I guess she was staying with Fendi.

Kash was silent as we exited the courtroom and headed toward the elevator. Up until this point, she hadn't been affected as badly as the rest of us. It took us a few minutes to get out of the courthouse. We walked toward the side of the building to avoid the crowd of people lingering in the designated smoking section.

I reached inside my bag, grabbed two cigarettes out of my pack and handed one to Kash. I lit my cigarette and passed her my lighter. Neither one of us were talkers. We smoked our cigarettes, lost in our thoughts. Both our fathers were locked up, and I wondered if that shit scared Kash as much as it scared me. I decided to break the silence.

"If you need me to step up and help you hustle, you know I got you."

Kash let out a slight chuckle. "I wish it was that simple, cuz. The niggas who work for us ain't gonna sit around and wait for me to find a new connect. On top of that, I don't have enough money to buy that amount of product."

"How long you think Ma is gonna go for us staying with her until she starts complaining."

"That bitch been started her bullshit. I've been throwing her bread without y'all knowing."

"Damn, Kash. You should have said something."

"For what? Y'all my little cousins. You know I'm a do everything in my power to make sure we good."

"Don't worry. I spoke to my father's lawyers and he's almost positive he's being released."

"Shit don't work that way, Gucci. They are about to try to dismantle the entire operation. I don't know how much longer I'm a be free. They are picking us off one by one."

"You bugging, Kash! Why would you say that to me? You act like my daddy ain't coming home."

"I'm a need you to wake the fuck up. It's do or die now. Ain't no one coming to save us. On top of these state charges, our fathers are facing a federal inditement. Niggas don't beat the feds, Gucci. Remember that if you don't remember anything else. I hate to say it, but I don't think we will ever see our fathers outside bars again unless they pull an El Chapo."

When we got back upstairs, my head was throbbing, and I was worried. Kash was talking crazy downstairs, and I wasn't prepared to ever think my father would die behind bars. I rocked back and forth through each case. I wished I knew how to pray because my family needed it. It took another thirty minutes for the judge to start calling the inmates. We'd been inside the courtroom so long, my Apple watch died, and they had no clocks inside the room. Jason had other clients he was defending, so I couldn't ask him what was up with my father's case.

I had long ago stopped paying attention to the cases in front of me. The metal from the shackles clanged against the floor as the sound of footsteps entered the room. The room grew silent. I didn't have to look up to know who it was walking into the room. There was only one person who had that much power in this city. I could feel his presence without having to lay my eyes on him. That was how strong our connection was.

Most people had never in life had the privilege of being in a real nigga's presence. The shit these rappers rapped about, my father lived it, and everyone inside this courtroom knew it. My eyes raised, and I studied my father, afraid to blink not knowing the next time I would be able to lay eyes on him. Just like that, he stole my breath. With his head held high and shoulders straight, he led the officer to the table. All eyes were on Deandre Snow, and from the smirk on his face, he knew half the courtroom was there for him. His case was high profile, bringing in reporters. A few hip-hop magazines had reached out to him wanting first dibs when he decided to tell his life story. He refused those requests because he wasn't about to become some washed-up king pen spending the rest of his life behind bars.

I couldn't blink. I had to take everything in about him, from his sharp lineup that framed his waves to the way he still moved like a king, despite having shackles wrapped around his wrist and legs. It seemed like a lifetime since the last time I saw my father. I almost forgot how handsome he was. He might be in his thirties, but he didn't look a day over twenty-five. He put me in the mindset of Damson Iris, the sexy-ass brother who played Franklin on Snow Fall.

My daddy smirked at the people watching him and looked over at us before he sat down, he blew a kiss in my direction. I caught it and brought it up to my lips like I used to do when I was a little girl. For years, my father taught me how to speak without having to use words. To anyone looking, they would have thought he was blowing his daughter a kiss, but nah. That was the kiss of death, his way of telling me to handle the bitch who was supposed to take the stand. That was one thing he didn't have to worry about. That bitch wasn't showing up today. I played stupid when I was talking to Jason, but I knew she wouldn't be a problem in my father's case. The prosecutor found a fiend who claimed they witnessed my father dump a body. Everyone knew that was a lie. My daddy was never the type to move sloppily in the streets. He had workers on his payroll to dump bodies.

I got the drop on her junky ass. She was hiding out in a trap house on the eastside. The bitch knew she had a target on her for going against the king of the streets. My father had some loyal soldiers who owed him for work they got on consignment. Lord knows I needed the money but, I used it to get rid of the witness. Once I put the ticket out on her head, it took less than forty-eight hours for me to find her. For a small fee, the niggas helped me hold her ass down and inject a hot shot of Heroin in her neck.

The prosecutor dropped the stacks of legal folders on the desk and cut her eyes at my father. He looked over at her, rubbed his hands together, and went back to writing on the legal pad in front of him. I couldn't help to stare at the woman who had no problem snatching all these black men's lives. Bitch wasn't even doing her job because she gave a fuck about the people affected by drugs. This hoe was mad because her husband got smoked doing his job.

"Your honor, I would like to motion for a continuance," the prosecutor called out, looking through the stack of files in front of her. Here we go with this bullshit. I swore I thought that was the only word that bitch knew. The prosecutor lacked organization and professionalism. Sitting in the courtroom all day, I heard the defendant's family members complain that she kept continuing the cases.

"Your honor, this is a bail reduction, not an arraignment. Now, I will say I've watched Prosecutor Jones go through each case today and refuse to do her job. If she is not capable of representing the case, maybe she needs to hire an assistant. If she paid attention in law school, she would know you can not request a continuance with a bond hearing. In the matter of bail, your honor, we are motioning for a bail reduction." Jason turned his head and stared at the prosecutor long and hard. His lips twisted into a smile, and he stood up, dusting an imaginary piece of lent off his suit.

"There is a conflict of interest in this case, your honor. What the prosecutor failed to mention is she knows my client from high school. I feel the prosecutor is a lover scorned, who is upset the man she crushed on for years repeatedly turned her advances down, and now she is seeking revenge by using the judicial system."

The prosecutor gasped at Jason's revelation and jumped out of her seat. "I have no prior relationships with the defendant, and I refuse to allow the defense to make a mockery of this courtroom."

"Judge, the charges are preposterous. My client is a law-abiding citizen with multiple businesses throughout the state. With these charges pending, there are hundreds of families out of work. This must stop, your honor. The state wants to prolong this case because all they have are the testimonies of drug addicts looking to shave time off their sentences." Jason pointed at the prosecutor, snapped his fingers, and walked back toward his table.

I tried to hold my smile in and not get my hopes up, but in my eyes, it was evident my father didn't belong behind bars. Fendi elbowed me in the side and moved toward me.

"Told you to chill, bitch." she whispered quietly so the bailiff wouldn't start tripping.

The judge looked back and forth between Jason and the prosecutor. His face remained straight as he read through a stack of papers in front of him. It was hard to say which way the judge would go with his decision. Even if he had his doubts of my father's innocence based on his prior rap sheet, he still couldn't hold that against him. That was not how the law worked. People had the right to a fair trial and are innocent until proven guilty.

"It looks like you two have not been able to come to terms in regard to a plea agreement?" the judge asked, looking up through his thick glasses.

"That's correct, your honor. My client is innocent. We will be taking the case to trial. The prosecutor has offered my client a reduced sentence if he testifies. Judge might I add Mr. Snow has stated he has no prior knowledge to these crimes, nor has he ever heard of the people she's referring to." Jason stood off to the side of the table where my father was sitting.

"Your honor, DeAndre Snow has terrorized this city for years. His reach goes far from police officials, politicians, and judges. The state needs a fair opportunity to build a solid case. Regarding bail, I request the bond to be revoked. Mr. Snow is a flight risk, your honor, who has access to enough money, and power to flee this country permanently."

This bitch was not giving up. The confused woman I perceived her for changed instantly before my eyes. Now, I understood why Kash said this was one of the worst prosecutors to go against. If felt like I was watching a tennis match. For every statement she made Jason was hitting her back just as hard. My father didn't seem fazed by the prosecutor. Every so often, he would write something on the note pad, tap Jason, and then go back to whatever he was writing.

"Allegedly, your honor, these crimes the prosecutor is attempting to persuade you to are nonexistent. I would also like to state if Ms. Jones doesn't step down from this case, I will personally present this to the bar for misconduct."

Prosecutor Jones neck snapped toward Jason. Her mouth twisted up in a snarl as she snatched a folder off her desk.

"Your honor, at this time I would like to present a federal motion for DeAndre Snow to be extradited to Forsyth County to await trial on the following Federal Cases."

"Kash, what the fuck is she talking about?" I asked. Kash looked over at me with a straight face, her gray eyes were frozen.

"We are fucked!" Kash replied.

The door of the courtroom opened and three men with USA federal vests entered the courtroom and stood to the side.

"DeAndre Snow, bail is denied. You will be escorted immediately to Forsyth County Jail where you will await trial. This matter is adjourned and continued until June twenty-first. The matter is adjourned."

The words *June twenty first* kept repeating in my head, which was three months away. I had to get out of this courthouse. This was too much for my mind to process. I knew Kash mentioned a federal case, but I had no idea that his case was this serious.

"Don't speak until we get home!" Kash said the moment we stepped foot out of the courtroom.

I had to stop walking and look over at her. My period must be about to come on because all these hoes were starting to work my nerves. "Bitch don't tell me what to do! I'm no stupid bitch, Kash. I wasn't gonna say shit in that courtroom."

I walked toward the parking deck, fuck waiting for them to catch up with me. Kash pissed me off acting like I was a child who didn't know how to conduct myself. At the end of the day, that was my father sitting inside that courtroom.

Once we entered the parking garage, we walked toward the

elevator so we could get to our cars. I didn't drive today, so I was forced to follow Fendi, who was running her mouth to Kash.

"Can y'all drop me off at school?" Dior asked out of the blue.

"Fuck that school shit, bitch. We need to figure out what we are about to do!" I screamed in Dior's direction.

"I understand you're upset, but I'm not your fuckin child, Gucci!"

"Y'all, chill the fuck out! Dior let's go. I'll meet y'all at Ma's." Kash grabbed Dior's arm and they both walked off, not saying another word.

"I'm getting tired of both them bitches! The fuck wrong with Kash talking to me like I'm a child, and don't get me started on Dior. The fact that she's still thinking about school when we are broke as fuck."

Fendi looked up from her phone and nodded her head. "We need to do something. Snow not being released was never in the plans for me. My mother's not gonna keep letting us stay there with no money."

Chapter Five

I barely could pay attention to what Ethel was talking about. Her ass stayed inside my liquor house every day. I could count on her to show up right after she left the game room. Today, that heffa must have hit because she had been ordering rounds for everyone since she sat down. My mind was focused on what was happening down at that courthouse. When I signed up to take custody of Gucci and Dior, I was told I wouldn't have to come out my pocket for shit. Now, Fendi was my child, so of course, I agreed to allow her to come back home. The icing on the motherfucking cake was when my son dropped his daughter, Kash, off along with the other girls. While the girls were getting situated, I pulled my son to the side and asked for my money. Wasn't any shame in my game. I didn't even raise my kids, so he knew the only reason I agreed to this shit was because of the money.

People could talk about me all they wanted, but they weren't around when my husband snatched everything from me, and my children turned their backs on me. I had two daughters across town living the lavish life, and I was in the hood struggling. Them bitches were probably turning in their graves at the thought of me raising their precious daughters.

"I'm telling you that nigga not posting no bond! I never thought I'd see the day big Snow would fall. Damn shame he got all your kids caught up in his web," Ethel said, sipping on her drink.

I couldn't stand Snow's ass, either, but I needed him home so I could get the money I was promised for taking on his headaches. The day my daughters came strolling into my apartment with Snow and his black ass brother, Dro, my family was flipped upside down. My daughters ended up dropping out of high school to chase behind them no good niggas. Now look at them. I done had to bury two children because of his ass, and my son was sitting inside the damn jailhouse, due to Snow's careless ways.

"Well, his ass should have had some money put up for situations like this." I ripped a piece of paper towel off the roll and wiped my counters down. Once I finished making sure my shit was clean, I sat down across from Ethel and lit a Newport 100.

"Ma, you lying! That nigga ain't have no stash?" Ethel said, leaning in closer to me. Normally, I don't tell my business. I would sit back and listen to these fool's problems, but this tea was piping hot, and I could no longer hold it in.

"Hell no, his ass ain't have shit! I had to come out of my pockets to bury the twins. Snow and his no-good ass brother ain't shit. Got me raising they youngins off my dime."

Speaking of my granddaughters, it was about time I had a

sit down with them heffa's. I hated to be the bearer of bad news, but I didn't allow bitches to live in my house and not make money. Their parents might have allowed that shit, letting them girls drive around in hundred-thousand-dollar cars, but not me. If I ain't play that broke shit with my own youngins, who the fuck were their spoiled ass's?

Since they arrived at my house, they have had their asses on their shoulders, walking around like the world was coming to an end. They betta be lucky I stepped up and got them instead of their other grandmother, Darlene, who was a known crackhead. My house might not be the mansion they were used to, but it was better than living with a junky. I put my hustle to the side and allowed two of them to share a room instead of putting all four of them inside one bedroom as I should have.

I ran the most popular liquor house in Greensboro. Every night, niggas and bitches were lined up to get drinks, food, and occasionally I had dancers. I used to rent their bedrooms to the niggas that wanted more than a lap dance. Now I only had one room to sell pussy in. They little spoiled asses had the game fucked up if they thought I was gonna stop making my money because they moved in.

My shit wasn't like the other liquor houses. It was exclusive. Only the top-notch dope boys and it-girls frequented my establishment. Them niggas loved that my house was in the cut off the highway. They had to know someone who knew somebody to even find my shit. That was why I needed these little bitches to get on board. The way I saw it, better I teach them the game than one of these no-good niggas.

That was where my daughters fucked up. They raised these

girls green as hell. Gucci's ass was running around with that nasty ass attitude. That girl thinks the world owes her something. I couldn't wait for one of these little trill bitches to run up in her shit. Her ass had life fucked up, and that was her parent's fault. The world didn't stop because her mama was dead, and her daddy was locked up. Welcome to America.

Snow and Prada kept Gucci separated from the streets in the suburbs, and that was why her ass didn't know shit about the streets.

Fendi's ass was just as stupid. I didn't know how many times I told her ass to make her sisters invest in her a little beauty bar. That girl could do nails just as good as any of the famous nail techs on Instagram, but Ma doesn't know shit. That little bitch thought Prada was her mama, and because Prada and Snow raised her majority of her life, she ignored my advice. Now, look at her running around my house trying to be the protocol daughter. Her sisters must not have told her about me. There was only so much I was gonna do for her ass.

Now, if they were smart, they asses would start stripping. When I mentioned that shit, they all turned their noses up like they were above it. That same night, a group of dancers showed up from South Carolina and walked out with a little over two thousand dollars each, and that was money they made from shaking their ass. Now, if my daughter and granddaughters decided to dance, none of these other bitches would be allowed to work. All money would stay in the house.

"Ma, let me get another drink!" Ethell slurred. Ethel ass ain't need nothing else to drink, but she was paying, so I was gonna keep my mouth shut. I grabbed the red plastic cup she was holding and refilled her drink. When I was finished, I made sure she paid me my money.

"Oh, shit, Ma. They said they denied Snow's bail! The fuckin feds snatched his ass up. Y'all niggas pay me my money. I told y'all they were putting his black ass under the jail," my customer, Roy, yelled out. The no-good niggas he was talking to started complaining as they began to hand him crisp hundred-dollar bills.

I swore gossip traveled so fast in this dam city. Any other day, I loved sitting around with my afternoon customers. All they wanted was to drink and talk shit. Today wasn't the day. Once I heard Snow wasn't bonding out, I knew now was the time to talk to the girls. I needed everyone out of the house before they got here. This was family business we were about to discuss. I would do for them what I should have done for they mamas. Teach them the game. Fuck all that love bullshit. See where that got my twins? In the grave. Now that the family was broke, I'd be dammed if I planned any more funerals. That shit cost me an arm and a leg.

"Y'all take these drinks and go. I'm closing now." I handed all my regulars cups filled with moonshine. These were my older customers who didn't like all that expensive liquor the younger crowd liked. Them niggas talked shit as they grabbed their belongings, but I didn't give a fuck. They would be right back tomorrow.

I walked my last customer to the door, waved goodbye, and slid the lock on my door.

"Alexa, play City Girls."

I loved all that ratchet shit they be rapping about. Couldn't tell me I wasn't twenty-five again after I got my BBL.

While I waited for my Apple music to load, I lit a joint and allowed the weed my granddaughter Kash gave me to calm my nerves. Once the music started playing, I grabbed my Fabuloso, broom, and bleach. I started with my living room and worked my way to the kitchen. Shit, I might run a liquor house, but this was still my house, so I made sure to take care of it. Men loved a clean house. Add some good food, liquor, and hoes, and them niggas wasn't moving.

I took a break from cleaning to prepare the fifty pounds of chicken wings I had in my sink. Once I finished soaking the wings in vinegar, I rinsed them off and seasoned them with my special blend of spices. I separated thirty wings and began the process of frying them for us to eat for lunch. I put the rest of the wings in the refrigerator to marinate for my customers this evening.

It took me an hour to finish cleaning my house from top to bottom. It wouldn't have taken me this long if I didn't have to clean up behind these little bitches.

Once I finished throwing the last load of clothes in the washer, I was tired as hell. The smell of my chicken wings frying on the stove filled the kitchen. I didn't like my house to smell like food, so I lit one of my Bath and Body Works candles that I picked up the other day at the mall. I walked over to the stove, lifted the top on my pot, and flipped the chicken over. They had begun to brown and would be done in no time. I was old school. I didn't believe in the air fryer things people were using. Give me a cast iron pot, and I was good.

The sound of keys jiggling at my door let me know the girls were home. Fendi stepped inside first, and I could tell by the blank look on her face the rumors were true. I turned back around and acted like I was checking the chicken. I didn't need anyone to see the smirk on my face. I noticed that Dior wasn't with them out the corner of my eyes. One by one, all three of the girls walked into the kitchen and took a seat at the table, looking defeated.

"Cheer up it's going to be ok. I got some drinks for y'all, and I'm frying some chicken wings for lunch. I know this transition has been hard on y'all. Whatever y'all need, I'm here for you."

I was laying it on thick, but I needed to gain their trust for my plan to work. I took the chicken out of the pan and placed it on some paper towels. When they didn't say shit, I shook it off and grabbed a bottle of Patron off the shelf and placed it in the middle of the table. That was why I acted the way I did. These little bitches were ungrateful. Here I was, cooking them lunch and offering they broke asses my good liquor, and they didn't have shit to say.

Fendi kicked off her red bottoms, grabbed a plastic cup off the table, and poured herself a drink. My first reaction was to curse her ass out when she filled the cup to the rim. I bit my tongue and walked back to the stove. It had been so long since I'd lived with anyone. I wasn't used to dealing with no messy bitches.

"Ma, can you make some fries with the wings?" Gucci had the nerve to ask. See what I mean? These little hoes were so used to living this designer lifestyle, they thought I was they mama or daddy. Well, technically, I was Fendi's mama, but damn.

"Damn, I knew I forgot something when I ran out to the store. Don't worry, baby. I'll make sure to get some fries before tonight," I lied. I had gone to Sams Club earlier this morning and had several bags of fries in my deep freezer.

"Hmm umm," she mumbled under her breath. She was her mama's child. Same nasty-ass attitude. I swore that child looked so much like my twins, it was hard to look at her ass sometimes. Gucci had the same gray cold cat eyes, perky nose, and pink pouty lips as my daughters. The only thing different was Gucci's ass was thick for days. My girls ain't never been that damn thick. She probably got that shit from Snow's side. His mama had a nice ass shape before the drugs got to her.

"I need a damn vacation! All of this shit is too much for me to deal with. First the twins, then they done locked Snow and Bishop up. We need to find Dro, now," Fendi complained. I cringed when she mentioned Dro. His ass was worse than his trifling ass brother. His ass was probably somewhere on a beach living lovely. I didn't mention that because they would swear, I was hating on his black ass.

I took the last batch of wings out of the oil and started to fill their plates high with my famous lemon pepper wings and walked the plates over to the table. Once I had the hot sauce positioned, along with a stack of paper plates and napkins, I poured myself a drink and sat my black ass down.

"Girl, I'm thinking I can start doing make-up until my father gets released. You're nice with the nails, and Dior a beast with the hair. Them bitches that come to Ma's to dance might go for that,"

Gucci said, sipping her drink and looking over at me.

Bitch thought she was slick, trying to act like she wanted my approval. That game she thought she was running she got naturally from me. If she thought she was manipulating me with that bullshit ass story, she was slower than I thought. Fendi ain't say shit. She looked over at me with them dam puppy dog eyes.

"Y'all about to help them hoes make money?"

These little bitches had me chain-smoking. While I waited for one of them to answer me, I lit another cigarette and sat back in my chair, looking each of them in the eye. If this was their master plan, they should be happy I was stepping up to help them.

"Ma, you act like strippers don't need their hair, nails, and makeup done. Think about it. Instead of them having to go all over the place to find someone to do each service, they can come to us." Gucci leaned over and grabbed my box of cigarettes off the table.

"Don't you think it's time you started investing in packs?" She rolled her eyes at me, but she still took a cigarette out of my box. Damn shame. I was about to have to start hiding my cigarettes in my own house.

"Facts. We would make a killing doing that shit. My DM's stay flooded with bitches trying to book me for nail appointments," Fendi added in, trying to change the subject.

They had a little bit of sense to them, but their plan would never work. They should have thought of this shit when their mama and daddy were throwing money around like it grew on trees. Their plan wasn't bad. The only thing they were forgetting was they spent money like it was going out of style and had never worked a day in their lives.

"I can present it to the dancers. It's not a bad idea! I just think y'all can do better." I said looking each of the girls in the eyes.

Kash's cellphone vibrated on the table. Before I could see who was calling, she snatched it up and walked out of the room. As I watched her bow-legged ass strut out the kitchen, I instantly thought about my son who shared the same walk. Now that his ass was locked up, I knew I wasn't seeing none of that money he promised me any time soon. What we weren't about to do was run my cell phone bill up with all the dam Jay-Pay calls.

A few minutes later, Kash walked back into the room holding a pink Balenciaga book bag. "My bad, y'all. I got to go make a drop! If y'all serious about doing makeup and nails, I can help y'all with the supplies."

Gucci and Fendi looked over at each other and started whispering. Fuck they broke asses. My attention was on my other granddaughter, Kash. Out of all the girl's, she was the only one who wasn't sitting around waiting for a handout. I liked that about her. As long as she didn't get in my way, we would be okay. Kash wasn't as spoiled as the other girls, and we had a closer relationship since I helped raised her when her no-good mama dropped her off on my doorsteps when she was a newborn. Bishop was sixteen at the time, and the only one of my children who lived with me.

"If y'all really wanna do this shit, I'll clear out one of the bedrooms so you can have space," I said, inhaling the Newport.

"Ma, can I bag these trees up?" Kash asked, unzipping the book bag.

"Do what you got to do. You know you could make a killing selling your shit while I'm open." Kash didn't respond right away. She was focused on the pound of weed she had inside a Ziploc bag. Her arched eyebrows were focused on the weed as she broke off small amounts and placed it on the scale. While I waited for her to finish bagging her weed, I thought of how I would break her to go along with my plan. She might be the only one who wouldn't go along with it, but desperation caused people to do shit they normally wouldn't do.

"Nah, I need to figure out who I can hit up for some work! The majority of your customers be geeked up," Kash said, causing us to all laugh.

"You ain't lying. They be sneaking and geeking like a mother-fucker. If you get some blow or perks, you'll make a killing while the liquor house is open," I added, taking a sip of my drink.

"That's not a bad idea, Kash! Now that we live here, all you would have to do is go downstairs. I think you should do it, especially with all the bullshit going on in the streets." Fendi was finally using the brain I gave her.

"I need some work to do that. This is all I got left from the last drop we did. My father ain't never introduce me to the connect."

"You could go to Sosa or Bag. You know them niggas is loyal to the family," Fendi suggested.

"I don't fuck with Sosa like that, and you know that. Call Bag and see if we can make some shit shake." Kash said shaking her head.

"What you mean we? I'll call him, but outside of that you on your own." Fendi shook her head. The conversation started to go left, and I had to grab my drink to calm down. Fendi's worried about looking bad for Bag and I'm trying to get some money generated in this house.

"On my own? Fendi, don't sit here acting like you have any real options to get money. You're right, though. I'm on my own cause I refuse to be a broke bitch waiting for a handout." Kash spat.

"Just because I'm not trying to be the next Griselda Blanca doesn't mean I'm a broke bitch!" Fendi spat.

Fendi and Kash glared at each other. Both of them had a point, but I wasn't saying shit. Out of the corner of my eye, I watched Gucci. She wasn't saying shit. All she was concerned with was the cup of liquor that she had refilled twice. "You need to slow down and put some food on your stomach before you get sick!"

"Why do you act like you give a fuck about what we do? As long as we hit you off, you're good, right?" Gucci snapped.

There it was that smart-ass attitude like her damn mama. "First of all, you can kill that attitude. There's only one bitch in this house paying bills, and I'm the one who gets to have a damn attitude. Y'all little bitches need to come down of your high horses and fast. If you think doing hair, nails, and makeup is gonna support y'all lifestyles do it, but what you not gonna do is put Kash down for getting in her bag. Now, if y'all think you gonna sit up in hurr and not do shit, this ain't the place for you. Yall need to use what God gave yall to get what you want."

"Ma, I ain't sellin no pussy if that's what you trying to suggest!"

"Little girl, did I ever suggest y'all sell pussy? Shit, I would never have y'all out hurr like that. What I'm saying is y'all come from me, and that broke shit not how we get down. When y'all bitch ass granddaddy left me for dead, I made shit shake. Not to talk about y'all mothers, but they should have had some bread stashed in case something happened to Snow and Dro. Now, I know y'all used to a certain lifestyle. Y'all don't know shit about the struggle. Y'all bitches grew up rich, and you talking to a bitch who got it out the mud."

"Ma's right y'all! I hate to say that shit, but we got to think smart. If Snow and my father don't get out, then what? Dro's ass is on the run, so he can't help us with shit, but if we can get enough bread up, we good. We take this city the fuck over." Kash spoke with so much fire the other girls nodded their head in agreement.

"I'm down if I don't have to sell no pussy." Fendi agreed.

Yes, two down and two more to go, I thought, looking over at Gucci, who now was slowly sipping her drink.

"Ain't a bitch badder than y'all in this city. Look how many more customers I have cause these niggas want to get next to y'all. These niggas ain't fucking with the clubs like that because of all the restrictions, and I'm the only liquor house that lets girl's dance. We cut all them hoes off, and we eat. The fuck y'all tryin do?" I threw it all out there. Shit, if Gucci ain't wanna get on the money train that was cool. I'm sure Dior would agree once she saw Kash and Fendi were on board. If I couldn't convince them, Kash and Fendi would do. Now if I could get all the girls to dance, they really could bring in some bread.

"My father would kill me if he found out I was dancing," Gucci said under her breath. This girl was crazy as hell worried about her damn daddy who wasn't getting out of jail.

"What your father don't know won't hurt him. Hell, yo mama danced at one point bet you ain't know that." I lied with a straight face. My daughter Prada would never dance. The girls didn't need to know that. It wasn't like the bitch was alive to tell them the truth.

"I highly doubt my mother would dance." Gucci sassed.

"Well, she did. Now if you don't want to fine. All I know is when your cousins and aunt start making money don't have your hand out." I looked over at her ass like she was crazy. She wasn't thinking straight, but I was about to get all their asses straight. "Now, listen. I usually charge the girls a tip out, but since we family, y'all don't have to worry about that. The way we gonna break this shit down, we all gonna eat, and when we get our money right, we can invest in y'all beauty bar and help Kash get back in the game."

"I'll try it. But if we don't make no real money I'm out." Gucci finally agreed.

"I'm down. I always wanted to dance, anyway." Fendi's ratchet ass jumped up when "Twerkalator" came on.

I slammed my hand on the table and raised my voice. "Sit yo ass down. We ain't playing right now."

Fendi rolled her eyes, plopped back down in the chair, and started sipping her drink.

"Y'all got to remember we ain't doing this for play play. We about to run this shit like a motherfucking business! I get the door and the bar. I'm upping the price on their asses. We only have ballin niggas and bad bitches come through, anyway, so they can afford it. Y'all get the tips you make. You can do private parties and all that shit. Now, Kash, I know you not dancing, and that's cool. You can help me with the bar if you not comfortable shaking your ass. If we do this shit right, we all gonna be straight. All money in this bitch is split among family."

"Ma, we gonna need outfits, and we broke," Fendi spoke up first.

"Don't worry about that. I'm a hit-up Desire. She makes all the girl's outfits. Y'all gonna need some dance shoes, too. We can hit this spot I know. I'm a make a few calls and promote this shit. We gonna do a lock door. I'm about to hit up some boosters. Make a list of what y'all need for hair, makeup, and your nails." Usually, when I did my lock doors, anything goes. A group of bitches willing to do anything equals a lot of money spent. My girls weren't ready for that just yet. I had to ease them into things.

"When we doin this?" Kash asked with an unsure look on her face.

"Tomorrow. Wait a minute, where the hell is Dior at?" I asked, realizing she was missing.

"School, Ma!" Gucci snickered.

"Aww, hell nah. Find my keys. Let's go get that bitch. We about to get this chicken."

Chapter Six
GUCCI

If someone told me a year ago I would be a damn stripper, I would have smacked the shit out of them. I couldn't believe I was about to go downstairs and shake my ass for the city. A chill ran through me as I held the perk Fendi gave me earlier. Tonight, I needed something stronger than liquor, and she told me this would help me loosen up. I placed the pill on my tongue and washed it down with the Henny I had in my cup.

I think everyone thought I was nervous to get naked. That wasn't my issue. My body was the least of my worries. I admired myself in the mirror. My stomach was flat with no pudges, my legs were thick smooth, and my ass was fat. My only issue was people being in my business. In a way, it felt as if I was betraying my father's trust. Snow had attempted to call me three times, but I had chosen not to answer. I was a mess, and I was terrified he'd notice. Everyone was trying to figure out what was going on with my father and uncle's case. I had to check a bitch the other night when she thought she was gonna question us about why we stayed with Ma.

Those hoes were about to be tight I planned on murdering these niggas pockets. Ain't a nigga in this city who wouldn't do whatever to fuck me. I wasn't being cocky, I was just being real. Niggas loved bad bitches.

I grabbed my Anastasia Beverly Hills brow wiz and quickly ran it across my arched eyebrows. The smokey nude eyeshadow and long individual lashes had me looking like a baby doll. Tonight, I wasn't going crazy with the makeup because I knew we were gonna be dancing. I finished my look with a nude coat of MAC lip gloss.

"Gucci, come hurr right quick before these niggas pull up," Ma screamed from her bedroom.

I grabbed my iPhone and looked down at the notifications flooding my home screen. I didn't bother checking them. We had been promoting tonight so hard my phone died earlier from the direct messages. I stopped at the dresser we shared and sprayed some Bond number 9 before I left our bedroom.

As I walked toward Ma's bedroom, I felt the pill kick in. My energy was on ten, and for the first time tonight, I felt relaxed. I paused at the door and admired Ma's room. She had it decked out in a queen theme with mirrors on her ceiling. This was the biggest room in the house. She knocked the walls down and combined two bedrooms. Fendi was sitting on Ma's king-size canopy bed, her long red weave fell in barrel curls down her back. "Dior you are killing it sis." Fendi said snapping a picture of Dior.

She was right. Until now, I had never seen Dior dressed so

sexy. I watched Dior admire herself in the full-length mirror. She no longer looked like a teenager. Baby girl was giving grown woman. Her gold strappy heels made her appear taller. The pink see-through crop top with the Dior Logo stopped right under her chest, exposing her washboard abs. She had on some light blue ripped booty shorts that cupped her round ass. The outfit was just the right amount of sex appeal for the pictures we were about to take.

"Y'all bitches about to kill it tonight!" Kash smiled as she inhaled a fat ass blunt. The blonde blunt-cut wig looked cute as hell against her brown skin. Kash didn't fuck with weaves or wigs, so I was surprised when she allowed Dior to put the wig on her.

"Nah, bitch. We all about to eat. Look at that ass!" I looked her up and down. Kash normally didn't dress sexually, but tonight, she had on a Versace bra and the matching panties with some see-through biker shorts and a pair of thigh-high stiletto boots.

"Y'all hurry up and take a picture and post that shit. Watch them niggas be lined up." Ma waved us over to where she had a ring light set up. When she said we were keeping all money in house, she wasn't playing. She refused to hire a photographer, so she went to Best Buy earlier and invested in a new camera and tripod.

"I can't believe we doin this shit!" Dior pouted as she stood next to me with her arms folded across her chest.

"Dior, stop bitchin. I ain't waste all this money for you to fuck this shit up Now, smile so y'all can post these pictures on your Instagram. All them damn followers y'all got, watch how the money come in tonight." Ma flipped her long box braids and pointed her finger at Dior.

The four of us posed in front of the camera like we were doing a professional photoshoot. Ma started following this designer on Instagram named Shane Justin and wanted to recreate one of his photoshoots, so we all lined up and strutted our most nasty provocative walks until she told us she was finished.

While Dior helped Ma edit our photos, I sat on the bed talking shit with Fendi and Kash.

"What y'all know about Sosa?" I asked casually, not trying to sound pressed. Ever since I ran into him at my mother's funeral, he had been on my mind.

"That nigga get to the bag, but all his bitches like to fight, so be ready," Ma's nosey ass said from her desk. I had to remind myself my grandmother wasn't a bake you some cookies type of granny. This bitch knew every dope boy in the city and who they were fucking.

"Girl, his ass crazy as hell, but she right, that nigga is next up after my nigga, of course," Fendi said with a smile on her face. That nigga Bag had this girl's mind gone. Ever since we moved into Ma's, she would dip off with his ass at the end of the night and return home with a fucked up head and a pocket full of money. I didn't know him like that, so I didn't know if she was being delusional or if that nigga was serious about her.

"Girl, bye. Sosa right up there with Bag. That nigga just low key. If I was twenty years younger, I would have both them niggas run a train on me." Our mouths dropped, and Ma looked at us like we were crazy. "Fuck y'all heffas looking at me like that for? If you don't know, them get money niggas like a freaky bitch. Ain't that right, Dior?" Ma burst out laughing and tried to high-five Dior, who shook her head at her. "Fuck you too, stuck up bitch! How much longer have we got on these pictures? I need to start prepping my chicken!" Ma asked, pouring herself another shot of Henny.

"I'm done I just sent the pictures to y'all emails. Let me know if you got them before I shut the computer down."

Once the email came through to my phone, I browsed through them. I couldn't front, we all looked good as hell. There wasn't one picture that wasn't a ten.

"Post that one, Gucci, cause I'm posting this one. You see a bitch ass!" Fendi said, leaning over my shoulder. Dior walked over to us and sat down next to me. She had her mouth turned up, and I knew she was about to start with her bullshit. "I'm not posting that to my page. I don't want my man tripping!"

Dior shook her head at the picture. Ma looked over at her like she was crazy. I had to bite my lip. At this moment, everything was hilarious to me.

"Hold up, I need a cigarette and a drink for this shit!" Ma shook her head, grabbed the box of Newports, and quickly lit a cigarette. "One of y'all pour me a drink while I school this girl!" she said, pointing at the fresh bottle of Hennessey sitting on her dresser. The bottle she originally was sipping out of was gone. Kash was the closest to the bottle, so she poured Ma's drink. I sat back and waited for Ma to rip Dior. How you gonna agree to dance but be scared to take some provocative pictures.

"How much money you got?" Ma asked as she grabbed the cup from Kash and took a quick sip. "Don't answer that shit.

You broke as hell. You just asked me for money for those damn school pictures. Now what yo goody two shoe ass needs to do is bag one of these get money niggas. The hell you don't got a ring on your finger. He shouldn't be on your Gram!"

Fendi leaned over to me.

"Is she quoting Cardi b?" Her ass was tipsy as hell, so her whisper came out loud as hell.

I busted out laughing, and Ma cut her eyes at us so fast, I quickly straightened up. Shit, I wasn't about to have her ass preaching to me and blowing my high.

"Oh, my God. Y'all, look!" Kash yelled from the floor-length window. We all ran over to the window, and I prayed it wasn't the police coming to snatch her ass up. My mouth dropped when I saw all the foreign cars lined up down the street.

"Bitch, we done brought the whole city out!" Fendi yelled excitedly as she started twerking to the music that was playing downstairs.

"Oh, a bitch about to make some money tonight!" I couldn't wait to get my hands on some money. This was the longest I ever went being broke, but from the looks of the early crowd, that shit was about to change.

"Come on, Kash, we got to go downstairs before these niggas start making a scene. Y'all bitches get your shit together. The dancers always come out at one thirty. Y'all got an hour and a half. Don't be late." Ma and Kash hurried out of the room leaving me, Fendi, and Dior behind.

"Come on, y'all. Come in me and Kash's room. I'm about to turn the fuck up before we go downstairs." Fendi's ass was already on ten, but shit, the way I was feeling, I might join her in whatever ratchet activities she had planned.

Thankfully, we all had our makeup, hair, and nails done and were already dressed in our first set of outfits. Desire, the girl who made the outfits, came through in the clutch. I couldn't stop admiring myself in Fendi's mirror. The hot pink bandeau net top was lined with a colorful Louis Vuitton monogram pattern. The shredded shorts in the matching Louis material had my ass sitting up just right.

"Shut my door. I don't need my mother in my business," Fendi said as she walked over to the little dresser next to her bed. The bag she pulled out was filled with perks, coke, and weed.

"Damn, bitch. Let me find out you the plug." I sat on the edge of her bed and began rocking back and forth to the sound of Future.

"Y'all don't need to be getting too fucked up!" Dior said with a frown on her face. I ignored her. If she wanted to shake her ass sober, that was on her. A bitch felt good, but I could always feel better. I was normally not a talkative person. The liquor and the perks brought out a different side of me.

"I'm serious, y'all. Don't be drinking no drinks no nigga's give you."

"Come on, Dior. We know what we doing. We ain't slow. Matter fact, here, drink some of this. You uptight," I tried to hand her my red plastic cup.

"I don't drink, and you know that!" Dior pushed the cup back toward me and folded her arms across her chest.

"You do today, bitch!" Fendi giggled from the bed, dipping her red stiletto nail into the bag of coke.

""The liquor will help you loosen up, Dior. It won't kill your ass. You won't be nervous anymore if you just drink it." Dior hesitantly grabbed my cup. She slowly brought it up to her mouth and took a quick sip.

"Nah, bitch. Gulp that shit down!" I said, frowning at her.

She took the drink to the head and passed me back the empty cup.

"You happy?' Dior handed me the cup and walked out of the room. She most likely was about to go call her broke-ass boyfriend and talk shit.

"Gucci, you want some?" Fendi asked, holding the baggie up toward me. I looked at the bag. It was no secret I did coke from time to time, who the fuck didn't? Please don't judge me until you mix the shit with some Patron your damn self. "Girl, you might as well take a bump and stop staring at the bag like you crazy. It's not like you never tried it before but hurry up if you gonna do it. I don't need Dior running her mouth to anyone about me giving you this shit."

"Let me see the bag and go lock the door."

I reached for the bag and waited for Fendi to come back from locking the door. The last time I tried coke was a year ago when we were in Miami. I promised myself it was gonna be a one-time thing. Fuck it. I was about to be on one tonight. I dipped my finger into the pure white cocaine that resembled snowflakes.

"Don't kill my shit. That's fish scale. You don't need too much to get you there," Fendi said, watching me. I followed her instructions and scooped a small amount inside my nail. I put it up to my nose and took a quick sniff and repeated the process with my other nostril. We did two more bumps and closed the bag back up. It took no time for me to feel the familiar drip that let me know the coke was working. As the thick mixture slid from the back of my nose down my throat, Dior banged on the door.

Fendi stopped at her mirror to check her nose while I pulled out my compact mirror to make sure I had no residue on me. I gave the bag back to Fendi and went to let Dior back in the bedroom.

Dior walked back into the room her face was relaxed. "Let me get another shot. I'm nervous as fuck!"

Dior approached me and grabbed the bottle off the dresser. She filled each of our cups before she started drinking hers.

"Girl, bye. We can dance, all our asses are fat, and these niggas love us. Fuck you nervous for?" I asked, sipping on my drink. The coke and perk along with the Henny had me feeling invincible.

"That's not the point. I'm scared as fuck of being on that stage and no one tipping our ass."

"Girl, Ma don't even have a real stage, so you don't have to worry about that."

"Yeah, that would be some embarrassing shit, but don't worry, I hit my niggas up and they already said they gonna show love! Fendi opened the baggie back up and took another bump of her coke. If I thought Dior wouldn't run her mouth, I would have taken one more hit to make sure I was good for the night. One thing about coke was that shit made you want more, and it felt good as hell while you were partying.

"I think we gonna be good. I done seen this ugly ass hoe that look like Young Thug make a bag in this bitch," I added, checking my Instagram page. The picture I just posted already had four thousand likes. It hadn't even been an hour, but a bitch was popping.

We all fell on the bed and laughed. It'd been so long since we had a moment like this, and it felt good. I wasn't thinking about my mama and aunt being dead, my uncle and daddy situation, or where the hell Uncle Dro was. I was feeling marvelous, and all I wanted to do was go downstairs and turn the fuck up.

"Let me get a perk, Fendi. I need something a little stronger than this Henny right now," Dior said, shocking the fuck out of me. Dior ran track and prided herself on living a healthy lifestyle, but for once, she was on the same shit as us.

"Oh, shit, bitch. You about to be on one tonight!" Fendi reached in the dresser and grabbed the baggie. Breaking a fifteen in half, she handed it to Dior. "Take this half first. When you ready, I'll give you the other half."

I lit the Newport I had gotten from Ma earlier and looked at Fendi with a smirk. "Yo ass high as hell. You ain't stopped talking."

"Bitch, I feel good as hell. Y'all ready to go downstairs? You know Ma about to call and see where we are at."

"Let's go get this money, bitch!" Dior said tipsily from the liquor.

"Hold up, Fendi. Break me another piece!" I said. While she

got her baggie out, I applied the bond number nine lotion she had on the dresser all over my thick thighs. Then I bent down in front of the floor-length mirror to make sure my pussy lips weren't coming out of this little ass outfit.

"Here!" Fendi placed the pill in my palm. I took a sip of my drink and was careful not to mess up my lipstick. We grabbed the money bags that matched our outfits. It was time to get this money.

Ma's living room was packed to capacity. Girls were twerking to Est Gee's "5500 Degrees" while niggas stood around smoking blunts and drinking premium liquor. I stepped into the living room and nodded my head at a couple of familiar faces. I was feeling the effect of the drugs and knew I had made the right decision upstairs. There were so many people packed inside the house, I knew I wouldn't have been able to do this sober.

"Y'all ready to do this?" Fendi yelled over the music.

"Fuck it, let's show these bitches who we are!" Dior flipped her long ponytail and grabbed our hands, pulling us toward the pole Ma had installed in the middle of the living room.

"Let's go. Y'all bitch's follow my lead and remember we are Snows. We don't show fear!" Fendi yelled over the music.

As we walked towards the pole, I purposely looked into each man's eyes I passed. I wanted to give them the impression that they had a chance with me. That was something I noticed the other dancers did when I watched them work.

Fendi and Dior reached the pole first and were bent over

shaking their asses in front of the pole. There was a crowd of niggas from the west side raining stacks on them.

I locked eyes with Bae, a boss nigga from the west side. He looked me up and down, nodding his head in approval. I smirked when he held up a stack of ones and mouthed *come here*. I don't know if it was the coke, the stacks of money in his hands, or the way his legs were spread as he casually bopped his head to the beat. I had never paid Bae much attention. We followed each other on social media, but that was about it. Tonight, I realized his big chocolate ass was fine. He had on a Forest Green Palms Angel sweat suit with an iced-out diamond Cuban around his neck.

"Rockstar" by Jayda Youngan started blasting through the speakers. When I got close to Bae he stepped back. The blunt dangled out of his mouth as he began raining ones down at me. Placing both hands on the cold floor, I bounced my left ass cheek slowly to the beat. Bae slapped a pile of one's on my ass, and that shit made me bounce my ass harder. I ran my hands across the back of my legs and pulled my ass cheeks apart so he could have a good view of my fat pussy print. Slowly and seductively, I rocked myself up in a standing position and turned around. Bae took a sip of his drink and started rapping along to the song.

Have you ever fucked a rockstar?

He broke the band on another stack of hundreds and let them rain like it was nothing.

Dior's flexible ass busted down into a Chinese split. She rocked her head and body back and forth to the beat as she played with her nipples, causing the niggas in front of her to go crazy. Fendi grabbed a trash bag and began throwing our money inside. There were a couple other dancers, but the focus was on us. Ma changed her mind last minute when they told her they drove up from Columbia South Carolina.

I continued dancing and looked around the room to figure out where we should go next.

"Gucci, look up at the bar. The Trap Boyz are here, and so is your boo," Fendi yelled over the music. I promised after tonight I was gonna teach her ass how to whisper properly. I looked over at the bar and noticed the Trap Boyz posted up throwing ones. In the middle was Sosa sipping straight from a bottle of 1942. The first time I saw him he was in a suit, but damn this nigga was looking like a whole snack. His locs were styled in rope twist, and he had on a pair of Amiri jeans that sagged slightly, showing the label of his Versace boxers and a Glock tucked in his waist. He kept it simple with a white wife-beater and a bust down Rolex on his wrist.

Sosa rapped along to G Herbos "2 Chains" and threw a stack of ones on the dancer in front of him. Before I could look away, his eyes locked with mine. A feeling of lust washed over me. He raised his hand and motioned for me to come to him.

Normally, any other nigga would have to approach me first, but Sosa was the one nigga I had been dying to run into. Shit, he was just as popular as me, and we definitely would be the cities Hove and Bey if we ever hooked up. I grabbed my dance bag off the ground and walked over to where Dior and Fendi were now dancing.

"Aye, Sosa just told me to come over to the bar!" I yelled excitedly over the music.

"Let's go. I think Bag is with him." Fendi bent down and grabbed the pile of money off the ground and started stuffing it inside the trash bag. She wasn't moving fast enough for me, so I started helping her. By the time we were finished, we had two garbage bags filled with money. As I threw my personal money bag inside the garbage bag, I looked over and noticed Dior still bent over shaking her ass.

"Let's go, Dior!" I nudged her and motioned for her to follow us.

"I told you this shit be lit!" I said when Dior walked over to us. She was the only one of us who had never gone downstairs when Ma was open.

"Girl, I was thinking you were capping, but nah, this shit is fun as hell."

Trying to get over to the bar was a task since the room was packed. Stepping over the girls and niggas dancing, I grew excited when we got closer. There were girls dancing for the Trap Boyz and they had an annoyed look on their faces as we approached.

"Aye, we good!" Sosa said, dismissing the light skinned dancer who wasn't trying to move.

She rolled her eyes at me, but she didn't cause a scene. That was a good thing because I was on one, and we were in my grandmother's house. I would have beat her ass and continued my night without a problem. While they picked up their money, I leaned over at the bar and had Kash pass me three bottles of water.

"That nigga's boss as fuck. You better get him, cousin!" Dior said, looking over at Sosa. I laughed. My eyes were locked on Sosa's face. That nigga was playa as fuck.

Once the dancers walked away, he grabbed my arm and pulled me closer to him

"I thought that was yo mean ass. What you drinking, ma?" Sosa asked, pointing at the table filled with liquor.

"You can pour me some Patron."

"What about your girls?" he asked, pouring me a double shot.

"They good." I took a sip and fanned my face. When Lil Baby's "On Me" came on, I spun around and started shaking my ass directly in front of him.

"Damn, that shit fat!" I heard him say under his breath. The sound of his deep voice did something to me. This nigga was about to be my man, and he didn't even know it. I threw my ass in a circle, and he pulled me back up confusing me.

"You ain't got to do all that," he whispered in my ear. I leaned my head back against his chest and wound my hips slowly in front of him. He was still throwing that paper without me having to work too hard. I appreciated that this was our first night dancing. I was low-key tired. I never expected this shit to be that hard, but it took skill to shake your ass, look cute, and pick up money without busting your ass in these tall ass heels.

I knew Sosa was getting to the money, but tonight, he was acting a fool. This crazy nigga wasn't even breaking the bands. He was just dropping the stacks on me. He started popping bands on me while he drank his 1942 from the bottle. Looking up, I noticed the out-of-town dancers had gotten naked. That shit was sad because the attention was still on us, and we hadn't taken off shit.

"Thank you, Sosa!" I bit my lip as I felt his dick get hard behind me. Thank God that niggas shit wasn't little.

"You good, ma. I just wanted to come and show love!"

As bad as I didn't want to, I excused myself so I could go change and use the bathroom. He nodded his head at me and went back to partying. I bent down to pick up my money, and then walked over to where Fendi and Dior were. They had two of the Trap Boyz stuck as they threw more ones on them.

"Aye, I got to use the bathroom," I yelled out to Fendi and Dior.

"Shit, me too. Let's hurry and get the money up!" Dior said, tapping Fendi.

Fendi leaned back and whispered something into Bag's ear. He nodded his head, smacked her on the ass, and walked back over to where Sosa was standing.

I rushed into Fendi's room and headed straight to the bathroom. Thank God we didn't have to use the bathroom downstairs, or I would have peed on myself trying to wait in that long ass line. I peed as quickly as possible. Shit, it was hard being high as fuck wearing heals and trying to get a g string down.

I flushed the toilet, walked to the sink to wash my hands, and stepped out of the way for Dior to use the bathroom.

"Bitch, hurry up, damn!" Fendi stood against the wall, tapping her foot impatiently as she waited for Dior to finish.

"I'm trying to get the outfit down!" Dior whined.

"Bitch, move Ill pee in the tub!" Fendi barked.

I swore that hoe didn't have any home training. I left out the bathroom and went back into our room. While I waited on them to come out from the bathroom, I freshened my makeup. We had been dancing nonstop for two hours, and I wasn't feeling the wet look my face was giving.

"Y'all hurry up so I can freshen your faces before we go back downstairs." I grabbed my makeup wipes, foundation, and eyeshadow. It didn't take me any time to remove the makeup and do a light beat. Once I finished applying my makeup, I walked over to my bathroom to brush my teeth.

While I was in my room, I removed my shoes and decided it would be best to change outfits while I was up here.

"I swear this dancing shit is like a drug," Dior said, walking back into the room. Dior removed her outfit, grabbed a pack of baby wipes, and started wiping her body down.

Kash walked in the room with another girl who looked young as fuck. "Aye, she's dancing, but she came by herself. Ma said let her get dressed in here."

We looked over at the girl who was standing behind Kash. She looked familiar, but I wasn't sure where I knew her from.

Kash walked out of the room to go back downstairs, and the girl entered our room with a scared look on her face. She didn't say shit to us. I couldn't tell if it was because she was nervous or stuck up. While I applied my makeup, I watched her through the mirror. When I first saw her, I thought she looked like a little girl, but now that she was getting undressed, I could see she was working with something. The girl dropped her dance bag on the floor and pulled her t-shirt over her head. Her titties were small and perky, but when she slid her joggers off and I got a look at her fat ass, I understood why she was here.

"Here, y'all!" Fendi walked back in the room with her little baggie and handed me and Dior the other half of our pills from earlier.

"Are those perks or xans ?" the girl asked, looking over at Fendi.

"These are 15s but—"

"Are they official?" she asked, cutting me off and walking closer to the bed.

"Yeah, they official!" I said, placing one on my tongue.

"I never tried a 15, but I'm down tonight. When I tell you these hoes worked my nerves. How much are they?" the girl asked, pulling a knot of money out of her joggers.

"Nah, boo. You can take half. If that shit works for you, I'll give you the other half. I ain't no hater, but they affect everyone differently," Fendi yelled over the music that was blasting from downstairs.

"I took a half earlier. The only thing it did was give me more energy. Don't be nervous."

Dior said.

"Watch, your ass about to be floating," I said, brushing through my hair.

"Damn. Y'all outfits cute as fuck!" the girl said, taking the pill and sitting down on the bed.

If I wasn't high, I would have cursed her ass out. She seemed cool, but not cool enough to be sitting on my bed. Our outfits were cute as hell. The three of us had slingshots on in different neon colors with diamond blinged-out U Bras.

"We got it from this lady who sells outfits. You can get one if you want," Dior said, being too damn nice. Shit, we weren't in the position to be handing out free outfits.

"Oh, nah. I'm good. I can't really waste no money right now."

"Girl, you good. Just pay us when you get it. Its mad money down there, and I know if Ma let you up here, you good peoples!" Fendi said, tossing an outfit at her.

The girl grabbed the Ziploc bag with the outfit in it and smiled at us. "Shit, let me hurry up and get changed. I'm so mad the girls I normally dance with left me. When I tell you this is my last time fucking with them, I put that on my mama. I'm out here trying to get it, and these bitches playing games. Mind you, they told me they weren't working at the last minute, but I go on Instagram and see them bitches in Raleigh at the club."

"Oh, I thought you were talking about one of them ratchet bitches downstairs."

The girl bust out laughing. "Hell nah. One of them hoes tried to steal my money last time I was here. Ma ass cursed them the fuck out and got my money back. I'm Star, by the way."

"I'm Gucci this is—"

"Fendi and Dior. Girl, everybody knows y'all. I just ain't know y'all dance."

Fendi's phone rang while Star was talking, and she answered it on speaker. "Yall hurry the hell up. Some more niggas just walked in, and they got money." She yelled over the base of the music.

When we got back downstairs, the house was more crowded than when we first went upstairs if that shit was even possible.

"Let's go get our drinks then we're about to work the room!" Fendi yelled, walking toward the bar.

Chapter Seven
SOSA

I couldn't remember the last time I was inside Ma's. A nigga didn't club, so the fact that I was standing here throwing ones was unusual for me. When Kash hit me up earlier today, I wasn't surprised. I knew Bishop had gotten knocked, and his camp wasn't fucking with her. I told her I would get back to her with a time and place for us to discuss business. I didn't decide to come to Ma's until I overheard my little niggas talking about the Snow Girls dancing. When they told me that shit, I didn't believe it. We were talking about the princesses of the streets, who rarely entertained niggas, shaking their ass. My nigga, Dee, pulled up the Instagram post, and I realized these niggas were spitting facts. Since I ran into Gucci, lil mama had been on my mind, so I decided to kill two birds with one stone and pop up. If a nigga in the city claimed they wouldn't wife her they were cappin. Most pretty bitches had been run through. I did my homework and didn't know one nigga who smashed. Snow kept her out the way, and that made her even rarer.

I pulled out my phone and shot Kash a quick message. My paranoia was fucking with me, and that meant it was time for me to slide. Whatever she had to say, she better come on with it. While I waited for her to text me back, I finished my drink. A bubble popped up on my phone

Kash: *Meet me upstairs in the private room in 10 minutes.*

Where I was positioned, I had a perfect view of the room. I could see who was coming and going. Kash was behind the bar serving drinks, and I couldn't front, I was interested to find out what she had to say. This was the first time I had seen her dressed provocatively. The tight black shorts hugged her slim-thick frame. When she turned around to grab a bottle off the shelf, I noticed her ass was hanging out. I knew a lot of niggas thought she was a dyke based on the way she carried herself. Kash was different. You ain't gonna catch her in a niggas face. She was about her bread. That shit was sexy as fuck to see her little ass barking out orders to her workers.

"Aye, I'll be right back!" I looked over at my cousin, Bag, who had a badass stripper in front of him.

"You good?" Bag asked, pushing shorty out the way. Ever since I could remember, my cousin had been overprotective of me. When my pops died, his father stepped up and assisted my mother with raising my little ass.

"Yeah, I'm goin to see what Kash wants. If anyone comes looking for me, let em know I bounced."

Bag was the only person in the streets I would trust to

know my exact location. He looked over at me with a knowing look and pulled me in for a dap. Bag's the only person I ever told that I fucked Kash. I'm not one to brag on my dick. But Kash was a different story. I was young when we fucked, and I couldn't hold it in.

"You wild, boy! Let me know when you about to bounce so we can roll out. We already on enemy territory. We ain't doing none of that disappearing shit tonight." That nigga swore the only reason I was helping Kash was to fuck.

It took me a minute to walk through the crib. Niggas were dapping me up left and right. Then, the bitches who weren't used to seeing me at Ma's were stopping me every couple of steps to try to shoot they shot.

I walked up the back set of stairs. I remembered how to get to the back rooms because I done slid back here a couple of times to get my dick sucked when I was younger. I'd give it to Ma, she made sure her shit was always clean. Before I entered the room, I pulled my strap out and peeked my head inside. The room had a fruity ass smell and various candles set around the furniture, giving it a dark sexy vibe. I sat down on the queen-sized bed and waited for Kash to come upstairs.

A few minutes later, I heard footsteps approaching the door. I had my nine on my lap, so if it was anyone other than Kash, they had a surprise waiting for them. The door opened slowly, and I could tell from the look on her face she didn't appreciate me having my burner out.

"You thought I would set you up?" Kash frowned and shut the door behind her.

"You already know this game is cold. Can't never be too cautious but fuck all that. What you got to say?" I asked, cutting straight to the point. Kash had been avoiding me for years. I thought we were better than that, but she proved otherwise. We fucked once back in the day. At the time, I didn't know she was a virgin until I was about to put my dick in. Shorty ain't say more than two words to me since then, and I was matching her energy.

"Damn, your ass is still rude as hell!"

"Stop stalling and say what you got to say!"

"Ain't no one stalling," she said, waving her hand

"What we doing? I know you ain't call me back here to give me some pussy."

She cut her eyes at me. It was dark, but I was still able to see her face flush and her body tense up. "You know I never fucked anyone after that!" she said softly, sitting down next to me.

"Damn, a nigga was that bad?" I asked laughing, knowing damn well that wasn't even an option. My dick game was crazy, and my shit had them bitches going crazy even when I was broke.

"No, you weren't. I just was so focused on the grind that a nigga was the last thing on my mind."

"I feel you. A bitch is the last thing on my mind, so what's up, Kash?" I pulled a sack of weed out of my pocket along with a cigar and began rolling it. I was not a mind reader, so I didn't want to assume what I thought she wanted. All I knew was her ass was close to me, the smell of her perfume was fucking with me, and after all them shots of liquor, a nigga was horny. I wasn't trying to take it there with her ass tonight, though.

I fired up my blunt and leaned back on the bed. Kash rolled over and grabbed the blunt out of my mouth. Shorty was tipsy, so when she reached for it, her titty popped out the little ass bra she had on. Our eyes locked, and she rolled her hazel eyes and placed my blunt in her mouth. She didn't bother to put her titty back in her bra. I could feel the passion and lust radiating from her.

"Fuck you rolling your eyes at? That shit might work with them other niggas—" Before I could finish, she shocked the shit out of me and leaned over and placed her juicy lips on mine. I grabbed her by the neck and pulled her little ass on top of me. She spread her legs around me and started grinding to the music that was playing through the wall speakers. My dick came to life at the sight of her pretty chocolate ass winding on top of me.

"This what you wanted?" I ain't wait for her to answer. From the expression on her face, I knew she was struggling with answering. Her little ass titty was staring at me. It was something about nipple piercings that turn me on. When I grabbed her A-cup breast, my big ass hand covered it. I brought it up to my mouth and sucked on it like it was a baby bottle filled with some good ass lean. I traced my tongue around her nipple in circular motions, the coldness of the metal bar made my dick harder.

"Fuck, Sosa!" Kash moaned, leaning her head back slightly. Her lips were stuck giving me a glimpse of the diamond grillz in her mouth. I couldn't help to grab her ass and smack it. Her shit was fatter and slightly heavier since the last time I felt it.

Kash looked up at me, her face was twisted with lust. This

must be some backed-up sexual frustration because I ain't never seen her act like this.

"Fuck me," she moaned in her raspy ass voice.

A part of me wanted to push her off me. A nigga was feeling her little cousin, yet here I was about to stick my dick in her. The blunt that dangled in her hand was seconds from burning me. I snatched the blunt and brought it up to my lips, inhaling the exotic weed slowly. Fuck it. I was single, and now that my dick was hard, I needed to relieve myself before I caught blue balls or some shit. I pushed her off me gently, stood up, and unzipped my jeans. Her mouth dropped when she saw my ten inches pop out at her. Yeah, I was a little nigga the last time we fucked, but this was a different Sosa. The moonlight was creeping in through the sheer curtains. I pulled off her shorts. I licked my lips. Her pussy was fat with no hair on it like she had recently got waxed.

I pulled a Magnum out of my back pocket, ripped it open, and slowly slid it down on my dick. If I had doubts, they were erased when Kash spread her legs, giving me the perfect view of her fat wet pussy.

Lowering myself down on the bed, I pushed her legs open wider and slid my dick up and down her slit. She wasn't lying when she said she ain't had any dick since the time I fucked her. It took me a minute to get inside her walls. When I finally did, I had to stop to prevent myself from nutting. After that, it was over with long hard strokes. I pounded into her little ass.

"Fuck, Sosa!" she moaned so loud in my ear I had to place my hand on her mouth to shut her ass up.

All I could hear was the bed rocking back and forth. My

mind was gone. I ain't had no pussy this good in a minute. The sight of her little ass titties bouncing up and down turned me on. Fuck that, I had to hit this shit from the back. I slid out of her tight ass pussy and almost changed my mind. This would kill any chance I had with Gucci. Fuck it the pussy was so good it was worth the risk. With one swift motion, I positioned her on her knees and pressed her back down, so it was arched how I liked it. I smacked her ass and watched it shake before diving back inside of her. I was a rough nigga, so I wasn't about to be in here making love. Nah, I grabbed the back of her neck and pounded into her. Her ass was a squitter, so a few minutes later, I felt her warm cum through the condom. Her pussy sucked me in deeper, and I busted long and hard inside the condom.

Once we caught our breath and fixed our clothes, I sat back down on the bed, and l sparked the blunt. Neither of us said anything. We just sat back and smoked.

"I can't believe I just fucked you," Kash mumbled.

"You always gonna love this dick, but chill. I know that wasn't your intentions, ma." I was trying to lighten the room before she got weird on me. Yeah, we fucked, but that was it. I had no plans of making this a normal thing.

Kash rolled her hazel eyes and grabbed the blunt out of my mouth and took a pull with her pouty pink lips.

"As you know, my people are locked down—" exhaling the smoke, she continued, "and I need a connect. I'm not trying to work for you or no shit like that, but I do need you to front me some work."

"Was that so hard?" I asked, grabbing my blunt back from

her. "I got you. Just make sure you have my money and we straight," I said, standing up. A nigga was high as fuck and tired after busting that nut.

Three Weeks Later

I rubbed the white hand towel across my forehead and tried to focus on the pile of money in front of me. I was at my trap house nursing a hangover, something I rarely got. My head was pounding from all the liquor I drank last night. Elle's ass was slamming shit and running her mouth, despite me advising her I wasn't in the mood. Once I was finished with this, I planned on going home and sleeping the day away. I grabbed a stack of hundreds and placed it inside the money counter.

"Any other time you can talk to me while you count your money!" Elle fussed.

Slamming the stack of ones down, I looked up at her. Since I walked into the trap, she had been on one. Her hair was pulled back in a ponytail displaying her flawless face. She must have come straight over from the gym because she was dressed down in Nike Yoga pants and a sports bra.

"I got a lot on my mind, Elle, and this ain't helping it." I frowned at her. Shorty was tweaking, walking back and forth slamming shit like I didn't tell her I had a headache.

"I don't got time to deal with your insecurities. Bounce!" I said, pointing at the door.

Elle walked over to the table with her fist balled tightly. I could feel the steam coming from her as she tapped her foot and looked me in the eyes.

"Oh, nigga, you gonna hear what I have to say. One of your bitches keeps playing on my phone. It's probably Jada's broke ass, or let's not forget Wynter, the bitch you took to Cali!" Elle screamed at me like she lost her mind.

"Yo, I just told you I had mad shit on my mind and you questioning me over a bitch. Damn, you made me fuck up my count." I snapped, pushing the pile of money away from me. I grabbed my Black and Mild out of the ashtray. I lit the black and looked Elle up and down. Might as well have this conversation with her. It was long overdue.

"You and your fucking insecurities is the reason you could never be my bitch! You keep making little remarks about Jada, but guess what? I bet you her ass would be doing everything to relieve my stress instead of adding to it."

Elle let out a harsh breath, rolled her eyes at me, and tugged on her ponytail. "Insecurities. Fuck that reverse psychology bullshit. Them hoes could never be me on their best day! Since they are so much better than me, call one of them hoes to come and hustle your shit."

I wiped my white rag across my forehead and didn't bother to respond to her ignorant ass. I wasn't about to go back and forth with her. I spoke my peace. It was her decision on what she wanted to do. It was not like I was holding a gun to her head, forcing her to deal with my shit.

My mind was on more pressing issues. Earlier today, my cousin, Pam, hit me up about something she overheard at work. She was a paralegal who worked downtown at the courthouse. I was the one who helped her when she was in college, so she always made sure to let me know when she heard any chatter downtown. Pam put me up on game, when she over-heard her boss talking about a snitch who had valuable information that could bring down the Trap Boyz. That shit had been on my mind since we spoke earlier. Elle and her feelings were the last thing on a nigga's mind.

"Right, Sosa. You think I haven't heard about you taking all these bitches out? Whenever I want to do something with you it's always an excuse!" she snapped.

Sitting back, I kept my face blank. The shit she was saying had me looking at her sideways. Elle was begging for my attention, and now she had it. While I smoked my black, I took the time to look at her, and I was not speaking on her physical. There were certain traits I didn't like in people. Jealousy, gossiping, and low energy... All the things I hated Elle was currently displaying. I didn't know what changed with us that had her so deep in her feelings.

I watched Elle walk away toward the counter where she had batches of crack drying. The smell of the dope was fucking with my head. "Open the window and air this bitch out." Instead of Elle opening the window, she turned to look at me over the shoulder and went back to cooking the work. I watched her grab a fresh pyrex, add some coke and baking soda, and place it inside the boiling water. Her ass jiggled with each step she took, and I could tell she wasn't wearing panties. Any other day, I would have had her bent over, but she killed my mood with her interrogations

While she cooked the work, I got up and headed to the living room to take a quick nap. I had taken a bc powder earlier and was waiting on that shit to kick in. With everything going on in the streets, I wasn't comfortable leaving Elle by herself, no matter how pissed off I was with her.

I didn't know how long I was knocked out for, but I was fully awake when I felt something wet land on me.

"So, this ain't you, nigga? Since you wanna play dumb?" Elle ran up on me and shoved her phone in my face.

It took me a moment to focus. "Back up out my face before I hurt you." I said. Elle backed up a little bit so I could get up. When I did, I removed my shirt and looked up at her. I couldn't read her fucking eyes. They looked sad with the tears, but I was no dumb nigga. I saw anger in them shits.

"I fucking hate you! I wish yo ass would die, nigga. Watch, you gonna get what you fucking deserve!" Elle was screaming, and she had tears falling down her face. I was still disoriented from being woken up out of my sleep that it took me a minute to figure out what the fuck was going on. I snatched the phone out her hand to see what had her bugging. It was a picture of me and this chick I used to fuck with at the Casino.

"You wanna play, nigga! Let's fucking play!" she screamed, running into the kitchen. The sound of pans slamming against the wall made me jump up. Fuck that phone and whatever she saw inside it. If she was fucking with my work I was going to show her a different side of me.

"Then you got the nerve to fucking sit in my face and lie to me!"

Fuck what she was talking about. The sight of my bricks splattered all over the kitchen had me ready to kill her ass. Elle stood in the middle of the kitchen looking like she was possessed. Her chest was moving up and down like she had just run a race, and she had tears running down her face mixing in with the snot coming from her nose.

"Bitch, you done lost your fucking mind! I don't give a fuck what you talking about. You playing with my money now." I didn't like to hit women, but this bitch was making it hard for me today. We stood glaring at each other before she snapped her head in my direction.

"Fuck you, nigga. I don't have to deal with your shit."

My eyes went toward the black garbage bag on the floor that had the remaining work in it.

"Oh, that's all you give a fuck about, huh?" she snarled. I ran toward the bag just as she charged toward it herself. Elle was little as hell standing at about four foot eleven inches, if I was guessing, so she wasn't able to do shit when I grabbed her by the back of her neck.

Elle kicked her legs in every direction. When that didn't work, she tried to bite my arm to get out of the chokehold. I squeezed my arm around her neck like I was a UFC fighter and rocked her back in forth.

"I can't breathe, Sosa!" she gagged, but I wasn't letting her go until I got my point across. She should have known fucking with my work was like fucking with her life. If she had been any other bitch, I would have broken her neck. I couldn't front. I was still tempted to snap that shit when I looked at the coke laying all over the room.

"You not my fucking bitch, Elle! Yeah, that's me in the fucking picture. I'm trying to figure out why that's your business," I snapped, letting her neck go and dropping her to the ground.

Her stupid ass was balled up gripping her legs and screaming all types of crazy shit.

"Oh, so now I'm not your fucking bitch, nigga? When I'm fucking and sucking your dick, am I not your bitch?" Elle screamed, wiping her tears with the back of her hand.

Wow, this was the type of shit I expected from Jada, but Elle shocked me with this one. It wasn't all about her ruining my product. I had the money stacked up to replace whatever I was short, but this bitch knew there was a drought, and it was hard as hell for me to get my hands on quality work.

"Get yo shit and bounce before I forget who you are to me." I turned around and grabbed a broom to begin cleaning the mess up.

"Nah fuck that. Ain't no bounce and leave," she screamed. Elle jumped off the ground and charged me, raining blows on me. "Am I not your bitch when I'm out here in these fucking trenches pushing your work? When you caught your first body, did I not ride down that dirt road helping you toss the gun and your outfit?"

That was it. I snapped and backhanded her across the room. A nigga was under so much pressure, and her stupid ass pushed me over the top.

"You talking about a bitch, Elle. A nigga trying to figure out who the fuck is snitching on me. Bitch, I'm starting to think it's you. Is it? Huh?"

The sound of her crying irritated me. She was in here

speaking about bodies, shit that you ain't never supposed to repeat.

"Fuck you, nigga. Now you putting your hands on me! Something you promised you would never do. Nah, I ain't snitching, fuck boy, but I hope they bury your ass under the jail," she spat.

I raced over to where she was and pulled my pistol out. With one swift motion, I flipped the safety off and put it under her chin.

"Elle if you ever repeat what the fuck you helped me do again, I'm a put you on a t-shirt. Do you fucking understand me?"

I waited for her to nod her head before removing my gun from under her chin. I walked over to the table, grabbed my phone, and hit one of the shorties I normally used to cook up. Baby girl had classes scheduled for the rest of the day, but when I added an extra thousand onto her normal pay, she told me she would be here in less than thirty minutes.

Elle grabbed her shit and scurried out the door without saying a word to me.

While I waited for ol girl to arrive, I pulled my out and went to my contacts. Before I left Ma's, Gucci placed her number in my phone. I ain't have shit to do today so I decided to hit her up. I clicked on her name and waited for her to answer. While I was waiting for her to answer, I began cleaning up the mess Elle made.

"Hello?" she answered. It sounded like either I woke her up, or she was just getting up.

"Stop playing like yo ass sleep. It's damn near three

o'clock." I raised the volume on my ear buds and continued sweeping.

"Who said I was playing? I'm tired as hell! Why you sound like that?"

"How I sound?"

"Like yo ass just got finished fighting or fucking. You breathing hard as hell."

I smirked. it was cute she picked up on a nigga's mood.

"Nah, baby girl. A nigga just had a minor setback, but I'm good now."

"Word, I feel you. That's all you can do. Shit, all I've been having is setbacks, but I'm sure you know that." Her voice drifted away. I did know what she was talking about, but I was not no gossiping ass nigga. If she chose to tell me her problems, then I would give my opinion.

"Sounds like we both need a getaway. You coming with me?"

The phone went silent, and I wasn't surprised. I was sure Gucci's ass wasn't used to dealing with a real nigga.

"Where we going?" she finally asked.

"I don't know, baby girl. We'll figure that out when we get to the airport."

Gucci giggled. "Sosa, I don't have clothes to go out of town. If you would have hit me up a couple of months ago, I would have been down."

What she was talking wasn't about shit. All that material-istic shit she lost could be replaced. I could have had any bitch hop on a flight with me, but I didn't want anyone but Gucci, and I wasn't taking no for an answer.

"You don't need shit but your ID! We'll shop when we land. I'm about to pull up. Be ready." I didn't wait for her to respond. Even if I had to run in Ma's and drag her ass out, she was going. My mind was all over the place, and Lil Gucci was about to be a nigga's peace.

Chapter Eight

I was lying down trying to focus on this week's episode of *Power* with Fendi and Dior. Every few minutes I would doze off and finally gave up on watching it. I was sleeping good as hell until they decided to have a movie date in our bedroom. Cocaine had proven to be an effective way, for me to cope with the nightmares caused by my mother's death. I was happy they did wake me up, otherwise, I would have missed Sosa's call. That was how hard I was sleeping. It was going on a couple of weeks since I had given him my number. I can't front after the third or fourth day of no communication I thought he wasn't fucking with me. I hung up the phone and couldn't help but smile thinking about taking a trip with Sosa. My mind was made up when he first asked, but I had to play hard to get. With everything going on in my life, I deserved a little vacation.

"Who got you cheesing, bitch?" Fendi tilted her head to the side and paused the TV.

"Bitch, pass me a shot before I give y'all this tea."

When neither of them moved I jumped out of the bed and did a little strut toward the bottle.

"Girl, spit it out we just got to the good part!"

I looked back at Fendi with a wide grin. "Nah, you ain't wanna pass me the bottle, so you gonna wait, but trust... This tea is piping hot."

I let out a little giggle and turned back around. Fendi and Dior started drinking early today, claiming they couldn't watch *Power* sober. I wasn't fucking with no liquor today, but after receiving that phone call a bitch was on one.

"Hurry up and make your drink! I hate when y'all do this shit. We getting to the good part,"

Dior whined. I grabbed the bottle of Patron from Fendi and poured some in the lemonade I had gotten earlier from Chick-fil-a. That shit was still nice and cold, so I knew it was gonna be busting. I took a quick sip of my drink. "So, this nigga Sosa wants to take a trip. He told me to just bring my ID and we can shop when we land!"

"Oh shit, bitch, and you better fuck the shit out his fine ass!" Fendi screamed.

"I don't know if you should go, Gucci. You don't even know him."

Fendi and I looked over at Dior like she had lost her mind. This bitch acted like I was in a position to turn down a free trip and some new clothes.

"Girl, bye. That nigga ain't about to do nothing crazy to her ass. That man has a line of bitches fighting for his attention. I say you go and put that pussy on a real nigga!" Fendi laughed, reaching for the remote.

Instead of feeding into Dior's scary-ass, I started getting ready for my trip. It wasn't like I needed anyone's permission to go out of town. I would be eighteen in a couple of months, and Ma didn't give a fuck what we did.

"Can y'all find me something to wear while I take a shower? I want to be ready when he pulls up." I knew one of them would get me together, so I jumped up, slipped my feet into my UGG slippers, and headed to the bathroom.

"You need anything else?" Dior yelled sarcastically from the bedroom. I was about to respond, but it wasn't worth it, so I let her have it. Dior could front all she wanted, but I knew her better than anyone else. Shit, we were raised in the same house all our lives. She wasn't mad that I was going out of town with Sosa because I just met him. Nah, she was in her feelings because I had met a nigga who was trying to level me up.

"Fendi, can you make sure my Fake ID is in my wallet and put it inside my Kelly bag?"

I put a little pep in my step. My mother always said if you're gonna make a man wait, make sure it was on purpose.

The bathroom we shared was smaller than what I was used to. Whoever designed the house said fuck it when they got to the bathroom. When I say small, I mean a little ass tub, toilet, and a sink with a mirror. I couldn't even fit a laundry basket inside. Another thing I couldn't get used to was the water took forever to heat up. While I waited for the water to warm up, I got a head start on getting my face together. We had been grinding hard all weekend, with little to no sleep. The bags under my eyes where the consequence.

Sosa didn't give me a time frame when he would be arriving. I hopped he was on colored people time. Instead of trying to do a full face of make-up, I focused on moisturizing my face so it would have a fresh dewy look when I saw him. My Tatcha Rice Wash Skin Softening Cleanser and the matching face mask was all I needed to get my skin back right. I stuck my hand inside the tub to test the water temperature. Now that it was perfect, I hopped inside and took a quick shower, making sure to focus on the body parts that mattered most. Thankfully I didn't have to shave. We all went and got waxed when we decided to start dancing.

The smile on my face expressed how impressed I was with Sosa. He was full of surprises. A bitch hadn't even put the pussy on him and was getting flewed out. I turned off the shower and grabbed my bath towel from the rack above the tub. Before I stepped out of the shower, I made sure to dry off. Wet bathroom floors are a pet peeve of mine. I grabbed my phone off the sink to make sure I hadn't missed Sosa's call. Thankfully, he hadn't called yet. I was trying to be ready by the time he pulled up so Ma wouldn't be in my business. Her ass had been cool since we were making money, but I would never forget how money hungry she was acting when we first moved in. Sosa equaled dollar signs, and I wasn't allowing no one to come up off him.

My new favorite perfume, Killian Love Don't Be Shy, had me smelling like money. When I got back into the room, I noticed the tacky ass outfit they chose for me to wear. That that low key hating shit. Why would they pick this basic ass dress for me to wear?

"Y'all couldn't do better than this dress?".

"Girl, you tripping. It's casual, and it's a body con. You about to be flying for who knows how long. Trust me, you want to be comfortable."

All my clothes were inside three trash bags. It would take me forever to sort through them. With so much going on, I hadn't unpacked for the sake of time. I settled on the nude dress.

Walking over to the full-length mirror, I slid the dress over my head, making sure not to fuck up the ponytail Dior did for me the other day.

"Dior, can you fix my baby hairs?"

"Ugh, I'll be happy when you leave so we can finish our show. Come on!"

Dior ran out of the room to grab her hair supplies while I looked for my Gucci Sandals. They were the only thing I had that would go with this dress.

"What you looking for?" Fendi asked.

"My Gucci sandals. I can't remember where I put them."

Fendi pointed toward the closet that had all her clothes neatly hung and boxes of shoes lined up at the top.

"You can wear my Tony Burch sandals. They'll go cute with that dress. If you want to grab some extra shit, go ahead." She rolled back on her stomach and continued texting whoever she was talking to.

"Nah, the shoes are good. He said we gonna go shopping

when we land. You know all my shit is at the old house, so I ain't letting him out of that one."

"Yeah, that nigga feeling you. I ain't never heard about him cashing out on a bitch who wasn't fucking him."

"Oh, I'm fucking him. Trust and believe that."

It took me a minute to grab the shoes off the top shelf, a curse of being four eleven. Fendi was right. The sandals complimented the dress. All I needed was Dior to fix my hair, and I was good.

"Dior I'm ready." I said sitting down on the edge of the bed.

"For what?" She asked playing dum.

"My hair. Fuck you mean for what?"

"You aint have to get nasty." Dior said.

"I said what I said." I rolled my eyes and waited for her to get up. I've been doing everyone's makeup since we started dancing. I never asked anyone to pay me. Even thinking about how much I've spent at Sephora makes me sick. "Mater fact you good. I'll do it myself. Make sure you keep the same energy when you want your makeup down." I said when she didn't get up.

"Dior go and do her hair. You know she big petty." Fendi interjected.

"Ugh. You get on my nerves. Why we got to change our routine because you're going out of town?"

"That show will be there when done." I said rolling my eyes.

Dior finally got up out the bed and walked over to where she kept her hair supplies. "I'm gonna put it up in a ponytail so you don't mess it up while you gone." She said walking back towards the bed with her edge control, edge brush, and this spray she made for her clients.

Dior started brushing my hair up into a high ponytail when my phone rang.

"Fendi, grab my phone!"

Fendi jumped off the bed and grabbed my phone off the charger. "Who is it?" I asked trying to look her way. Fendi waved the phone childishly with a stupid grin on her face.

"He's outside!" Fendi said, holding my phone up.

"Text him I'm coming!" As soon as I said that Dior started brushing my hair roughly. At first, I thought I was overreacting. When I felt her pull a little too hard, I had to say something. "Girl calm yo ass down. Stop jerking my head Dior."

Dior dropped the brush and walked back towards the bed with a nasty attitude. Me and Fendi locked eyes. I don't know what's going on with Dior but for the last couple of days she's been real snappy.

"Dior you on some real-life hating shit. How you gonna stop doing my hair, and you know my ride outside?"

Dior acted like she didn't hear me. Instead of responding crossed her arms and looked straight ahead at the tv. It took everything in me to remain calm instead of going off. She's lucky I needed her to finish my hair. "Dior can you please finish my hair."

"Dior go ahead and finish her hair. Dam you bugging I'm about to stop giving you pills cause they got you tripping." Fendi said.

"I'm not tripping. She's you know what never mind." Dior

129

got up and walked back over to where I was sitting and picked up the brush.

"Nah say what's on your mind." Tapping my foot on the ground, I waited for her to hurry up and finish my edges. A few seconds later, she drooped the brush, sprayed some of her special spray on my hair, and we were done.

"I'm still scared ok! Every night I have nightmares about what happened."

"Aww baby. It's ok if you not ready to be alone, I'll sleep in hear while Gucci's gone." Fendi walked over to Dior and pulled her in a hug. I turned around and joined the group hug.

"Girl I'm not leaving forever and I'm a bring you back something cute boo." Dior smiled

I grabbed my phone from Fendi. The last time I took a flight, it was cold as hell, so I made sure to grab my black ripped jean jacket. Grabbing my Kelly bag, I looked around the room to make sure I wasn't forgetting anything. I grabbed my nude Mac Lip gloss, applied a couple of coats, then slid on my Chanel shades.

"Girl, go ahead. You look cute, bae!" Fendi said, waving her hand toward the door.

"Yeah, go ahead and leave so we can get back to our show! Love you, hoe," Dior yelled.

"Love y'all! I'll hit the group chat when we land."

As I walked down the stairs, I tried to calm my nerves. *Would Sosa want sex?* Of course, he would. He wouldn't take me on a trip and not expect some pussy.

Ma and Kash were sitting on the living room floor counting money and smoking a blunt. They stopped counting when I walked into the room. "Look at you looking all snazzy. Where are you going?" Ma asked, blowing a cloud of smoke in my direction.

"I'm going on a trip," I said, hoping her ass wouldn't start bitching. For the most part, she didn't give a fuck what we did but, I never knew with her ass.

Ma raised her perfectly arched eyebrow and nodded her head in approval. She clapped her hands and looked me up and down with a proud look on her face.

"Oh, you're good! Who's taking you on a trip, Ms. Thang?"

The doorbell rang, taking the attention off me. Kash hopped up out of her seat since she was closest to the door.

"Hey, what are you doing here?" she asked, holding the door cracked slightly.

"What's good, Kash?" Sosa gave her a head nod and pushed her out of his way before he stepped inside. His blue fitted was turned to the back, and his hair was still twisted in the rope twists he had the other day. I loved a man who could dress. His purple Balenciaga t-shirt matched his jays, and the light blue ripped jeans balanced the outfit. We were about to have a good time tearing the mall down wherever we went.

"Sosa, what do I owe the pleasure?" Ma asked, shooting me a knowing look.

"What's good, Ma! Damn, shorty. Why you so sexy?" Sosa asked, pulling me into a hug. Damn he smelled good as hell every time I'd been in his presence. His cologne was always on point.

"Don't y'all look cute together. Now, Sosa, that's my grandbaby."

"Ma, she good!" Sosa grabbed my hand and pulled me in front of him.

"Aight, now. I don't play about my youngins." Ma sat back down and resumed counting the pile of money. Kash stood in the middle of the room with her arms crossed over her chest. "Kash, why the hell you standing there? we got to get this money together! I'm tired. I ain't gonna be up all day fooling with this shit," Ma snapped.

Kash was doing too much, and I had no idea why she was acting weird. She muttered something about unfairness under her breath and walked back over to where Ma was sitting.

"You ready?" Sosa asked, breaking me out of my thoughts.

"Yeah, let's go!"

If Kash wanted to be petty, that was on her. Since she wanted to ignore me, I did the same. I hugged Ma and followed Sosa out of the house.

Sosa held me hand as we walked towards his Black Tomahawk Jeep. The sun was shining, and the air had that crisp *just rained the night before* smell.

When we got to the car, Sosa shocked me when he opened my door and helped me inside. This was the first time I had seen him smile so much. As soon as he hopped inside the car, he removed his t-shirt and threw it in the back seat. The white wife-beater hugged his muscular frame. Bae was tatted the fuck up. It seemed like each tattoo told a story of some sort. They all connected from his neck, back, and down his arms. I couldn't help but stare at him.

"You trying to make a nigga blush?" Sosa asked, giving me the side-eye. He whipped his truck out of Ma's driveway and adjusted the volume on the stereo. While he got himself situated, I took the time to study his car. I could tell a lot about a person by how they kept their car. Nine times out of ten if their car was nasty I knew their house was the same. Sosa's car was neat as hell. It still had that new car smell mixed with his cologne and a light scent of weed

"You ever been to Vegas, superstar?" Sosa asked. I was unable to respond to him. I was fascinated with his full lips. His cologne had me hypnotized, and I couldn't think or move. We were coming up to a stop sign when he leaned over and grabbed the back of my neck. We stared into each other's eyes, our mouths were inches away from each other. "Stop playing with me."

He leaned forward and pushed his tongue inside my mouth. The fruity taste on his tongue attacked my tastebuds. I couldn't move. The way Sosa gently sucked on my tongue had me in a state of shock.

If this nigga kisses like this, I know he fuck good.

The kiss deepened, and we only separated because the old bitch in the brown beat-up Volkswagen kept blowing her horn.

"Answer my question, ma!" Sosa demanded, glancing over at me.

"Nah, I ain't never been. I heard it's lit, though."

"Yeah, we about to find out."

I was confused when we headed in the opposite direction from the Airport. Sosa pulled over in front of a blue trap house, and seconds later, a dark skin fat nigga walked out holding a brown paper bag.

"What's good, Sosa? Miss Lady!" the man said, reaching

inside the car to dap him up. I smiled at him and started checking my Instagram while they did whatever they were doing.

"What's good, Chuck? This shit better be cold. Last time my shit was warm." Sosa reached for the brown bag and handed Chuck four crisp hundred-dollar bills.

Sosa pulled off and handed me the brown bag. Whatever was inside the bag was so cold the water was seeping through.

"Bust the top on the bottle and hand it to me, beautiful."

I didn't ask any questions. When I opened the bag, I saw Wockhardt Promethazine Codeine Syrup on the prescription bottle. I twisted off the cap and handed it to him. "Grab a Styrofoam cup from the black bag in the backseat." He demanded.

I reached behind me, grabbed the cup out of the bag, and handed it to him. Sosa poured some in the Styrofoam cup and handed me the bottle back. While I screwed the cap back on, I looked over at him. "You drink that straight?"

"How else I'm 'posed to sip it?" He placed the cup in the cup holder and headed toward the highway.

"I thought you were supposed to mix it with sprite or some shit," I said, peering inside the cup at the thick syrup.

"Yo ass been watching too many rap videos. Don't nobody do that shit no more." Sosa reached for the cup and took another sip and lit a blunt he had in the ashtray. Curiosity got the best of me, and I reached for the cup to see what the hype was about. "Take it easy with that shit or yo ass gonna be fucked up."

If his ass only knew I wasn't some square rich bitch. This

wasn't my first time trying lean, but Sosa didn't need to know that. Previously when I tried it, we mixed the syrup, with Sprite and Jolly Ranchers. The lean wasn't as bad as I thought it would be. It tasted like some strong ass cough medicine. Sosa nodded his head at me, and I took a bigger sip, hoping it would help calm my nerves.

While he was sipping, he turned NBA YoungBoy's "Smoke Strong" on, and the car seat rocked from the base. By the time we arrived at the airport, I had a nice little buzz from the lean and Patron I had earlier. Sosa pulled his car up to the short-term parking.

Sosa grabbed my hand and lead me through the airport so we could purchase our tickets and board our flight. I noticed a bitch grilling us as we walked past.

"Do you always get this much attention?" I asked once we passed the girl.

"A lot of bitches about to hate you once they find out I'm taking you out of town."

I just smiled knowing he could have called any bitch in the city, but he called me. There was something about a hood nigga giving me his full attention that did something to me. I didn't know if it was because my daddy was a dope boy who spent countless hours bleeding the block or what. I would sit up late at night waiting for him to come home, no matter how much my mother protested. The entire time we checked in, I gazed at Sosa. I loved watching him walk. He was bow-legged, and for some reason, I found myself fantasizing about what his dick felt like to the point my panties were now wet.

Sosa went all out with our last-minute tickets. He told the

ticket agent we were flying business class, and it didn't matter how much it cost, just to get it done. It was shit like that which had me fantasizing about him fucking the shit out of me when we got to Vegas. We boarded the plane before the other passengers and were escorted to our seats.

"Damn, these seats are so comfortable!"

The seat adjusted into a semi-bed position, giving me plenty of legroom. We got settled and adjusted our flat screen TVs to a movie we both agreed on. A flight attendant comes over to us. The young stewardess was pushing a tray filled with orange juice, champagne, and bottled waters.

"Would you guys like a Mimosa while we wait for the other passengers to board?" she asked, her voice dripping with happiness.

"You want one?" Sosa turns to ask me, still gripping my hand. I nodded my head, hoping the stewardess didn't card me. I didn't know if Sosa was aware of my age. He never asked, and I wasn't volunteering that information. Sosa pulled out a stack of crisp hundreds and handed the stewardess two bills. "Let us get two of them thangs, shorty."

"Sure, no problem!" she said, smiling at the generous tip. Once she passed us our drinks, she continued down the aisle to the other guests.

This was how my life was supposed to be. Catching flights and drinking champagne with a boss ass nigga. While I waited for the flight to take off, I gazed out the window lost in my thoughts. I looked over at Sosa to make sure he hadn't fallen asleep. He was playing a game on his phone. "You straight? You can order some food, or we can eat when we land. It's up to you." Sosa asked.

"Yeah, I'm straight. We can eat when we get to Vegas. Thank you for this. You don't know how bad I needed to get away."

"This ain't about nothing! But I hear you. We both needed a getaway."

"To new beginnings!" I held my champagne flute up, and we clicked them together.

"For sho!" his ghetto ass said.

I couldn't tell you what happened after we finished our drinks. One minute we were watching TV, the next I allowed myself to embrace the sleepiness and get some much-needed rest.

Vegas

"All passengers please fasten your seat belt as we prepare to land. The temperature shows eighty-five degrees. Welcome to Sin City," a cheerful voice projected through the plane's speakers waking me up.

I looked out the window and noticed the scenery had changed. Fields of dark red mixed with scattered houses filled my vision. I quickly snapped a picture from this angle. I had the perfect view of the desert below us. Yawning, I looked over at Sosa who was still knocked out.

Damn, he looks so peaceful. Sosa's eyes were closed tightly, and his head was tipped back. His locs spread out across his shoulders. What stood out the most to me was the smile on his face. That was so cute, and I was tempted to snap a picture to show him when he woke up. I gently shook his shoulder. "We are about to land."

With half-closed eyes, he looked over at me. "Damn, I slept the whole flight. A nigga needed that shit!"

He stretched his arms back before sitting up.

"Me too. I feel like I ain't sleep since I started dancing."

"Yo ass been grinding it be like that?" he asked. The plane began to descend toward the ground, and my stomach jumped. I held my breath, closed my eyes, and grabbed Sosa's hands. "Let me find out yo ass was scared to fly?"

I couldn't answer him right now. All I was focused on was landing without some freak accident happening.

"Ladies and gentlemen, we have landed in Las Vegas, Nevada. Thank you for flying United. Enjoy your stay," a cheerful voice said through the airplane intercom. That was when I released Sosa's hand and opened my eyes.

"Boy, shut up!" I stammered. Damn, I got to get it together. My heart was still racing, and I found it difficult to form my words correctly.

Sosa shook his head, gave me a little smirk, and bent down to tie his shoes.

I took the time to send everyone a group chat to let them know we arrived safely.

Me: We just landed 😬

Dior: Oh, shit that was quick

Kash: 👀

Chanel: 👑

Me: 😭😭😭 Sosa flewed me out. We in Vegas I'll hit y'all later.

I powered off my phone before they could ask any more questions. We exited the plane and bypassed the lines of people forming at the baggage carousel. Sosa grabbed my hand and pulled me back to him. "Hold up, shorty! It's hot as hell outside. Let me order the Uber first."

"Do you need me to do anything?"

This was our first time going out of town. Hell, this is our first time chilling with each other, so I didn't know if he already booked where we would be staying since this was a last minute trip.

"Stand there, look beautiful, and be my eyes while I order our ride."

I guess our ride was close because he grabbed my hand and lead me out of the airport. The section where we had to catch the Ubers was on the other side of the airport, so it took us some time to get to it.

Sosa held the door open for me like a true gentleman. The minute we stepped outside, the intense dry heat smacked me in the face, and I instantly felt the difference from the heat back home. It felt hotter out here, but it was dry, so hopefully, I would be able to beat my face when we went out and not have to worry about it melting.

There were lines of Ubers, and Lyfts. Without Sosa having to point to our car, I knew which one was ours. The Uber driver hopped out of the black Escalade and held the door open for us to get inside.

The air condition car was refreshing, and I didn't want to seem pressed like I had never taken a trip, so I sat back and relaxed, even though I wanted to check out the scenery. This was the first time I saw real palm trees, and they were beautiful.

Neon lights flashed from the hotels. As we drove down the strip tourists were casually walking, and I was ready to join them.

"This shit is so dope. which one are we staying at?" I asked, leaning into him. Sosa pulled me on his lap and kissed my forehead. "Psalms."

He leaned back and rolled the window down, and we both gazed out of it.

"My man, stop at one of these dispensaries before we get to the hotel," Sosa called out to the older black man who was driving.

"Sure, young man. You can add it on in the app, and we can go to whichever one you want." The man looked back at Sosa waiting for his instructions.

"Nah, boss. I ain't about to be Googling dispensaries and adding trips. Is this enough for your troubles?" he asked, breaking the man off with a couple of hundreds.

"Damn, youngin. You made my night. I don't smoke refer, but I know everyone goes to that mega dispensary off West Desert Inn. I can't recall the name, but I can get you there. Them fools call it the Walmart of Weed."

"It's whatever, my man. That shit not too far from where we going?" Sosa ass had some nerve making this man drive out his way and then wanna complain about the time.

"Nah, it ain't out the way at all. Y'all kids good. You can connect your Bluetooth if you need to."

"We good, boss."

A few minutes later, we pulled up to Planet 13, and the driver pulled around to the front. A security guard stood at the front of the building checking IDs. I had my fake ID with me in case they tried to card me but wasn't trying to take that risk.

"You coming in or you waiting?" Sosa asked, looking over at me.

"Do you, boo!" I jumped off his lap allowing him to get out of the car to handle his business. While he was inside, the driver was suggesting different places we should go to eat and different attractions the city offered.

Twenty minutes later, Sosa exited the dispensary. The women waiting in line were breaking their necks trying to get his attention. He wasn't paying them any mind as he walked toward the car holding a big ass bag in his hand.

"Any more stops before we get to the Palms?" The driver looked back at us through the rearview.

"Yeah, a nigga hungry as hell. What fast food restaurants y'all got in the vicinity?"

"I hear from them accents y'all must be from the south. I was raised in Virginia. When we first moved out here, my wife had me eating In & Out Burgers for a month straight. If y'all wanna try it, there's one on the way to the Hotel."

"You want that or something else?"

"That's cool, boo! I just wanna get to the room, smoke, and take a shower."

"That's cool, bro. Take us there and then we good."

The driver pulled the car out of the parking lot and headed to In & Out.

When we pulled up, the double lines were backed up with cars. That was a good sign that the food would be on point. Sosa pulled out two vapes from the bag. He kept one and handed me the other. Out of respect for the man, I rolled my window down. I had never smoked a vape before, so I wasn't sure if it would leave a smell in his car. We waited in the drive-thru line and puffed on the vapes that had some good ass weed inside.

"The Animal Style fries are what everyone comes for and the Milkshakes. You can't go wrong with that," the driver said, easing toward the menu.

Sosa peered at the menu before looking over at me. "What you want?"

"I'm getting whatever you order." I was high as fuck and had the munchies.

Sosa nodded at me and leaned closer to the window to place his order. By the time he was finished, he had ordered six double-double burgers, four animal-style fries, and two large Strawberry Milk Shakes. The girl behind the counter handed Sosa the big-ass white bag filled with food.

The drive to the hotel took no time, and when we finally pulled up, I was in awe. There were two big ass towers, one with the name Palms, and the other had Palms Place on the front. When we got to the circular driveway that was filled with Maybachs, and most importantly, a van that had Money Team written on it.

"Y'all going to the hotel side or the condo side?" the driver asked.

"The condos, boss!" Sosa began gathering the bags, and I grabbed the tray with our drinks. After, we said bye to the driver and headed toward the hotel entrance. The lobby was empty except for a couple of people walking toward the elevator and the two employees behind the desk. While Sosa handled checking in, I grabbed a book that had different things to do in Vegas.

"Come on. Let's go to the room!" Sosa said, walking up on me. His hands were full, but he still made sure I was walking in front of him. The elevator was a couple of feet away from the lobby and had two elevators that went to different floors. I had no idea what floor we were going to, so I stopped in between them and waited for Sosa to press the button.

The elevator doors closed, and Sosa walked up to me and started sucking on my neck. Each time the elevator dinged alerting us we were passing a different floor my pussy grew wetter. This man knew what he was doing, and he had no problem showing me what he wanted. I was not gonna say all he wanted was sex because if he wanted that he could have gotten that back home.

"This our floor, ma." He removed his mouth from my neck and the elevator door opened on the thirtieth floor. We walked down the long hallway looking for our room. "This us right here."

He slid the key card in the lock, and a few seconds later, the light on the door went from red to green.

We entered the room, and my mouth dropped. I don't know

what I was expecting, but this wasn't it. This was a whole ass condo, equipped with a kitchen area, living room, and bedroom. I dropped my bag on the couch and started exploring our space. Sosa sat down on the couch and kicked his feet up like this shit was regular to him. The bathroom was to the side of the bedroom and was bomb as fuck. The toilet was separated from the rest of the room with a privacy door. His and her sinks with a nice ass white bench where in the middle of the room, and to the left was a glass door that led to a standing shower with a twelve head, and a big ass jacuzzi sat behind it. Satisfied with the bathroom, I walked back into the living room where Sosa had the food spread out on the table.

"This shit good as fuck, ma!" he said in between bites. My stomach rumbled at the sight of the juicy burgers and French fries with some type of sauce on them. Everything else could wait. I was about to murder this food.

When we were finished eating, I grabbed my toothbrush out of my purse and walked toward the bathroom. Looking in the mirror, I decided to freshen up a little. The shower was calling me. It had been months since I had the pleasure of bathing in a quality space. I pulled my dress over my head making sure not to fuck up my hair. I walked back into the living room to grab my scarf out of my purse. Sosa looked up from rolling his blunt and licked his thick lips.

"You see something you like?" I teased him.

After I tied my hair up, I walked over to where he was sitting and grabbed the vape I had been smoking from earlier. I could feel his eyes on me, and I can't front, I loved that shit. I was no shy ass bitch, and I was aware of who the fuck I was.

"Of course!" he said. We locked eyes, and I could see the hunger he had for me. I took a deep pull, making sure to twirl my tongue extra hard. As I exhaled the smoke, I noticed myself in the ceiling mirror. My perky titties sat up, and my nipple bars glistened. Getting them pierced was the best decision I ever made. Nigga's loved that shit. While I smoked, I twirled my nipple bar. This nigga had me horny as fuck, and we hadn't done shit yet.

"Go get some ice out of the freezer. Grab that bottle out yo purse and bring us two cups."

Oh, we about to get lit.

I had forgotten that we snuck the bottle of lean through the airport. Sosa's crazy ass poured it inside a Pedialyte container when we got to the airport and sealed it with some clear tape so they would think it was unopened.

My shower was gonna have to wait for a little bit. I wanted to be faded when I got this dick. I grabbed my purse and brought it over to the kitchen area so I wouldn't have to run back and forth. I shook the bottle, grabbed our cups and some ice, and brought the drinks back over to Sosa.

"We can smoke in here?" I passed him his cup, and out of instinct, I opened the balcony door.

"Ma, we can do whatever the fuck we want in here. We grown."

"I hear you, bae!"

By the time we finished smoking and drinking, I was fucked up and feeling good. I wasn't too fucked up to forget to wash my ass, though.

"I'll be right back." I leaned in kissed Sosa and got up to take my shower.

I connected my phone to the Bluetooth and Summer Walker's voice filled the room. The shower took no time to heat, and when I stepped inside, the water pressure was perfect. I grabbed the body wash and looked down at the label. This shit was gonna have to do until we went shopping.

When I was finished, I pressed the button on the wall to turn the shower off, grabbed the plush white towel off the stand, and dried off before walking into the room.

Sosa had his shirt off and his locs were pulled back in a ponytail as he focused on Sports Center. It was weird that he was watching that shit with no volume on.

"Damn, I thought yo ass was dead," he said, looking up from the TV.

"Nah, it just felt good as hell!" I smiled, dropped my towel, and grabbed the vape off the table. I switched my hips slowly and walked toward the balcony. The warm air felt good as hell against my skin. I didn't bother to cover up. We were so high up, I doubted anyone could see me. "It's so beautiful here. Look at all the lights."

I turned around and Sosa was standing at the door in his Versace boxers. He had his iced-out Sosa chain on, but that was all he needed. Bae was raw like that. He walked up behind me and pulled me back to him. We were so close I swore our hearts were beating as one. No words were spoken as we looked down at the bright lights below us.

"What you trying to do tomorrow?" He grabbed one of the chairs behind us and pulled it toward where we were standing.

His big ass hands grabbed me by the waist and pulled me down into his lap. I couldn't answer him. I felt his dick growing under me, and a bitch was scared. His hands traveled up my stomach, and he lightly started rubbing circles on my nipples.

"Can I touch you?" he asked in his low raspy voice.

"After I touch you." I stood up and turned around, getting down on my knees in front of him. His dick was fighting to get out of his boxer briefs. I had never done anything like this, but I couldn't help it. This man was that damn sexy to me. I didn't know if it was the lean or the weed, but I wanted Sosa in the worst way.

"Word." he smirked down at me.

I nodded my head, reached inside his boxers, and pulled his dick out. My mouth watered. His dick was beautiful, long, dark, and thick with a nice mushroom head at the top. I spit on it and allowed it to drip from my mouth onto him. Slowly, I eased my mouth down and didn't stop until his head hit the back of my throat.

"Fuck, bae," he moaned. That turned me on, and I started going harder. Sosa grabbed my head and started guiding me up and down. As my mouth came back up, I used my hand to jerk on him. I looked him in the eyes and spit on it again, staring the process over.

"You coming like that, Gucci?" He grabbed my hair rougher this time and force my head back down as he fucked my mouth. I ain't gag or nothing. I took that shit like a real bitch.

"Turn around, ma." He released my hair and pushed me down on my knees in front of him. He kissed me from the top of my neck down my back, smacked my ass, and mumbled something under his breath. My ass cheeks spread, and I felt his hot breath blowing on me. Sosa didn't even look like the type to eat pussy, but he was killing my shit. His tongue licked me from front to back, and he was sucking on my clit like a baby sucking on a bottle.

"Fuck, bae!" I screamed, cumming. He licked that shit up and stepped back, leaving me trying to catch my breath. Sosa grabbed me and pushed me toward the railing. I pressed my hands on the glass, arched my back, and spread my legs wide. He walked up behind me and rubbed the tip of his dick, rubbing up and down my pussy.

"Damn, this shit tight as fuck!" he moaned, pushing inside of me. He rocked back and forth, rubbing his hands on my nipples. I froze. He felt like heaven inside of me. "This my pussy. Don't play with me."

I couldn't speak. This nigga had me bent over as he dug into me deeper. My ass smacked against his stomach as he drilled my shit. The sounds of my moans and him talking shit enhanced my experience. The raw dick hit different, on God. I was coming back-to-back, and I knew this nigga was feeling my shit. I hadn't had sex in over a year. This was the third time I ever had sex, and the first two times didn't feel like this. My stomach clenched as Sosa pounded into me. Bliss took over me. My body started shaking as my juices poured out of me. I hopped off the dick and Sosa had a confused look on his face. I smirked and got on my knees. His hard dick was sticking straight toward me with my juices glistening all over it. I licked my juices off him before deep throating him. I swore his dick got harder and grew another inch. I was ready to ride the nut up out of him. Sosa's eyes were closed. He was biting his bottom lip as I worked my mouth up and down. My pussy was ready to feel him inside her again. I released him and stood, up wiping my mouth. I pushed him down on the chair. My mind was gone as I climbed on top of him, spread my legs, and place my feet on the side of the chair. I placed my hands on his chest and grabbing his chain gently, I bounced up and down slowly until I caught my rhythm.

Sosa leaned up and grabbed me by the back of my neck and pulled me in for a slow, long, nasty kiss.

"This my pussy, Gucci?" Sosa growled in my ear.

"Yes, daddy," I moaned.

"Come for me, baby girl." Sosa picked up his speed and began drilling my pussy. We fucked like two dogs in heat. Wasn't nothing gentle or slow. This was raw as we both battled for control. *Smack! Smack!*

Each time his hand met my ass, I would speed up. Closing my eyes, I opened my mouth slightly. Tears formed in the corner of my eyes as the urge to pee came over me followed by me coming long and hard. Sosa looked down at his stomach that now was covered in my juices with a smirk on his handsome face. He grabbed my waist and bounced into me. My pussy sounded like he was mixing macaroni and cheese. Seconds later, he came long and hard inside of me. We were so high that he didn't pull out, and I didn't try to stop him.

Chapter Nine

SOSA

I woke up the next day to Gucci's little ass snuggled in a ball next to me. The sun was shining through the sheer white curtains. Yawning, I slipped my hand from around her and got up to take a piss. It was going on one in the afternoon. Between us fucking and the time difference, I wasn't surprised we slept late. My stomach was fucked up. I closed the bathroom, door turned the fan on, and took a shit. While I was doing that, I ordered us some room service to put something on our stomachs before we hit the mall.

The alert on my phone let me know our food would be arriving in thirty minutes. Which gave me time to take a shower. I couldn't front, this bathroom was nice as hell. The entire condo was dope, but the bathroom was a vibe. When I got back home, I was gonna hit my contractor up to install one of these showers in my house. It felt like a nigga was getting a personal message from the shower jets alone.

Out of the corner of my eye, I watched Gucci walk into the bathroom and close the door to the toilet area. Her little ass was bad as hell, and I was feeling shorty's company. Since we landed in Vegas, she was on some chill shit and was going with the flow. I was skeptical at first, taking her out of town. Wynter left a bad taste in my mouth during our trip to Miami. Shorty was in my pockets hard as hell and ain't wanna do shit but spend my money and post me on her IG. Whenever I took a bitch out of town, I knew I was gonna spend bread on her. A nigga loved to shop, and I ain't the type to have someone window shopping while I blew a bag, but Wynter had the game fucked up when she kept dropping hints about wanting to go to Hermes and Chanel. I knew for a fact shorty didn't shop at those types of stores. She killed the mood, and by the third day, I sent her ass back to North Carolina by herself. The way Wynter was acting, I halfway expected that out of Gucci. Her ass came from hood royalty, and I knew Snow had her ass spoiled. She hadn't shown me that side of her, and with that fire ass pussy she blessed a nigga with, I was about to blow some bands on her pretty ass.

"Yo, hurry up. We about to go shopping. I got room service on the way," I said when she stepped out of the bathroom.

"Damn, I forgot we ain't have no clothes." Gucci walked over to the sink, brushed her teeth, and applied some purple cream all over her face. Whatever that shit was, it was doing the damn job because she ain't have no dark spots or none of them blackheads that most of these hoes had on their faces. Last night, I was so fucked up I ain't even peep how thick shorty was. She was Cornbread fed all natural. Only God could make a body that perfect. Baby girl was bow-legged with the thighs to match and a fat ass that looked like two basketballs. She turned around and my eyes traveled down the front of her body. Even her feet were perfect. She had white polish on her toes. Thankfully, her feet were little as hell. I didn't know how many bad bitches a nigga met with them quarterback feet.

Gucci stepped in the shower and grabbed the rag to wash my back. Her little nasty ass started stroking my dick. It was a wrap. I turned around and pinned her onto the wall. My dick was hard as hell and my shorty's pussy was wet for daddy.

"When's your birthday, and how old are you?" I asked. I remembered someone saying shorty wasn't eighteen, but I wasn't sure since Ma was her grandmother and had her dancing. The last thing I needed was a charge or to beef with Snow for fucking his underage daughter.

"Next month I'll be eighteen," she moaned, kissing on my lips as my dick slowly entered her. Damn, this bitch got some good pussy. It was virgin tight, letting me know she wasn't no hoe. The way her pussy was gripping my dick, I knew if a nigga had been inside this pussy, he ain't break her ass in. Groaning, I sucked on her tongue and tasted the mint from the toothpaste.

Baby girl had me tripping. I should have verified her age before taking her out of town and sticking my dick in her, but it was too late. Her walls were warm, tight, wet, and causing me to slowly lose my mind. "You on birth control?"

"No, I don't be fucking!" she said, her gray eyes wide with passion. I was fucking the shit out this girl raw, and that was completely out of my character. Her pussy got wetter with each thrust I took. Today, I wasn't holding shit back. Last night, I took it easy on her. Today, I wanted to see what this pussy could do. I bit down on her neck and pried her legs open, allowing me full access to her.

"Damn, this pussy good as fuck!"

The water fell down my back as Gucci whimpered underneath me. We locked eyes, and she grabbed my neck, spreading her legs wider. She moved her waist, matching me stroke for stroke. Her pussy was so good I had to pull out to prevent myself from busting. There was a bench in the shower, so I pushed her on her knees. With a smirk on her face, she turned to look back at me while she played in her swollen pussy.

"Remind me to go get you a plan b."

She smiled and nodded her head then placed both hands on the wet shower wall. I grabbed my dick and slowly pushed inside of her. Once my dick was inside, I stooped to look down the perfection in front of me. Her waist was tiny as fuck in comparison to the way her ass and hips stuck out. I smacked her ass and started drilling her while she threw her ass back at me. I had to get control of her little ass because she was going crazy on the dick. Placing one hand on the wall behind me, I placed my foot on the bench and grabbed her waist to balance me. It was crazy shorty was seventeen and built better than all my other bitches.

"Sosa!"

"Yes, bae?" I bit my lips.

"I'm about to cum!" Her face twisted up in pleasure as I went in and out faster. I couldn't speak. I focused on her ass each time I slid my dick out. I got glimpses of her cum all over me. I stopped for a second and then slammed back inside of her, feeling the nut coming from deep within me. Her walls snatched a nigga deeper, and her pussy got wetter. I couldn't help it. The shit was too good to pull out.

"Sosa!" she screamed, releasing all over me, and for the second time in my life, I nutted deep in some pussy.

We finished up in the shower, and as we were drying off, there was a knock on the door. Gucci's ass was moving in slow motion, so I wrapped a towel around my waist and headed to the door.

Two Spanish maids stood in front of me, fidgeting and squirming. My dick was still semi-hard, and neither of them had bothered to look up since I answered the door. I looked them up and down and laughed. These bitches looked like they were ready to say fuck their job and join our party.

"Room service!" The one on the right blushed when our eyes connected.

"Y'all can put it over there."

They grinned at me and pushed the cart inside the room. I stepped to the side and admired their wide hips as they passed me. They started removing the platters from the cart and placing them on the table. I ordered so much food, we received complimentary Mimosas.

"Were done, papi, and if you need anything else, let me know!" The woman slid a card into my hand and licked her lip. I wasn't fucking with them, but I did accept the card and handed both of them a tip.

"Damn, you ordered the whole menu. I'm a be big as hell by

the time we get home." Gucci walked out of the bathroom looking like a different person. I didn't mean that in a bad way. She removed the fake hair she had in and was rocking her natural hair. It was curly as fuck and reached a little below her shoulders. She had the dress on from when we arrived. Yeah, I got to take Lil baby shopping. I knew she wasn't used to this type of shit.

"I ain't know what you liked, so I got a little of everything."

She was right, though. A nigga did go overboard. We had cheese eggs, cheese grits, sausage, bacon, hash browns, fruit platter, steaks, some pancake-looking shits, and Belgium waffles with three different types of syrups.

"You want a little bit of everything?" she asked, grabbing two plates.

"That's straight, ma." I sipped on my drink while she hooked our plates up. She ain't even know it but shit like that had her winning. A nigga loved to be treated like a king, and her doing this shit without me asking reminded me she was raised differently from my other bitches. Her daddy was the king of kings in the streets, so I was sure she watched her mama cater to her daddy.

I grabbed my phone off the table. My phone had been dead since we been in Vegas. "You brought yo charger, ma?"

"Yeah, it's in my purse." She turned around and pointed toward her bag that was sitting on the chair next to the bed.

I got up and grabbed her charger out of the purse and plugged it in the outlet close to the table. She had one of the long-ass chargers, so I was able to put it next to me. It took a few minutes for my iPhone 12 to charge. I swore as soon as I saw the Apple logo come on my screen, the messages started dumping in. This shit didn't make no damn sense. My team already knew what it was. My right hand was handling shit while I was gone.

The phone started ringing, and Elle's name popped up. I noticed I had thirty missed calls from her and numerous messages. I wasn't about to read through all them shits. I accepted the call and put it on speaker. I ain't have shit to hide. "Fuck you blowing my shit up like you crazy for?"

"That's how you do, nigga? You taking bitches on trips and shit?"

"Don't worry about what the fuck I'm doing. Worry about if you got my fucking money, bitch." I hadn't forgotten about that little stunt she pulled the other day. That was part of the reason I was able to go out of town. I met with my connect twice a month, nothing less and nothing more. With everything going on in the streets, niggas were more paranoid than usual. It would have looked crazy if I hit him up after we just re-upped, so I let the shit slide and told everyone to take the next couple of days off while I figured shit out.

"Bitch! That's how you coming, nigga? Don't sit there fronting cause you got yo little groupie around you."

"Bae, which syrup you want?" Gucci yelled out, unfazed about what Elle was saying.

"Blueberry!"

"Wow, so it's true. You took that little stripper bitch out of town?" Elle screamed in the phone. Shorty was breathing hard as hell like she was seconds away from losing her shit.

"He sure did! Watch yo mouth when you speak on me, hoe! I'm with all the shits," Gucci yelled out.

"Sosa you got me on speaker in front of her?"

"Elle, I don't got time for this shit. You already know what it is!" I wasn't about to keep going back and forth with shorty. Elle fucked up when she fucked with my work. She was lucky I ain't get none of my cousins to slide on her.

"Fuck you, Quavon! Why the fuck you out in Vegas with a bitch? That shit is mad embarrassing. Then you let her post you. What happened to you don't do social media?" Elle violated when she said my name. We never used our government names on the phone.

Before I could respond, Gucci's switched her sexy ass over to the table with my plate, placed it down in front of me, and snatched my phone out of my hand. She placed her hand on her wide hips and started going in.

"Girl, what type of weak bitch begs a nigga while another bitch listens?" Her face was twisted up with a stank look as she waited for Elle to respond.

"Little girl, give Sosa the phone back!" Elle snapped.

Gucci's busted out laughing. "Bitch, he don't want you. Whatever y'all had, that shit is done. Since you seem a little slow, I'm a do you a favor and let that shit you said slide."

"Bitch, you think I'm playing with you. Ask about me, hoe!" Elle screamed into the phone.

"Girl, I don't give a fuck about none of that shit! I don't check on irrelevant hoes, but since you sound fanned out, I know your dumb ass done asked around about me. Act like you know my name is Gucci Snow, bitch! Whatever you and Sosa had, it's a wrap, hoe. All that tough shit you spitting, keep that energy! I'm a find you when we land, and don't bother calling this number back cause I'm a block you soon as we hang up!" Gucci disconnected the call and passed me my phone back.

"Make sure you block that bitch! I hope you ain't think I was playing?" she said, taking a seat and digging into her plate.

Chapter Ten
GUCCI

I held Sosa's hand as we strolled through The Shops at Crystals, feeling like a million dollars. I was back in my element. It had been a minute since I had the luxury of hitting my favorite designer stores. I left my money at home when Sosa called. He said I didn't need shit, and I was holding him to that. The way I was throwing this pussy on him, I had no doubt the sky was the limit when it came to me shopping. On top of that, Sosa was big on fashion himself, so I knew bae had me.

"What you over there thinking about?" he asked, pulling me toward the escalator.

"You!" I looked back and smiled at him.

"Nah, yo ass over there plotting. I ain't gonna keep you in that room our whole trip."

"Boy, wasn't no one thinking that. I fucks with you! Most niggas wouldn't do this for a bitch they just met, so I appreciate you."

Sosa grabbed my arm and pulled me into him when we got off the escalator.

"As long as you solid, you ain't got to worry about shit. Now, let's blow some bands, ma!" He hit me with that cocky ass smile and pulled me toward the Balenciaga store.

My mouth watered when we entered the store. I had a bad shopping habit, and I hoped Sosa was ready. I was nothing like the other bitches he fucked with. Them hoes just started getting money, I come from that shit. We walked over to the wall that held the sneakers, and Sosa stopped at the women's section.

"These shits fire. I ain't seen no one with these." Sosa picked up a pair of nude speed sneakers with the word Balenciaga written in black.

"Yeah, those fire, bae." I was already imagining what I would get to go with them. They were cute as hell. They were the sock-looking sneakers. I grabbed his hand and led him over to the men's section where they had a man's version of my sneakers.

"Look, bae!"

He grabbed them out of my hand and was in deep thought.

"Before I tell them to grab them out the back, you see anything else you want in here?"

I looked around the store. I only fucked with Balenciaga for their sneakers and bags occasionally. A hot pink hoodie caught my attention on the other side of the store. I walked over and grabbed the last one. It was cute and had the *This Is The New Balenciaga Logo* written in black on the front of it.

"Now I'm done," I said, handing him my hoodie.

Sosa paid for our shit while I scrolled through my phone looking at the malls store directory.

"They got a Fendi store?" Sosa asked, walking up on me. He was so tall he could see what I was doing as soon as he got close to me.

"Yeah, we can go there. I wanna get a bathing suit for that pool party later."

While we strolled through the mall, we discussed our childhoods. It was crazy we were both from the same city but had such a different upbringing. Sosa got everything he had out the mud, and that made me respect him.

"So how did you cope with your father being murdered?"

"That shit was hard, especially since that fuck nigga killed him in front of me. Then after that shit, I shut everyone out. Couldn't trust no one."

"They killed my mother and aunt in front of me and Dior." He stopped walking and looked over at me with a confused expression on his face. "I never told anyone that. My uncle thought it was best to not mention it to anyone so only the family knows."

"Damn, ma. I ain't know you were going through all that. I know how that shit feels. You start questioning yourself, blaming yourself because you ain't save them. Don't let that shit fuck with you, Gucci. There was nothing you could have done to stop that shit. From what I heard it was a planned hit."

"You don't understand, Sosa! My cousin blames me for their death."

He pulled me toward a bench that was outside the Fendi store. I hated to bring up my past because that shit was dark.

For the past month, I buried that night deep in my mind talking about it was almost like reliving it. The drugs and liquor helped take my mind away from things I couldn't deal with.

"Ma, if that shit is too much for you then we can leave it alone, but whoever was behind that shit is gunning for all the top money-makers in the city, and I'm included on that list. I can't keep you safe if I don't know what I'm dealing with."

"His name was Ace!" I blinked back tears as visions of that night flashed through my mind. Maybe one day I would be willing to speak about what happened that night, but I wasn't there yet.

Later that evening

After we left the mall, we came back to the room ate and got ready for the pool party one of Sosa's homeboys, who lived out here, was throwing. The jetlag was something serious. This was my first time being in a different time zone. It was a little after six. My body was still on eastern time, but I wasn't about to miss a pool party because I was tired. I sipped on my Red Bull as we walked through the lobby. People kept stopping us thinking we were celebrities and shit. I had on a cute Fendi print swimsuit with some black ripped jeans shorts and sandals to match. Sosa was rocking a pair of Gucci swim shorts with the matching slides and a black wife beater.

Our Uber was thirteen minutes away, and I noticed a fly-ass

photo opportunity. Since we had been out here, we hadn't taken any pictures.

"Excuse me, miss, do you mind taking a picture of us?" I asked one of the hotel employees who was walking past.

"Sure, you wanna take them right here?"

I looked over at Sosa.

"I don't give a fuck where we take them!" Sosa said, leaning against the wall.

"Yes, that's fine!" I handed her my phone and stood in front of him. He held my waist and then we switched it up and did some different poses.

"Get your phone. That's our Uber!" Sosa released me and sent a text to our driver, letting him know we were coming.

I thanked the woman and grabbed my phone. We hurried out the hotel where there were several cars parked near the entrance. Sosa guided me toward a Lincoln Continental that was parked on the side of the building.

The driver wasn't as talkative as our last driver, and that was cool with me. I scrolled through the pictures we took and paused when I got to the one that had the palm trees visible behind us. "Bae, do you mind if I post us on the Gram?"

Sosa looked up from his phone and glanced at our picture. I held my breath because some niggas were funny about bitches posting them on the Gram. Sosa was a popular nigga, who I've seen in the Greensboro Shade Room several times.

"I ain't got no bitch. Do you, ma!" He went back to texting whoever he was talking to.

I went back and forth between two pictures. They were both cute as hell. The first picture had Sosa biting his bottom with his head tilted back as he squeezed my ass while I looked back at the camera. Both pictures were giving, so I posted both with the caption *Life is Gucci $$$*. I made sure I added our location, The Vegas Strip.

We entered a more residential section of the city called Summerlin. All the houses were pastel colors with manicured yards, palm trees, and other plants I wasn't familiar with.

"How do you know the person who's throwing the party?"

"My nigga, Jay. He moved out here from Raleigh a couple of years back. We do business together, and that nigga's been trying to get me to come out here and check him on the personal tip." He grabbed a black rubber band off his wrist and pulled half his hair back off his face.

"Oh, that's why y'all weed be good as hell! You got the west coast connect."

"Exactly, ma!" Sosa winked and pulled me closer to him. "When we get there, I'm a chop it up with him about some business shit. His girl cool as fuck. I'm a need you to chill with her and her peoples until I'm finished."

"Sosa, I don't do bitches I don't know!" I whined as we pulled up to a house with tall ass palm trees and LED lights bordering the lawn.

"Toughen up. Nobody gonna fuck with you." I rolled my eyes but decided to drop the subject. Up until this point, our trip had been going good, and I didn't want to fuck our vibe up. "Right here, my man!" Sosa pointed toward the house.

We hopped out of the Uber and walked up a driveway that was lined with exotic cars. Est Gee's "Special" blasted from the backyard, and the smell of food grilling was in the air. Sosa pulled open the white gate, and my mouth dropped. Niggas were standing around kiddie pool filled with baby oil, and two girls were wrestling naked as the men tossed money at them. There were chicks inside the infinity pool twerking. Some had on bathing suits, others were naked.

"My nigga, Sosa!" A dark-skinned man with a low cut and grills walked up to us and pulled Sosa into a hug.

"What's good, my nigga? You doin it big out this bitch." Sosa smiled and looked around at the massive yard. He wasn't lying. The outside of the house was beautiful. I could only imagine what the inside looked like.

"I keep telling you the west coast and the property taxes low as hell. You better get up on it. My girl done talked me into buying the house across the street and turning it into an Airbnb. I'm Jay, sweetheart, since this nigga don't got no manners!"

"My bad, fam. This my shorty, Gucci."

I shook his hand, and a pretty girl walked up to us. She was tall as hell and looked very familiar. Then it clicked to me that she was the Instagram model, Italy. Italy was a known stripper who had turned into a video vixen. Now, she was up there with all the other popular girls who made their money posting pictures.

"Bae, we need some more turn up! Oh, hey Sosa, and who is this you have with you today?" she asked, talking fast as hell.

"What's good, Italy. This my girl, Gucci. Gucci, this Italy!" I smiled when he referred to me as his girl. I didn't know if he slipped up or he meant it, but it felt good that he was claiming me.

"Oh, my God. You're so pretty! Damn, I was worried when Jay said Sosa was bringing his girl, but you gonna fit in fine. Bad bitches only. Come on, girl. You can come with me. I know you don't want to be bored with men talk!" Italy had a slight accent, making me wonder where she was from. Her skin was golden brown, and she had long sandy blonde hair that stopped at the crack of her ass. I couldn't tell if she was wearing a weave or if it was her natural hair.

I laughed and allowed her to grab my hand and lead me toward the group of women sitting under the Gazebo.

"I'll be right back, ladies!" Italy breezed past them. She had long legs, so I was struggling to keep up with her.

We walked around to the back door and entered the house through the kitchen. They had a nice modern décor with stainless steel appliances.

"Come on up to our bedroom. I need to grab some coco for the party! How long have you and Sosa been dating?" She asked, leading me up the white wood floating stairs.

"To be honest I didn't know we were dating."

We both laughed as we continued through the upper level of the house. The carpet was a white color, and all the furniture I had seen so far was white, letting me know they didn't have any children.

Italy pushed a white double door open, revealing their master bedroom. A built-in fireplace sat in the middle of the room with a white bearskin rug in front of it. I could tell quality furniture when I saw it, and I knew they spent a grip on the white marble bedroom set.

"Me and my girls are about to get in the pool. If you want

to join us, you can put your shorts over there with the rest of their things." She pointed toward the vanity table in the corner.

I walked over to where their belongings were and removed my shorts. They had a floor-length mirror where I checked my reflection and applied some lip gloss while Italy rumbled in her dresser draw.

"Girl, your body is sick. You should start modeling. I make a killing on Instagram. I can definitely point you in the right direction."

"That would be cool. I dance right now, but I've been wanting to break into Instagram modeling for a minute. My followers are up, but nowhere near your level." I turned around and watched Italy grab a plastic baggie of coke out of the dresser.

Italy placed the bag next to her and focused on her reflection in the mirror. Her makeup was perfect, and her hair was laid to the gods, but I understood. I was the same way, always fucking with myself to make sure my appearance was straight, especially when I was gone off that powder.

"I used to dance, but once I took off on Instagram, I said fuck that shit. It was too much work for me. With hostings and modeling, all you have to do is show up. How long have you've been dancing?" she asked, looking over at me.

"Not long at all. I haven't technically worked a club, just an after-hours joint, but the money is lit, and I don't have to deal with unfamiliar bitches."

"Girl, don't sleep on the after-hours and private parties. Them bitches outside came up dancing for Jay and his peoples.

Have a seat, girl. I got to get Jay his shit before he has a heart attack."

I was funny about people sitting on my bed, so I chose to sit at her vanity. Italy disappeared into his and her closets and returned a few seconds later with four pints of lean.

"Don't worry, it only gets better for girls who look like us. Once I post you on my page, I guarantee you your followers will be up by the time you leave. I'm a hit my connect over at the Shade Room to get some exposure. You party?" she asked, pouring some of the coke on her dresser.

Fuck it. This bitch had more to lose than I did if it was ever to come out what was going on in the bedroom. Sosa didn't know that I fucked with coke, and I wanted to keep it that way, but there was no harm in doing a line before we went back outside. Italy rolled a hundred-dollar bill tightly and slowly inhaled one line in the right nostril and repeated the process with the left. I slowly got up and walked over to the dresser and watched her separate six additional lines.

"Three for you, three for me. I only do this on special occasions, but I don't like everyone in my business. Keep it on the low because I don't want them bitches outside in my business. Fuck around and be on the Shade Room!" Italy laughed and moved out of the way so I could get to the lines.

"Trust, I won't be saying shit. Sosa doesn't know I fuck with this shit." I bent over, pressed my finger against my nose and inhaled the first line. This was some pressure because the shit Fendi had didn't compare to this. I killed the other line and walked over to the mirror to check my nose. The familiar drip that I had grown to love slid down the back of my throat.

"You want some more before I put it up? We got to hurry up before one of them nosey bitches come looking for us," she asked, pouring us both a drink from the personal bar she had in her bedroom.

Fuck it. I was about to be on cloud nine. The way the coke made me horny, I was about to turn Sosa's ass out when we get back to the room.

"Fuck it, go ahead!" We bent over and enjoyed the coke. When we were done, Italy's eyes where slightly red. "Let me get that off you."

I leaned forward and wiped her nose. I was not a hater. Italy was cool as hell and had been showing me love, so I wasn't gonna let her play herself.

"I feel so good. I got a lot going on back home. It feels good to be able to relax."

" Fuck with me, girl. All me and my bitches do is get money and have fun. If you ever want to come back out here, let me know. Fuck around and might come out of retirement for one night. Let me check your face before we go back downstairs." Italy grabbed my face, and all of a sudden, she leaned forward and softly kissed me.

"Girl, I had to do that. Your lips were calling me. Let's go back downstairs before I fuck around and cheat on my man. If you and Sosa are down, we can hit the club up I used to work at."

She shocked the hell out of me with the kiss. I had never been interested in women before. Her lips where softer than a man, and now she had me curious. Nah, I wasn't gay. That was the coke fucking with me. I followed her back down the stairs, and I watched her ass shake the entire way.

Once we got back outside, more people had arrived, and the girls where now walking around giving niggas lap dances. Sosa was in the corner sitting with a group of men playing cards. He looked up at me and blew me a kiss.

"Come on, girl, let me bring Jay these bottles of lean."

While Italy talked to Jay, Sosa motioned for me to come over to him.

"You good, ma?" he asked while he focused on the cards in his hands.

"Yeah, I'm straight. Italy was talking about all of us hitting the strip club later."

Sosa's threw out his hand.

"Y'all niggas ain't fuckin wit me, boy," he shouted. "We can do that, bae."

He smacked me on my ass, and I walked back over to Italy, who took me to meet her friends.

We walked over to where four women, who looked to be in their early twenties were sitting. I could tell none of them were broke from the bathing suits they had on and the bags sitting next to them. They were talking and giggling when we walked up, but once we got close, they got quiet. I hoped they weren't on no bullshit because I would hate to cause a scene at Italy and Jay's home.

"Ladies, this is Sosa's girl, Gucci! Gucci, this is Mya, Cali, Dream, and Chyna!" Italy was speed talking as she introduced us. Everyone smiled and waved except for the girl with her hair pulled back in a long braid. I couldn't miss the shade if I wanted to. She looked me up and down, rolled her eyes, and went back to smoking the hookah that sat in the middle of the glass table.

"Girl, how do y'all do it? It's hot as hell out here. I had to take my wig off our first night," I said, sitting on one of the egg chairs.

"This ain't shit. The summertime is brutal! A bitch can't keep a wig to save my life when it gets hot," Italy's homegirl said, looking up from the blunt she was rolling.

"Nah, Dream. That's because you keep going letting your cousin do your shit. Don't listen to her, girl," Mya said.

"Chyna, pass me and Gucci them Daiquiri's. I need a drink. We about to get lit."

"Damn, Italy. Do I look like your maid?" Chyna snapped, putting the hookah down and reaching for the tray with the frozen drinks. I waited to see if Italy was gonna put her in her place, but she never did.

"Here, girl. Try this. It's my secret recipe." Italy winked, handing me a white drink.

I took a sip, and it was busting. The taste of coconut and pineapples exploded in my mouth. Whatever type of liquor she used blended in perfectly to the point I couldn't taste it.

"This is good as hell. You got to tell me what's in it so I can tell my grandmother. She'd make a killing selling these shits."

"Your grandmother's a bartender? Girl, with all that designer you rocking, you can't help her out?"

Italy cut her eyes at Chyna. "Chyna, chill out!"

"Nah, she good, Italy. Not that I have to explain shit to you, but my grandmother chooses to run her establishment."

"Oh, I get it. She must be one of the forty-year-old grand-mothers." Chyna let out a nasty giggle.

"She's fifty-three, but she looks younger than you. Do you wanna see a picture since you all in my business?" I asked with a blank look on my face.

"No need to get hostile. I was just making conversation." Chyna rolled her eyes and started whispering to the girl sitting next to her. I hated bitches like Chyna. The ones who tried to shade me and then hide their hand. I could feel her eyes on me as she whispered to the girl. Chyna was cute, but her attitude made her ugly.

"Girl, why Kitta called me the other day trying to get me to dance with her? Y'all heard of this club called Exotics?" Chyna asked.

"I heard of it, but I've never been. I already know it's gonna be some bullshit, so come with it. I been told that bitch to stop fucking with the clubs out here. Ever since the pandemic hit, them shits be hit or miss." Mya shook her head and inhaled her blunt. The other girls agreed with her, and I could tell that pissed Chyna off. From the short time I had been around her, I could tell the bitch thought she was better and knew it all.

"I make money wherever I go. Slow nights or whatever, so I can't relate." Chyna giggled, and the Cali girl high-fived her.

"That's because you fuck with them white clubs. You ain't got no competition. Your ass can't take that half-assed dancing to know black club and eat." Mya blew the smoke in Chyna's direction.

An hour had passed of me getting to know these ladies and

everyone was cool except for Chyna and Cali. I finished my drink and reached for another one. They were so good, and it helped to cool me down. My mouth was dry as hell from the coke, and I needed something in my mouth to stop me from twitching.

"Damn, you killing the drinks. Italy, next time you have a get-together, make sure everyone goes in on the bottle." Chyna looked over at me and rolled her eyes.

"Bitch, my nigga could pay for these lil drinks and your thirsty ass. Girl, you're a birdbrain and a fuckin hater sitting out here running yo people's business, and for what? To make yourself look better. Cause obviously you don't got it like that. Bitches who get money don't do all this."

The bitch wanted a reaction from me, now she got it. I didn't give a fuck where I was at. The one thing I couldn't allow was for another bitch to try to stunt on me.

Chyna's mouth dropped. She had this dumb ass look on her face like she was shocked I ripped her.

"Italy, you gonna let her talk to me like that? You don't even know this girl, yet we've been friends for over ten years, and you didn't once check her. I swear you always get pussy when it comes to Jay's people."

"Nah, Chyna. That's what we not gonna do. Don't mention my man. Gucci ain't did shit to you. Since the girl sat down yo ass been on ten," Italy corrected Chyna.

"Wow! Italy, you showing your true colors today. Cali I'm out let's go." Chyna snatched her bag off the chair and stormed off, not bothering to wait for Cali to respond. Cali was a do girl. I could tell by the way she dick rode Chyna.

"Bye y'all," Cali mumbled as she quickly followed behind Chyna, who was halfway across the yard.

From where I was sitting, I couldn't help but watch them leave. Chyna was a wack bitch, so I wasn't surprised when she stopped at Sosa's table. Whatever she said to him, he wasn't checking for her because he waved his hand and went back to playing cards. She stood next to him for a couple of seconds before she got the picture and left.

"Girl, don't pay that bitch any attention. She's mad you're here with Sosa, and he ghosted her." Mya said, passing me the blunt.

My head turned so fast I felt a deep pull in my neck. I wasn't blind to the fact that Sosa was a very popular man. For some reason, I was more pissed off that he would allow me to sit around a bitch he fucked with and not put me up on game.

"They used to fuck around?" I frowned at the thought of sharing Sosa with a bitch like Chyna. She wasn't an ugly chick by far. She was the stereotypical west coast girl, clueless. In the hour I was around her, all she did was brag about how much money she made. I wasn't doubting what they said. He was a man at the end of the day, and Chyna was a pretty face with a fat ass.

"That wasn't about shit. She ducked off with him when we were in Miami. Girl, they fucked around a couple of times when we went to Greensboro. Please, don't mention it to Sosa. I don't need my man mad because I'm running my mouth." Italy said.

"You good. She must not be that important if he didn't feel the need to bring her up. Thank you for the heads up. I'm a watch her ass!"

"I feel you on that. As fine as his ass is, I'd be mad, too." Mya said, sipping her drink.

"Enough of that bull shit let's take a selfie." Italy pulled out her camera, and instantly, the girls started checking their appearances.

"Hold up Italy, where's your tripod so we can all get in the picture?" Dream asked.

"It's behind the bar, let me go get it." Italy got up and walked over to the bar. A few seconds later she returned with a portable tripod.

I was happy she changed the subject. The last thing I wanted to do was discuss Sosa and Chyna. These girls were connected to people I needed access to. At the end of the day, Chyna was a bitch they rocked with and didn't owe me any loyalty. I positioned myself in between Mya, Dream and Italy, as we posed for the pictures.

Thirty minutes later, we were munching on some good ass barbeque when Italy started screaming.

"Look, bitches. We made it to Shade Room! I'm trying to get Savage Fenty to pick me up. This is the exposure I needed." She held her phone up and started popping her ass to the song playing.

Your girl made it to the Shade Room. That was major. Of course, the reason we were posted was because of them, but I was the baddest bitch in the picture. I scrolled through the comments that were filled with fire emojis and different people trying to figure out who I was. The caption read

Italy and friends turning up at exclusive Vegas Pool party.

"Girl, what's your IG so I can tag you in my story? My notifications are going crazy. Everyone is trying to figure out who you are." Italy held her phone, showing me the numerous inquiries on who I was.

I gave her my Instagram handle. Sosa, Jay, and the basketball player, Jahmere, walked over to us. I wasn't aware that there were celebrities in attendance at the party.

"Italy you got my girl going viral?" Sosa grabbed me and kissed me on the side of my neck.

"That's what happens when you're fine as fuck." Italy smirked.

"Enough of that shit. No more videos. We about to turn up. This ain't for the Gram!" Jay looked each of us in the eye before pouring himself another cup of lean.

Chapter Eleven
SOSA

Four months had went by since I returned from Vegas. My days and nights were spent hunting that nigga, Ace, and dodging a Federal Inditement. Vegas was the distraction I needed. A nigga had a chance to get away and regroup. The streets had been quiet for a minute. No home invasions, and the Feds hadn't done any recent sweeps. Alongside the other bosses in the city, we held a meeting with all active soldiers on our team. We all had one common enemy and used our recourses to find him. Them young boys went crazy when we announced the two hundred- and fifty-thousand-dollar bounty on that nigga's head.

Tonight, I was cooling in my condo downtown. This was the first day I had the chance to sit back and relax. My phone rang with an unknown number. Normally, I wouldn't answer, but my curiosity got the best of me.

"Who dis?"

"Sosa, please don't hang up. I know you not trying to talk to me, but please, give me a minute!"

Wynter was the last person I wanted to speak to. Her voice was shaking like she had just got finished crying. I let out a deep breath and debated if I should hear or out or hang up the phone like I had been doing. Wynter was a bitch I was fucking with hard at one point. Shit was going good up until the point some money had come up missing. The only two bitches that had access to my crib at the time were Elle and her. The fact that Elle was moving off jealousy made me question her loyalty. I had no reason to doubt Wynter up to this point. I fell back from both of them since I couldn't prove who took my shit. "You got two minutes."

"I don't know how many times I have to tell you I didn't steal from you. I love you. Why would I jeopardize what we had for some money?"

"If this is what you called to discuss, I'm a hang-up. Whatever we had, you ruined that shit. I can't fuck with a bitch I can't trust." I kept shit real with her so she could get the picture. Whatever we shared was dead, and she killed that shit. The same went for Elle. It was a wrap for her, too. Ain't no coming back from that type of shit. A bitch that would steal from me would set me up, and I didn't have time for that. In my line of work I can't afford no losses.

Wynter let out a deep breath and cleared her throat. "I'm never going to apologize for some shit I didn't do. You think because Elle plays that good girl role that she's above a lot of shit. When the time comes that you see that shit, remember this conversation. I was calling you because I don't have anywhere to go, and I can't do shit with this baby in my stomach. Now, if you want to turn your back on me, that's fine, but this is your baby, and I need your fucking help!" she screamed into the phone.

Here she went with this bullshit. Wynter had been running around the city claiming she was pregnant for a minute. I never bothered to reach out to her because I knew what I did with my dick.

"Lower yo voice when you speaking to me. We both know that baby you carrying ain't mine."

"I don't know what I ever saw in yo ass. If I had a doubt, do you think I would be blowing you up? I wasn't fucking no one but you. I know that's hard for you to believe, but it's the truth!"

"Yeah, aight! Hit me when you drop, and we'll do a DNA test. Until then, don't hit me for shit." If I thought, there was a possibility she was carrying my seed, I would have stepped up. It was easy for me to dismiss her. She was acting like I didn't know who the fuck she was. I did my homework on any bitch I stuck my dick in. Wynter and her ratchet ass family were known for scamming niggas. I was about to hang up on her stupid ass until she shocked the fuck out of me.

"We can do the test now. I don't care about the risk of losing the baby." Her voice cracked as she continued. "I'm not ready for no baby, and I'm too far along to get the abortion. Please, Sosa. I can't do this shit alone! I know you think I'm sheisty. Pick a fucking doctor, and I'll be there!" she screamed and then hung on me.

Shorty had poured her heart out to me. Those were tears of

desperation. I could hear it in her voice. The only thing that moved me about what she said was I could choose the doctor. I had to sit back and think of the times I fucked Wynter.

After two blunts and deep concertation, I couldn't think of a time when the condom broke, and that was on everything I loved. The only bitch I had ever ran up in raw was Gucci, and then it dawned on me. We never got that Plan B. We hadn't spoken much since we got back from Vegas. I was not the type to chase a bitch. Plus, I had a lot of shit on my plate. From what I heard, shorty was blowing up with that stripping shit, but we had some shit that needed to be discussed.

I needed to see her reaction when I asked about the Plan B. With the sneaky bitches I had in my life, my trust level was non-existent.

After a few seconds of waiting, the call connected to her bent over shaking her ass.

"Hey, Sosa. I'm working right now. Let me hit you back later," she said over the loud music. Wherever she was damn sure wasn't Ma's. It looked like she had graduated to shaking her ass in an actual club.

For some reason, that shit irked the fuck out of me, I didn't know if it was because she was being reckless saying my name or what. Them niggas she was dancing for could have been anyone, and with that nigga Ace walking freely, I wasn't feeling that shit. Then her ass was naked, and from the red tint of her eyes, I knew she was fucked up.

"Fuck them niggas. Take yo ass somewhere quiet now."

Gucci rolled her eyes like me hitting her up was a problem.

That was some shit I wasn't used to. My hoes always broke their necks when I called, so to have her dismiss me was new. While I waited for her to gather her money and walk off, I lit another blunt to calm my nerves. Gucci was on some other shit, and it wasn't sitting well with me that I was feeling her little ass.

"You got to chill with that shit! When I tell you I'm working, respect that. I don't blow your shit up making demands." Her gray eyes narrowed as she tapped her foot, waiting for me to respond. "I know you ain't do all that to not say shit." She folded her arms across them perky ass titties I loved to suck and rolled her eyes in annoyance.

"Are you done?" I smirked. Anyone else I would have cursed out, but she got a pass.

"Yeah," She mumbled.

That was what I thought. She must have forgotten who the fuck I was. "Did you ever get that plan B?" From the stupid ass expression on her face and the way her mouth dropped, I had my answer. A girl walked up, handed her a cigarette, and walked out of what I was guessing was the dressing room. There were clothes, makeup, flat irons, and a bunch of other shit spread out on the counter.

"I forgot, but it's straight. If I'm pregnant I'm not keeping it no way," Gucci said nonchalantly.

I should have been happy by her response. If Wynter was pregnant with my baby, I wasn't trying to have two kids within months of each other. That was two baby mamas a nigga would have to deal with for eighteen years. This shit was crazy as hell. A nigga didn't even like kids, and now I had two possibly on the way with a scammer and stripper. My mama was gonna have a field day with this one.

"Hit me when you leave work so we can talk."

"You gonna come scope me when I get back to Greensboro? I rather talk in person." She positioned her phone in front of her bald pussy, and images of her fucking me filled my mind.

"Yeah, I need some pussy. Hit me when you get back!"

" It's gonna be late when we get back. I'm in Charlotte. Make sure you answer!" Gucci blew me a kiss and disconnected the call.

When I hung up the phone, I started comparing Elle with Gucci. Elle was the closest thing I had to a girl. Out of habit, I always compared any bitch I fucked with to her. Elle was the type to ride with me even if I was right or wrong. I had to remember I was fucking with a young bitch. I was not used to having to wait to get my dick wet. Gucci was in the streets damn near as much as me and that was a turn off.

I ain't have time to go back and forth all night. I needed to handle this Wynter situation before it slipped my mind. I shot my cousin, True, a text to find me a doctor who did an early DNA test. True lived in Raleigh far enough from Greensboro where I didn't have to worry about Wynter trying to pay someone to tamper with the test results. True hit me back and let me know she would find someone who could see us ASAP. I slid a thousand in her account through my Cash app for her troubles.

. . .

Later on that Evening Carolina's Diner

I headed toward the airport to meet up with my cousin, Bag, and this older cat named Ray, who ran High Point. We chose the diner to meet because of its location. Not too many people traveled this far for food. All anyone was gonna see were truck drivers stopping through.

I pulled into the parking lot and parked next to Ray's old school box Chevy. That nigga was one of the most cautious hustlers I had seen in my life. I picked up on a lot of shit for him. If I didn't know better, I would think he was the typical older bachelor who collected disability. That nigga was a beast. He'd been in the dope game for years, served his time in prison like a G, and came home and took back over his territory. Most niggas didn't even know his ass was still in the game. They weren't gonna see him unless he wanted to be seen.

I walked past Bag's Black Camaro and was happy his ass was on time for once. As soon as the door swung open, the smell of bacon frying, sausages smoking, and coffee filled my nose. An older waitress named Anne stood behind the counter yelling out orders to the kitchen. We'd been coming to this spot for years, so I knew everyone on a first-name basis.

"What you getting today, baby?" she asked, leaning against the counter.

My stomach growled, reminding me I hadn't eaten since earlier. I looked up at the special board hanging from the wall and scanned the menu to see what I wanted. Their food was busting, so it didn't take long for me to decide what I was in the mood for. I had a taste for a big southern breakfast, so I went with the meat lovers omelet stuffed with diced ham, bacon, crumbled sausage, & cheddar cheese.

"What's good with you, Ms. Ann?" If my mama did one thing right, she made sure I had manners. Most people didn't see this side of me, but this woman was old enough to be my grandmother, so I showed her respect.

"I'm okay, baby. Can't wait to get off and go home to catch up on my stories." Ann placed a stack of napkins in the dispenser and then reached for her notepad to take my order.

"Let me get the meat lovers omelet with a side of cheese grits, home fries, and sausage."

"Coffee or Orange Juice?" she asked, scribbling on the pad.

"Both." I winked at her and headed toward the far back where Bag and Ray were seated inside a booth.

Ray sipped on a cup of coffee while he flipped through the newspaper.

"What's good, youngin?" he asked, never looking up from the paper.

"I can't call it!" I dapped both of them up and slid into the booth next to Bag.

"Yo peoples came upon any information on that nigga Ace?" I asked, getting straight to the point.

Ray folded the newspaper and leaned closer to us. "I don't believe in coincidences. No one knows shit, and if it wasn't for the Snow girl telling you that bit of information, we would still be in the dark. Now, it's mighty funny this nigga slides through, kill the twins, hits their stashes, and Snow is locked up the same night that shit went down. What does that sound like to y'all?" He looked between me and Bag.

"That shit sounds like an inside job. Ain't no way someone gonna hit them motherfuckers if they ain't have a connect to the inside."

"Now, you think the whole time we chasing a ghost in Miami that no one ever heard of, yet, they targeting all the niggas in North Carolina that's getting it. I spoke to my people in Tennessee. Same shit happening out there."

Miss Anne walked over to our table with another waitress with our orders. "I apologize, gentleman. I don't mean to interrupt, but I didn't want to wait, and your food get cold."

"You good, Ann. You know you owe me a date from eighty-nine. I ain't forget." Ray winked at Ms. Ann, who waved her hand at him.

"Raymond, you was a whore back then, and I'm sure not much has changed. Here y'all go, babies. If you need anything, let me know." She smiled at me and Bag, placed our plates down, and walked off. The other waitress placed Ray's food down and scurried behind Ann.

I picked up a piece of crisp bacon and chewed, thinking about what Ray said. "You know, what's crazy to me is ain't no one heard from that nigga Dro since all this shit went down."

"Bingo! Now y'all niggas are thinking. With Snow out the way, who benefits the most from it?" Ray clapped his hands and nodded his head.

"Damn, that shit crazy, and if that nigga gets all of us hemmed up, then he can take over everything," I mumbled, mad that I hadn't been thought of that shit.

"You think that nigga would kill his wife and abandon his daughter for that shit?"

"Niggas will sell out they own mama for a chance to have that much power. Who's to say the bitch is even dead? Either she wasn't down with it, and he murked her ass before she could get to his brother, or she was in on the shit, too." Ray bit into his pancake like he didn't drop a bomb.

"Nah, she dead. My shorty replayed the story to me. That nigga Ace murked everyone inside that house. If she wasn't on her shit, she would have been in the stars with them."

We all continued to eat lost in our thoughts. If Dro was behind this shit, then he was a marked man. "Someone needs to go holla at Snow. He's the only one closest to his brother who can point us in the right direction. I ain't about to sit around playing checkers while this nigga playing Chess."

Bag looked over at me, and I already knew what type of shit he was on. "Fuck you looking at me for?"

"Nigga, you got the best connection to that nigga, Snow. His daughter." Bag shook his head and bit into his T-bone. I loved my cousin to death, but sometimes, he didn't think. The last person we needed getting involved in this was one of the girls.

"Nah, that ain't gonna work. This situation too close to her. Females are emotional." I took a sip of my drink and placed it back down on the table. If Gucci wasn't so connected to the situation, she would have been the perfect person to get me to Snow. They weren't doing phone visits right now. Everything was over the phone through this app called Webex.

"Nah, youngin. He got a point. You know his daughter is on

his list. It ain't nothing for you to get her to get him on the phone and then step in private to speak to him. Who you think she gonna choose? Her Uncle or her Mama and Daddy?" Ray dropped his napkin onto the plate that was empty except for the ketchup and egg yolk stains and waited for my answer.

Chapter Twelve
SNOW

"Have you changed your mind?" the old man asked. His shifty eyes danced around my room. He whistled and then took a seat on the rusty stainless-steel toilet in the corner of my cell. The black silk suit blended in with his coal-like skin. He took a bite of a bright red apple that had specks of gray mold on it and continued to look around my cell.

The first thought that crossed my mind was I was going crazy. The twenty-three-hour lockdown had finally gotten to me. This wasn't the first time I'd seen the creepy old man. Twenty-three hours before I was arrested, he appeared the same way and warned I would lose everything before the next sunset. I dismissed the crazy-ass dream and promised myself to lay off the Henny for a minute.

Some days I would never forget. January fifteenth was one of them, and it would haunt me for the rest of my life. The business trip I just returned from in Peru went better than expected. With the new ticket, I was about to flood the streets with ninety-nine percent uncut cocaine. Niggas wasn't fuckin with me because my coke was too raw. "Life Was Good" by Future and Drake was playing while I sipped on my Yak in the backseat of my Maybach. My driver paused the music and commented on the sky. It was dusk, and the sun was setting. In my thirty-nine years of being on this Earth, I never witnessed the sky that blood-red color. The sound of sirens came out of nowhere. I wasn't worried because the car was clean and any guns inside it were registered. The pigs snatched me up for an old body from years back. My first murder to be exact. It had been twenty years since I murked the nigga responsible for getting my mother sprung out on heroin, my bitch ass father. I was transported to an unknown location and spent seventeen hours inside an interrogation room. The cocky-ass officer dropped a stack of photos on the table and walked out of the room. My heart broke the moment my eyes landed on the pictures. My beautiful wife laid in a pool of blood with her twin Chanel, beside her. Through my tears, I saw a sequence of numbers that made me freeze. That was the third day I saw the numbers six six six. First on my plane ticket. Then, the squad car had the numbers written on the side of it, and when the detective showed me the picture of Prada's lifeless body the time stamp revealed the same numbers. At that moment, I knew it wasn't a dream. This was my reality. The deal I made years ago was now coming back to haunt me.

"You know when you went to see that old hag in South Carolina none of the other Ancestors would touch you. They turned their backs on you, and I gave you everything you wanted. Fame, power, and enough money that your grandchildren's children would prosper. When I did that, you didn't have to wait for an answer. Now tell me, did you change your mind?" the old man interrupted my thoughts. His voice sounded like nails scratching slowly against a blackboard.

My mouth felt dry as I struggled to breathe. The air grew stale and smelled of dead flowers.

"Nah, I paid my debt to you in blood when I killed my father. I did everything you requested. I don't owe you shit."

The man's eyes narrowed. His mouth twisted into a sly grin. "You do know it doesn't work that way." His laugh sounded like a pack of hyenas. I swore every time I saw this nigga it felt like I was speaking to the devil himself. In the past I've seen him in my dreams, this was the first time he appeared as clear as day. Whatever power this nigga held, it always felt like my soul was slowly leaving my body when I was near him. "I want the girl permanently. I wouldn't take too long to come to a decision. You aren't the only family member I can do business with. Say the words, and you can go back to your life like this."

He snapped his fingers.

What the fuck? I was no longer inside my cell. I blinked, and I was back home. My hands gripped the silk sheets. This shit can't be real. My eyes traveled down my body. I was no longer wearing the cheap prison jumpsuit. Instead, I was dressed in a pair of boxer briefs. The smell of bacon and coffee brewing downstairs made my stomach rumble. Damn. I missed waking up to the sun shining through my bay windows.

I blinked again and was back inside my cell, drenched in

sweat. My heart was racing as I stared around the empty room and tried to catch my breath. The deal I made years ago when I was a desperate corner boy willing to do anything to rise to the top had come back to haunt me. When I went to visit the voodoo queen back in the day, I halfway believed the bullshit she was saying. Now I knew everything she predicted was coming to pass. My sudden come up in the dope game, Prada's murder, my freedom being snatched away, and my daughter wilding out was not a coincidence. When I found out my daughter was stripping and getting high, that broke my heart. The streets talked and even, with me being locked up I still heard everything. I had eyes everywhere and knew Prada's snake ass mama had the girls dancing.

Ninety days and sixteen hours I'd been on a twenty-three-hour lockdown. The only time I was allowed out of my cell was to shower and when the other inmates slept. The alphabet boys were playing no games when it came to this bullshit case they were trying to build. Sloppy was one thing I'd never been which was why they were trying to hit me with a conspiracy charge. If they could get someone from my team to crack that was all they needed to place me under the jail. What they failed to realize was there were only two people who knew that type of information they needed. My brother and my wife, who was now gone. I was praying Dro was alive because I needed him now more than ever.

It was killing me they denied my bond. I had to get back to the streets to save my business and my daughter. Stupid ass pigs had me marked as a high-risk escape. They were trying to break a nigga. I ain't never been a weak nigga. I preferred being isolated. It gave me a chance to think. With all the issues I had in my life, socializing was the last thing on my mind.

Being on lockdown gave me a chance to sit back and see where I went wrong. Before my incarceration, I was living every dope boy's dream. Ya boy was the plug. Years of hugging the block finally paid off. I elevated from selling grams out of The Grove to supplying every major city in North Carolina, South Carolina, and Tennessee. God blessed me when he gave me the last name Snow because that was who I was on the streets, The Snow Man.

I lived a crazy life filled with sex, money, and murder. Thanks to my connect in Ell Callo Peru, I was able to provide my family with the luxurious lifestyle they deserved.

God had a way of humbling you real quick. I went from living in an eight thousand square feet mansion to sleeping in a room big enough to hold a bed, toilet, and sink. When the lights were off and the dorm was quiet, I was faced with the bitter truth. I failed my family. All that materialistic shit wasn't bringing back my wife, and that was what hurt a nigga most. That woman was my rock. We went from getting free lunch in middle school to hugging the block and then traveling world in private jets.

I replayed the crazy-ass dream back in my head a hundred times until the guard brought me my tray for breakfast. I eyed the brown tray. I wouldn't feed this type of shit to my dog, let alone ingest it myself. Slop was what I called the runny eggs, gray lumpy grits, and this hard-ass roll that looked like a cross between a biscuit and dry-ass cornbread. My real breakfast was on its way, but food was the last thing on my mind. I needed answers on how to get this old nigga off my back and my life back on track. The only person who could answer those questions was hundreds of miles away in a small town in South Carolina.

Thirty minutes later, like clockwork, there was a tap on my cell door. My back cracked when I stood up. The flimsy mattress was doing a number on me. I walked to the door and reached for the bag of Bojangles that one of the guards I had on payroll named Thompson brought me every morning. Thompson was a younger CO that grew up in the hood. He wasn't uptight like the other officers and had no problem accepting a payout to make my time easier behind bars. Thompson wasn't the only officer I had on my payroll.

"What's good, Snow? My bad if your food isn't as warm as usual. Old lady Taylor was on duty when I came in. You got a visit at nine this morning. I'm a take you so you can have your privacy."

Old Lady Taylor, as we called her, was the true definition of a bitch. Forty years old, balding, ain't never been married, and lived at home with her cats. The highlight of her miserable life was coming to work and fucking with people.

"You straight, man. Ain't no one stunning that old hag. Give me a couple of minutes to kill this, and you can come back to get the bag."

"No problem, Snow." He turned to walk away.

Then I remembered this was the first visit request since I'd been locked down. I didn't like surprises and needed to know who was attempting to see me. "Thompson, what name is on the visit sheet?"

I looked through the small window and watched him flip through the clipboard. He might be on my payroll, but that didn't mean I trusted his ass. It's one thing to accept the food he brings, that doesn't mean I had to trust him with my safety.

"Gucci Snow," he said before he walked away.

It surprised me that Gucci took this long to reach out to me. There was some shit we needed to discuss, so I was happy she set up the visit. I hurried and ate the Cajun Chicken Filet Biscuit combo.

When Thompson came back to get the bag, I had him take me to the shower area so I could get myself together. My baby girl was going through enough. I didn't want her worrying about me.

Entering my room, my eyes scanned everything to make sure my shit was how it was before I left. These niggas knew better than to enter my room, but there was always one knucklehead who loved to play with fire. My sneakers were lined up against the wall, the books I got from the commissary were how I left them, and my hygiene products were still in the same spot. After I threw on a fresh pair of boxers, socks, a wife-beater, and a new uniform, I felt better about myself. Now, all I had to do was wait for the visit. Time moved slowly in here. I ran my wave brush through my hair and waited for Thompson to come back to get me.

Keys jingled outside my door. I placed my brush under my pillow and stood up so Thompson could escort me to the visitation. The door swung open, and he allowed me out of my room.

Inmates nodded their heads in respect as I strolled through the hallway. The other guards would be dicks and handcuff me, but Thompson allowed me my freedom.

The spot where they held the virtual visits was on C block, one level up from where I was housed. The room was empty except for the tables they allowed inmates to use. I stared at the screen on the tablet and waited for Gucci to join the meeting.

"Hey, Daddy I miss you so much!" Gucci's beautiful face popped up on the screen. That girl looked just like her mama. Same gray cat eyes, pouty lips, and perky nose. The only thing she got from me was my silky hair texture.

I nodded my head at Thompson so he could leave before I spoke to my daughter. Something was off with her, and I couldn't place it.

"Fuck you doing stripping?" I ain't have time to waste. The visits lasted for thirty minutes, so I got straight to the point. Yeah, I needed to speak to her about the shit I needed her to do, but I had to address the elephant in the room.

Gucci bit her bottom lip and looked away from the phone. My baby girl was forgetting who the fuck she was. A nigga had been so busy trying to protect her from the streets that I made her a target. She didn't know shit about getting it out the mud like me and her mother.

"Nah, don't get quiet on me. If shit is that bad, then go to your uncle, open your fucking mouth, let him know what you need." I was referring to Prada's younger brother, Bishop, who I left in charge when I got locked up. If my brother Dro wasn't missing, then he would have had that position. No one had heard from him to my knowledge. I hated to say it, but if that nigga ain't shown up by now, he was most likely dead. He couldn't stay away from home for an extended period of time. My brother loved Greensboro. The only time he left was for business and to get him to do that was like pulling teeth.

"Daddy!" Gucci let out a deep breath before she continued. "Uncle Bishop got knocked a couple of days after Mama's funeral," she whispered.

Nah, that couldn't be right. I wasn't hearing her correctly. My fist slammed on the table. Everything was falling apart, and a nigga couldn't do shit. This type of information was what I pay Jason for. As soon as Bishop was bagged, I should have been the first person informed. Bishop was a vital member of my team. If he was locked up then that meant there was no money being made.

"Where the fuck you at?" I noticed her background for the first time since we had been on the call. The closet door was open and rows of sneakers and fitted hats lined the shelf. This girl done bumped her head if she was discussing family business with one of these bottom feeder hustlers around.

"Daddy I'm at my man's house. I've been meaning to write you, but things have been crazy. I lost my ID in Vegas, and the county wouldn't allow me to schedule a visit without it."

"Let me holla at him real quick," a deep voice said in the background. I ain't wanna believe the rumors that my baby girl was on that bugger sugga. That was the only explanation for this carless ass move.

"Girl, have you bumped yo motherfucking head? You know better than to bring one of these little niggas into my business."

Before I could finish cursing her ass out, a black hand snatched the phone from her.

My eyes narrowed. This nigga had some fuckin balls. If I wasn't locked up, I would have smacked the shit out of him. All them young niggas knew my daughter was off-limits.

"Nigga, you fucking my daughter?" My voice was no longer calm and gentle like it was when I was talking to Gucci.

Sosa wasn't the worse nigga she could have chosen, but his ass still ain't good enough for my little girl. I watched this little nigga rise in the streets. Even schooled him when he first got on the scene on how to conduct himself. He reminded me of a younger version of myself, and that was why I would never approve of him and my daughter's relationship. That nigga was knee deep in the streets, and I ain't want that Karma coming back to my baby girl.

"Better me than one of these fuck niggas. You know how I rock, OG," he said nonchalantly.

"Yeah nigga, that's the problem. I know how you motherfuckin rock. I taught yo lil ass the game."

Sosa continued to smoke his blunt. "I ain't on no fuck shit when it comes to her, Snow."

"Nigga, my daughter is out here stripping and she's fucking you. If you gave a fuck about her, you would of deaded that shit." We locked eyes. Game recognized game. That nigga wasn't doing something I had done a million times in the past, saying whatever to fuck a bad bitch. When you loved a woman, there's certain shit you won't tolerate.

"Snow, you know my character. Out of respect for you, I'm a

keep shit hot. I ain't asking you for your permission to fuck with your daughter. We ain't that serious. I fuck with shorty. On my Earth, she was stripping when I meet her. I been tried to holla at her about taking that makeup shit serious, but she ain't wit it. What I'm tryna do is make sure she doesn't end up like everyone else in your organization. In order for me to do that, I need your help."

Little nigga had some balls on him coming to me about my daughter. I was curious about what he had to say, so I entertained the conversation. Now that Bishop was locked up, I needed someone on the outside I could trust. Over the years, Sosa proved his loyalty.

"Baby girl, step out so we can talk business," I said to Gucci, who was sitting next to Sosa shitting bricks. This part of the conversation she didn't need to hear. I never discussed business around my daughter. The less she knew, the better. The way the Feds were coming, I needed to keep her separated from what I had going on.

Once Gucci left the room, we continued with our conversation.

"Aight, lil nigga. You did all this to get me here so talk." I leaned back in the chair and kept my eyes on Sosa, looking for any sudden changes in his body posture.

He looked me in my eyes and let out a deep breath.

"High Point and South Side had a meeting with me, and we tried to come up with who is behind this shit," he started speaking in code. High Point was an older cat named Ray who coped work from me, and South Side was his cousin Bag. Every nigga who worked for me had code names, it was something I had come up years ago to prevent the police from infiltrating my organization.

"Baby girl disclosed to me what happened the night at the spot we were playing cards. Nigga had a hand full of Ace's."

My jaw clenched as the rest of my body locked up with rage. Ace was the nigga responsible for my family's massacre. I wanted that niggas head, and it would be my bullet that would end his life.

"Continue." I let out a deep breath. There wasn't much I could say. Most likely the Feds were recording this conversation, but it was a risk I had to take.

"Hight Point put us up on game. Ain't no way that nigga could know the ins and out of everyone else's hands unless someone rigged the game. The only thing that makes sense is there was someone on the inside. Weather is crazy as fuck out here. We think it might Snow." He locked eyes with me.

I didn't speak right away. I had to process what he was saying. The dream I had earlier replayed in my mind. *I wouldn't take too long to come to a decision. You aren't the only family member who I've done business with.* There it was. The missing piece to the puzzle. No one knew where my family laid their head but my staff, which I vetted myself, and the people who lived there. I didn't want to believe my little brother would snake me like this. I needed more information before I sicked the dogs on him.

"Before y'all make any moves, I need you to do something for me. No one knows what I'm about to tell you, and I expect it to stay that way."

"Understood!" That nigga ain't flinch, and from the fire in his eyes, I knew he was ready for war.

"Tell my daughter to come back in the room and get something to write on." This was my last chance to make shit right and I prayed I was making the right decision.

Chapter Thirteen
GUCCI

Why do I feel like I've seen this before?

We drove down the deserted highway, and a feeling of déjà vu crept over me. I remembered everything from when I drove down this same road years ago. The cream-colored house that sat in the middle of a dying cornfield. We were the only cars on US-1 every so often, a truck would pass by us. My father's visit shook me to the core, and old memories resurfaced.

The car was quiet. Neither of us had spoken since we left Greensboro. When my daddy told me to leave the room, I stood at the door listening to the conversation. I was tired of everyone treating me like a little kid. Anything regarding my mother's death was my business. A part of me wished I would have walked away. Uncle Dro was my favorite uncle, the one I could go to about anything. To hear he might have destroyed our family had me running to the bathroom and throwing up everything I ate the night before.

I cleaned my face, brushed my teeth, and took a hit of coke to help calm my nerves. I went back to the living room and waited for them to finish talking. My nerves were all over the place, and I was questioning everyone, especially Dior. Did she know about her father's betrayal and was she part of it?

Sosa had me come back in the room, and that was when my father told me he needed me to go to South Carolina. As soon as the word left his mouth, I knew what this was about. There have always been rumors in the streets that my family dabbled in black magic. We wrote the directions down, and the visit came to an end. Sosa had so many questions, and I couldn't answer them. I guess he was still pissed about it because he hadn't spoken a word to me since we left.

Sosa looked over at me. His eyes were filled with frustration as he tugged on his locs. Normally, he kept them twisted up, but I guess he needed a retwist because he had them down, and his new growth was showing. The silence was killing me, and his cold stare wasn't helping things.

"I'm a need you to keep it real with me and tell me what I'm walking into?"

"How much do you wanna know?" I wasn't trying to tell him more than he needed to know. If it was up to me, this would have stayed a secret, but my father involved him in our family's business.

"Everything. You can start with who this woman is that can help us figure out who has a target on our back and why no one can know about her?"

I let out a deep breath and looked out the window, wishing this trip was for pleasure instead of business. The air smelled like salt water, and the closer we got to Hilton Head, the salt-water smell got stronger. I always knew when I was getting close to a beach location once that smell hits my nose. When I turned back around, he was shaking his head.

"I'm a tell you some shit that might have you side-eyeing me and questioning everything." I paused. When he didn't say anything, I continued. "You know the rumors about my family. Some of them are true. We aren't devil worshipers, but my father has an agreement with the witch doctor we are going to see. I don't know much about that agreement. The first time he took me to see her all I remember was the lady seemed to know things she shouldn't."

"Fuck you trying to say? Tell me this some bullshit so I can turn back around. I don't got time to go on a witch hunt, ma."

"Nah, if my father told you to go see her there's a reason for it. I know it sounds crazy. Imagine how I feel having to tell you this. At first, it was just a secret between me and my dad, but then my mom started going." I paused to gather my thoughts. Sosa looked over at me, and I let out a deep breath before I continued.

"All I know is my mother and father took trips to see this woman every couple of months for years. On the last visit, something happened, and I don't know what it was. When they came back, my father and mother argued for hours. That was the worse argument I ever heard them have. When they were finished, my father and uncle left, and then the Haitians ran into our crib a few hours later."

Sosa's mouth dropped, and his hand gripped the steering wheel. It didn't matter if he believed in what I was saying, but I knew the truth. My family had done some fucked up things to get where they were in life, and this woman held the secrets on how we could get back on top.

"I've heard of niggas fucking with a witch in South Carolina. My nigga, Bam, told me he heard of a lady when he was locked up that a lot of street niggas fucked with. I thought all that shit was cap. Now I'm seeing this bitch might be the key to everything. I believe in none of that shit, but it doesn't mean other niggas don't. If she's as connected as you say, that bitch gonna lead us to Ace. We can do it the nice way or by force."

"Nigga, are you crazy? Did you not just hear what I said? This woman is powerful. She read my fucking when mind when I was a little girl. Some shit that would have been impossible to guess, she knew."

"What she guess, ma?"

"That's beside the point. When we get there, don't do anything stupid. If you don't believe in voodoo that's cool, but I know the truth. My family ain't get where they are by hugging the block. There was a lot of bloodshed, and it wasn't just on some street war shit."

Sosa laughed. He could think this was a joke if he wanted. A lot of niggas dabbled in black magic to get put on. I saw it more in South Carolina, Florida, and New Orleans. It was the best-kept secret in the dope game. If you think niggas go from the projects to multimillionaires off their ability to navigate the streets, you're crazy. Anyone can grab a pack and flip it. Most niggas end up dead or behind bars. It was a devilish game to win. You had to be willing to sacrifice anything or anyone.

"We gonna have to stop for gas before we get to Hilton Head. I wanna be able to bounce if shit goes left."

I wanted to ease his mind, and hopefully, in the process, I could calm my nerves.

"From what I remember, she's not a threat. She's weird as hell, but she's old and deadly. From what I remember, she said she turned her husband into a cat. Crazy, right?"

Sosa laughed and squeezed his hand around his gun tighter. I was trying not to feel offended that he felt the need to have his gun on his lap around me. I could see him riding like that in the city, but we were driving on a country road. The only thing around us was farmland, cows, and horses. Now that he knew the truth, I wondered how that would change things. People were ignorant when it came to anything they couldn't understand or see.

"You too trusting, ma. You got to stop that shit. I don't give a fuck who it is. We don't know how far this nigga Ace's reach is and who's working with him. I always hold shit down, but a nigga can never be too cautious."

Damn. This nigga was spitting knowledge, and all I could think about was how I rode his face last night. I ain't wanna come off as weak, so I bit my tongue. It was obvious that Sosa was playing no games when it came to our safety. He was right. That nigga Ace was a problem. He stormed our estate like it was nothing. My father had all types of high-tech security, and the one place he couldn't gain access to was the panic room. If Ace had the time, I believed he would have burned the house down to ensure none of us survived. The mention of Ace's name sent chills down my body. I needed Sosa to handle this nigga because something in my spirit told me he was coming back for me. Fuck that. If bae wanted a rider, I was gonna be that. I reached inside my new Hermès Kelly bag that Sosa copped me and pulled out my baby nine.

Sosa glanced over at me and nodded his head in approval. "Now you thinking, bae. I need yo head in this. I've heard old heads talk about an old lady that was a voodoo priestess or whatever they call that shit."

"My heads in this, but this woman isn't a threat. My family has been dealing with her for years. Trust me, were good. Let me find out you scared of an old woman." I laughed. Why did I say that? His crazy ass slammed his foot on the breaks, stopping in the middle of the highway. Thank God there were no cars behind us.

"Baby girl, don't ever twist yo lips to question how I move in these streets. Unlike you, I ain't have a mama and daddy to protect me. That paranoia is the reason I wake up on the green side of the dirt every day." He looked at me long and hard before he pulled off.

"First of all, you don't know what I've been through. Yeah, I might have grown up sheltered, but that doesn't mean my father didn't teach me everything I know. If he told us to go see her, it's for a reason." I wasn't about to argue with him. My daddy told us to go, and we were going to do just that. I got that Sosa was hesitant. Even though I seemed not to be bothered, deep down, I was somewhat worried. The last time I went with my father, I had nightmares for weeks. The gram of coke I had in my purse was calling my name. I needed to numb myself to deal with this situation. I tried to search for nearby gas stations. We must have been in a dead zone because I wasn't getting any signal.

"Let me see your phone. Mine isn't getting service."

Sosa reached for his phone and glanced down at the screen. "My phones not getting service either. Chill out. We ain't got that many stops before we hit Hilton Head."

That wasn't the answer I wanted to hear. I pretended I wasn't bothered that he didn't want to stop. Sosa didn't know about me doing powder, and I planned to keep it like that. To be honest, that nigga drank lean all day, so he should be the last person to judge me.

"Man stop pouting when I see an exit we'll stop." Sosa said.

After driving for what seemed like forever, we were eight miles north of the Georgia border. Sosa exited the highway and followed the signs until we pulled up at a gas station.

"You want me to pay for the gas and you pump?" I asked, removing my seatbelt.

"Yeah and grab us some snacks." He handed me the money, and I jumped out of the car and ran inside. I paid for the gas first and grabbed the bathroom key off the counter. I would grab our snacks once I was finished.

The bathroom had a slightly fishy odor, tissue was all over the floor, and little gnats flew around. Any other time I would have walked out, but I had no other option but to deal with it. I locked the door with a piece of tissue and fumbled inside my purse until my hands touched the blinged-out heart compact mirror I used to stash my shit. Dipping my pinky nail in the baggie, I scooped as much as it could hold and brought it up to my nose. I repeated the process a couple of times and knotted the bag back up so it wouldn't spill. The mirror was dirty, so I used my cell phone to check my nose and applied some lip gloss before I walked out of the nasty bathroom.

"Damn, you bad as hell," a voice said from behind me. I could see his reflection through the drink refrigerator. He was a little cutey and seemed to be around my age. Sosa was outside, so I wasn't going to fuck with it. I thanked him grabbed us both a Snapple and walked over to the register. There was no way I was eating after hitting the coke, but I made sure to grab Sosa a couple of Slim Jim's and a bag of chips to hold him off. That nigga ate like there was no tomorrow. The guy that spoke to me paid for my things and walked out of the gas station before I could thank him.

"You welcome, gorgeous!" he called out as I hurried to Sosa's car. Sosa looked at me when I got in the car, and I avoided his eyes.

"I didn't know what you wanted." I took my drink out of the bag and handed it to him.

"You good, ma." He turned the music up and pulled out the gas station and jumped back on the highway. We were driving for about forty minutes before he turned the music down and asked, "What we supposed to do now, shorty?"

"All it says is go east and follow the signs until we get to the bridge."

A part of me was hopping when we arrived the woman wouldn't be there. This situation only proved how crazy my family was.

By the time we entered Hilton Head, the sun set, and the streets were dark. I didn't know what was up with this town, but they didn't believe in streetlights. I hadn't seen one since we got here.

We got lost, and we couldn't make out any of the street names. Sosa made a left and almost hit a little girl. She had on a dingy white dress, no shoes, and was struggling to hold a straggly white dog. My heart dropped, and thankfully, we didn't hit her. Sosa pulled over to where she was and yelled out to her. "Aye, princess! It's late as hell for you to be wandering out here alone."

The little girl looked up at us with a nervous expression on her face. The dog started barking and was fighting to break free.

"Sosa, she's scared, baby," I whispered to him. She looked like she was about to run at any second.

"Chill, I got this. Watch me work," he whispered. "Baby girl, do you know where I can find a pink house? There's an old lady that lives there it's on a dead-end street." Sosa flashed the little girl a warm smile, and her face relaxed.

The little girl placed her finger on her chin while she thought. "The witch doctor, Madame Boudet?"

Sosa looked over at me for confirmation and I shook my head yes. The little girls face dropped, and she grabbed her dog and walked off fast as hell.

Sosa shook his head and drove behind her at a snail's pace. "I'll pay you if you tell me how to find her."

Sosa pulled a stack of money out of his pocket and held it up.

The little girl stopped. Rocking back and forth, she looked over us. "My mama said the lady is evil. If I take that money and something happens to you, God would be mad at me."

"Ain't nothing gonna happen to us, sweetheart. All we needed to do is talk to the lady."

The little girl blushed with her fast ass. Her mama needed to teach her not to be talking to strangers. I guessed Sosa's charm worked even on little girls because she damn sure accepted the money and directed Sosa how to get to the woman's house.

After a few turns, we pulled onto a dead-end street, and there was the pink house. It seemed duller than I remembered as a little girl.

"Are those birds?" I asked. I had never seen birds fly at night, and they seemed to be hovering over the house.

"Nah, baby girl. Those are bats," he responded, driving up to the house. Sosa ain't give no fucks. That nigga chose violence when he parked his car on the lawn. He hopped out the car with his gun in his hand. I jummped out to try and tell him to move the car when the door opened.

"Hello, Gucci long time no see."

It felt like I was seeing a ghost. She had half her locs up in a bun, and the rest hung down to her ankles. Her skin was smooth with no wrinkles, almost like hadn't aged a day since I last saw her. I knew that was impossible. Madame Boudet smiled at us. The gold cap on the side of her front tooth sparkled. "I was wondering when you were going to come see me. You've been causing a lot of issues in the underworld, my dear."

She held the door open wider for us to enter, but my legs weren't moving.

Sosa stepped in front of me with his forty on his side. "Who's inside the house?" Sosa asked not moving.

"I'm alone. Oh, and Sosa baby, make this your first and last time parking on my lawn."

"How the fuck do you know my name?" Sosa gripped his gun and grabbed my hand, pulling me toward the house with a crazy look on his face.

Madame Boudet wasn't fazed by his question. I knew she was crazy when she busted out laughing.

"I haven't had someone talk to me like that in years. Watch yourself, boy." Her face went blank, and she no longer was smiling.

"My father sent us to talk to you. He didn't mean any harm," I tried to defuse the situation. Sosa wasn't aware of how powerful or dangerous this woman was. He wasn't thinking rationally and was trying to handle her like she was a street nigga.

"I hope you got my money. I don't do shit for free. Y'all hurry up and come inside before you let these blood suckas in my house," she snapped at us.

I looked at Sosa and mouthed, *Let me handle this*. Right now, we needed her on our side. Sosa walked in the house first. He had the safety off his gun and made sure to check each room before coming back to the living room and locking the door.

While he did that, I couldn't help to look around for the cat that was here the last time.

"He's on the wall. Wouldn't stay out of my business."

Madame Boudet took a seat on the Artic blue couch and motioned for us to join her. She grabbed a pack of Virginia Slims, removed a cigarette, and lit it. "I had such high hopes for you, but with all the black magic surrounding you, this was to be expected."

I hated when a person talked in riddles, and the fact that she was holding whatever she knew over my head drove me crazy. The idea of her telling Sosa about my recreational drug use made me want to run out the door. My heart was racing, and I desperately needed a shot of something strong to calm me down. If I would of known the coke I did earlier in the bathroom would have me this jittery, I would have waited to do it. Instead of calming me, it had my senses overactive. My eyes kept bouncing around from the cat skulls dangling over my head to the vial on the table that looked like blood. The house was creeping me out,

"Baby girl, you have something on your nose. The bathroom is down the hall to the right. Take your time. Me and Sosa have some things to discuss in private." She looked at me like she could see straight through me.

Chapter Fourteen
MADAME BOUDET

I knew they were coming before Snow placed the thought in their head. That was how strong my aura was. Since a little girl, I was blessed, or should I say, cursed, with seeing the future. Gucci ran toward the bathroom like she had fire ants on her. The girl might be fooling everyone around her, but I knew the truth. This was only the beginning of her self-destruction. One thing I never saw, and it confused me, was Sosa. Nowhere in the bones I read the night Snow sold his soul to the devil did I see a knight in shining armor. I'm sure you were wondering why I cared about the Snow family and how I'd become tangled in their spider web. Snow reminded me of my late husband. We had a strong belief in reincarnation when it came to the spiritual realm. Years ago, when he showed up at my doorstep, I was convinced he was my ex-husband reborn.

When I was around twenty years old, many moons ago, I had veered off from my original path. Not all Voodoo Queens were evil. Some were chosen to heal and guide. That was the path I was supposed to take, but that wasn't in my cards. My first husband, Blaise Boudet, was the only man I ever loved and the only husband I didn't kill. The Mafia put a hit out on him when they saw how powerful he was. Rumors were floating through Louisiana that he was untouchable because he was protected by black magic. Now, those old white devils didn't like that, but the funny thing was, he wasn't protected. After they killed him, I went on a witch hunt and made all of them pay for breaking my heart in ways I wouldn't mention. Once word got out that I had successfully executed the Rossi family, my price went up in the streets. Had hustlers coming from as far north as Chicago to request my services. The power of voodoo could only take me so far. I went underground and relocated to Hilton Head where I'd managed to keep a low profile until Snow entered my life twelve years ago.

"Do you love her?" I asked, focusing my attention on Sosa.

"I ain't here to discuss my love life. Snow needs whatever you did for him back in the day reversed." Sosa tapped his foot against the floor as he spoke, his gun rested in his lap. The boy wasn't trusting, and I didn't blame him. There were too many snake niggas in this game.

"You kin to any Geechees?" The boy was protected, and he didn't know it. He was too dark to be creole, so my next guess was the Geechees who ran South Carolina.

"Lady, you ain't getting it. Whatever you selling, I ain't buying. All them other niggas might believe you hold some type of power, but that shit ain't working on me. I respect yo hustle, and I ain't here to stop it. You not getting in my head. I know your type."

"You think it was a miracle that gun jammed when you were a little boy? You're a street nigga. You don't believe in those, or maybe you thought it was luck on your side," I threw that in nonchalantly. Sosa was the type who thought he knew everything. Unlike them fake two-bit hustlers who made money selling candles in the French Quarters to tourists, I was the real deal. Little nigga had some nerve questioning me, but he was gone learn. I promised that.

Sosa cut his eyes at me, never once opening his mouth to respond, but that was fine. He didn't have to he got my point.

"You don't have to answer my question. I know who you are now. I'm getting old, but it always comes to me. Now, do you have any other questions before we get down to why you are here? This doesn't work unless you believe, and I charge one thousand by the hour, so I suggest you use it wisely." Now, it was my turn to give him a condescending smirk. Checkmate, little nigga. That tough shit might work in the streets, but now he was in my world.

"Snow thinks his brother is behind his wife's murder and his incarceration. Some old man came to visit him, and he said the man slipped up and said he wasn't the only one in his family he's done business with."

I took a deep pull of my cigarette and thought about what the boy was saying. Hmm, this was something new to me. If Dro made a side deal, I wasn't aware of that. I was not the only root doctor, and if he did make that type of deal, it wouldn't be something I was privileged to know. That didn't mean I couldn't find the truth. It meant it was going to take some digging.

"Go knock on the bathroom door and get the girl. We need her to find the truth. You need to do better in watching who you are with." I hissed, chastising him like a woman would do her child.

"She's grown," he mumbled under his breath. It took everything in me not to crack him in his back with my broom. I couldn't stand these youngins. They had no respect for the elders. My generation didn't either, but we hid that shit.

"Your ignorance will be your demise. You know the Feds are lurking even when you can't see them, correct?" I leaned forward in my chair and waited for his reaction. A part of me wanted to kick his ass out and be done with the foolishness. This wasn't my battle, yet here I was, fighting alongside them like a fool.

"Gucci bring yo ass out so we can hurry this shit up." Sosa, didn't get up from his seat but that was ok. He still did what I asked.

We didn't speak while we waited for Gucci to bring her ass out that bathroom. It was funny that Sosa didn't see what was right in front of nis nose. She walked back in the room, and her eyes were dilated, but it was not my place to put her business on blast like that.

"What I miss?" she asked, taking a seat next to Sosa.

"She ain't say shit worth repeating."

"Gucci, shuffle this deck of cards. Y'all bringing negativity into my house, and I don't need that." The sage that I lit wasn't doing the trick. This girl had something dark surrounding her, and I was starting to think the ancestors had the wrong Snow girl. Like I said, this wasn't my business, so I did what was asked of me.

"The family is surrounded by black magic. Snow wasn't the only one to make a deal with the devil. The difference between him and his brother is he's willing to sacrifice anyone to get what he wants."

"What does that mean? Can you answer our questions? This is too much. I can't understand these riddles." Gucci was fuckin with my flow. Her demand would have the ancestors who praised her second guessing their decision to protect her.

"It means your damn uncle has struck a deal to gain control of your family. Your father is no longer calling the shots, and if you don't get your shit together, things will only get worse. You need to step back from what you are doing."

"I've tried to be patient with you. Where are Dro and Ace, and how can we find them?" Sosa stood up from his seat and walked toward me. His gun was visible, and his face was twisted into a scowl.

Chapter Fifteen
SOSA

I had done a lot of crazy shit in my life, but I never pulled a gun on an old lady. After hearing her talk, I grew tired of her games. Dro dealing with the Haitians was a problem that had to be dealt with right away. She would only know all of this if she had communicated with him. I don't believe in voodoo, so that's my only explanation. After we left South Carolina, a nigga was more confused than ever. This shit Snow had going on was foreign to me. I would never allow myself to believe in that Voodoo shit they had going on. That proved that these niggas weren't built like me, so I did what I did best. I dropped Gucci off at Ma's and focused on my business. When Dro resurfaced, I would be ready for him. Until then, I had a business to run.

I was so caught up in the bullshit with the streets I had forgotten about Wynter and this supposed baby situation. My cousin came through with a doctor who performed the DNA test. I had the results sent to my mama's house.

With the envelope in my lap, I headed to scoop Wynter up. I wanted her next to me when I read the results so we could dead this situation once and for all.

I pulled on my blunt and stared down at the test results in big bold letters. The probability of paternity was 99.8%. Wynter rubbed her hand on her stomach, which was starting to show, and smiled like she had won the lottery. She shook her Cookout cup that was filled with Ice and started chewing it slowly. "I told you this was your baby!"

Wynter had life fucked up if she thought I would ever take her word for a baby being mine. She lucked up with this shit, on God. "I don't give a fuck about what you told me. Out of all the niggas you fucked, I'm the one who slipped up. Damn," I mumbled, mad as hell. Having a baby with Wynter's ratchet ass was about to be a headache. I grabbed my cup of Yak and took a sip to calm down.

"Listen, baby daddy. I don't want us arguing. The past is the past. What we need to talk about is what you about to do!"

"What the fuck you mean what I'm about to do? Bitch, get that meal ticket shit out your mind right now. We about to get this shit straight now. I aint yo man. The only thing I'm concerned about is my seed."

"Wow I never thought you would be a dead beat. It was cool for you to nut in me but now you don't want to help me. Like I said, I'm a need you to step up. I'm not raising this baby by myself."

I had to catch myself. This was exactly why I never wanted to deal with getting one of the bitches I fucked pregnant.

"Watch how the fuck you speak to me. Don't let none of

this shit confuse you on who you are to me. Boosting and scamming ain't no fuckin job. Dead all that shit. Once you have the baby, you can do whatever the fuck you please."

Wynter let out a high-pitched laugh. "A baby you didn't want. Please, stop with this daddy of the year attitude. Since you have all the answers, if I stop scamming, then what?"

"I don't fucking know. Go sign yo ass up for school!" I pulled out of the parking lot and headed to one of my traps on the east side. Last thing I wanted to do was bring Wynter's ass along, but I wasn't trying to drive the opposite direction to drop her off.

"I was thinking you could let me run your daycare," she said that with so much confidence that I hated to burst her bubble. This girl had no real job skills that I knew of. If she thought I was letting her anywhere near the daycare, she done lost her mind.

"Nah, that ain't gonna work."

"Why not? It's perfect. I don't want to leave the baby while I work. This way, the baby can be with me."

I ain't want her ass nowhere near my business, but she had a point. With her working there, the baby could be with her. Yeah, I wanted Wynter to work, but I wasn't comfortable with anyone outside my mama watching the baby until it could talk. "I'll speak with the director and get you a position in the office. When you find out what you having?"

"Soon. I want a girl." She smiled at me and laid her head back. It didn't matter what we had. As long as the baby was healthy, I was good. This was the first time I found myself imagining what the baby would look like. As I drove, every so often, I would find myself glancing at her stomach.

School was letting out when I pulled up to the trap. The school bus had the stop sign out. Once the children were off the bus, I pulled up to where Duke was standing. Duke was a lil nigga with an old soul. He wasn't the biggest nigga. I'd say he was five foot four inches at the most. What he lacked in height he made up with heart. That nigga had the same green joggers and white tee on from when I hit him off the other day. He was no bummy nigga. When the time came, he would get fresh, but right, now he was in grinding mode. I had eyes on the trap. When Dro or Ace decided to come at me, I would be ready. The only time I heard of Duke leaving was to walk around the corner and get a plate from one of the restaurants. Other than that, he lived in the trap.

"Boy, you ain't playin no games, is you?" I dapped Duke up and took the money he handed me in a pink book bag.

"Hell no. My lil bitch pregnant, and you know how that goes." He nodded his head at Wynter, who I was sure he was familiar with.

"You doing right. Stack that paper and stay out the way. Ain't nothin else you can do."

"Appreciate that, fam. I'm a get me some sleep until lil ma come drop the work off."

I dapped Duke up and watched him walk back into the spot before pulling off. A nigga was tired as hell my damn self. My mama used to say when a woman was pregnant a man had symptoms. I wondered if that was my baby kicking my ass.

"Where you want me to drop you off? A nigga tired as hell and about to take it down."

"I was hoping I could come with you. I need somewhere to stay, my aunt just put me out."

I slammed my hand on the wheel. This was the shit I was talking about. One night of pleasure had turned into a new fucking bill. I was not tripping. A nigga money was straight, so I could easily set Wynter up with a crib. I ain't want her thinking shit was sweet. Once she stepped up and proved she was serious about working, I would revisit the idea.

"I got an apartment so you can stay out by the airport. There's furniture there and shit. No one knows about it, so keep it that way."

"I promise you can trust me," she said that with so much passion I had to laugh. I would never trust her with any valuable information. That was why I was letting her stay at my duck-off spot instead of my main house. The only person that knew where I rest my head was my mama, sister, and cousin, and it was gonna stay that way. I hit the volume on the radio and headed toward the crib. As soon as I got into my song, Wynter leaned over and turned the volume down.

"Man, what?"

"I need to go get my clothes."

"Nah, a nigga tired. We can go shopping in the morning. You not bringing none of that shit over here. Yo peoples got roaches."

Turning the radio back up, I headed toward my apartment. Wynter ain't say shit because she knew it was the truth. She would complain about how nasty her aunt was on multiple occasions. The last thing I wanted to do was take her shopping, but it is what it is. Thunder exploded in the distance. The sky was a dark gray, and I could smell the rain in the air.

"Hurry up!" I slammed my door and hurried toward the building. I ain't have time to be getting wet. When I looked back, I noticed Wynter's slow ass was still in the parking lot. The baby had her moving in slow motion. Since she was carrying my seed, I waited for her instead of continuing to the apartment.

"Thank you for waiting for me, but can we hurry up? The baby is on my bladder!"

"Fuck is that supposed to mean?" I asked, looking over at her.

"Boy, come on. I got to pee." Her face twisted in discomfort as she bounced foot to foot. My apartment was toward the back. Each floor had seven to eight apartments. A set of wooden steps lead up to the next floor. When I chose this condo, I wanted something off the ground. I made sure to purchase the condo directly under the one we were going to. If shit was to ever pop off and niggas tried their luck, I wouldn't have to worry about no nosey neighbors trying to play hero. By the time we got to the fourth and last floor, Wynter was out of breath. I slid my key card, and the door popped open. Wynter pushed past me like she knew where she was going.

"The bathroom is the third door to the right."

My condo was clean and smelling like fresh lavender, thanks to the maid service I used once a week. It didn't matter that I didn't live at this spot. I made sure when I popped up, everything was to my standards. The apartment was bare, except for the black leather sectional, eighty-inch flat screen hanging from the wall, and a bedroom set. I kicked my sneakers off, sat down, grabbed my remote, and turned the TV on. Wynter had mentioned something earlier, and it popped into my head. I would never be a deadbeat that wasn't in my nature. I grew up without a father. I would never intentionally cause my child that type of pain. So, I stayed to learn more about her pregnancy. My eyes were heavy from lack of sleep. I kicked my feet up and laid back.

A couple of minutes later, Wynter walked back into the room and took a seat next to me. "This is nice, Sosa. I appreciate you letting me stay here."

"You straight, ma." There was an awkward silence. I wasn't about to sit here and hold a conversation I was tired as hell. The bean I popped last night was starting to wear off, and I needed a couple hours of sleep before I hit the block. My forty was poking me, so I took it out and laid it next to me.

"You got food in here?" Wynter reached for the white throw blanket that was folded on the couch and placed it over her legs. Through squinted eyes, I looked over at her, trying to remember if I had my mama go food shopping at this spot.

"Go check the kitchen. There might be food in there. If not, order Uber Eats. I'll take you to Walmart when I get up."

That was all I remembered because sleep took over me, and I was out.

The smell of food cooking and the soft nudge on my side woke me up. My eyes went to the balcony in front of me. The dark sky let me know I had been asleep for a minute. Wynter must have thrown a blanket over me because I ain't have it on me when I went to sleep. I reached for my phone and checked the time. It was a little after eleven. The missed calls from Gucci would have to wait. I was still tired and most likely would be going back to sleep. Wynter walked back in the living room with a big ass plate of T-Bone steak, Lobster tails, mashed potatoes, and Asparagus. Damn, I ain't even know I had all that in the kitchen. The aroma coming from the steamy plate made my stomach grumble.

Wynter placed her plate down and took a sip of her red juice.

"I didn't know if you were hungry, but there's a plate in the microwave." She cut the steak with her knife and did a little dance when she put it on her tongue. I wasn't gonna ask her to stop eating, so I got up to grab my plate. The kitchen was wiped down, and the dishwasher was running. At least she wasn't nasty. I put the microwave on two minutes. I loved my food hot. The microwave dinged, and I grabbed my plate, fork, and a can of Cheer wine and walked back to the living room.

I placed my food down, said a quick prayer, and stuck a forkful of mashed potatoes in my mouth. The potatoes were busting, so I knew the rest of the plate was gonna be straight. "I appreciate it. Nigga don't eat home cooking unless my mama or granny cook it."

"All them bitches you got and they don't be cooking for you?"

"Nah, they don't." I kept my answer short. I ain't no hoe

nigga that was gonna discuss my other hoes with my baby mama.

My plate was halfway cleared. I saved my steak and lobster tail for last. The steak was restaurant quality, almost to the point I suspected she might have ordered it and put it on the plates. "Aye, you need to go to culinary school or some shit!"

"I mean, I never thought of it. I love to cook, but I just can't see myself working in nobody's restaurant."

"Who said you would have to work for someone? I'll help you open some shit. I put that on our seed!"

Wynter's face lit up, then it balled up as she rubbed her stomach. "You good?"

I placed my plate down and walked over to where she was sitting.

"Yeah, the baby just kicked. Wow, this is the first time!" Smiling up at me, she grabbed my hand and put it on her stomach. Leaning forward, I jumped slightly when I felt her shit move. My eyes were on her stomach. Every so often, it would ball up. My baby was inside going crazy. Seemed like when it heard my voice, it started moving faster.

"The Doctor told me at the end of the month, I can find out what I'm having. You want to come with me?"

"Yeah, I'll make sure I'm there."

Wynter looked up at me and smiled. All a nigga wanted to do was feel my baby kick and get some rest. I pulled her little ass on top of me, and I chilled with her the rest of the night.

Chapter Sixteen
GUCCI

I was sick as hell when I woke up. My throat was dry, my eyes were stuck together, and my stomach was on fire. This was the second time I tried to get out of bed and wasn't able to. My phone was next to me, but the bright light from the screen was fucking with me. Damn. It was six in the evening, and there was no way I was going to work tonight. A sharp pain shot from my stomach to my back, and I tasted throw up in my mouth. The only thing on my mind was making it to the bathroom before I made a mess that I wasn't willing to clean.

I ran to the bathroom and wrapped my arms around the cold porcelain toilet. The bile exploded out of my mouth. As soon as I thought I was done, another wave came behind it. Once my stomach calmed down, I slowly stood up and walked to the sink. I washed my face, brushed my teeth, and avoided looking into the mirror. That was how bad I looked.

I walked back into the room and got right back into

the bed. The window curtains were closed, and it was dark in the room. You know I was feeling bad when I didn't bother to check my messages or jump on Instagram.

A few minutes later, Dior and Fendi walked into the room with bags from Hooters. The smell of the wings turned my stomach, and I buried my head under the covers.

"We brought you a plate." Fendi snatched the covers back and held up a Styrofoam container filled with lemon pepper wings, and hot fries.

"I can't eat right now. Put it in the kitchen for me." I closed my eyes and tried to get comfortable, which was hard with both of them on the bed.

Dior took a bite of her wing and then looked me up and down. "Damn, yo ass look like death! I hope you don't have Covid."

"Nah, she looks pregnant if you ask me! I hope you making that nigga strap up cause his ass is fertile as fuck right now." Fendi grabbed her drink and took a sip before she passed me her phone

"Girl, what is this?" I asked to save face. It was obvious what the picture was, but a part of me did not want to accept what I was seeing. Fendi's phone was on The Greensboro Tea page. The page exposed people on the regular. This particular picture belonged to TheColdestWynter, and the caption read, *We can't wait to find out what we are having!! What's understood doesn't need to be explained!* In the picture, she was sitting up in what looked like a bed. Her stomach was out, showing off her baby bump. The hand in the picture was what had my attention. I recognized that death before dishonor tattoo.

"Read the caption! If that's your boo, I figured you would know," Fendi's messy ass said taking a bite of her cheese fries.

The tea page had the question, **Is That Sosa's Hand? Who wants the Tea?**

I was furious to see people tagging me in the post. I gave Fendi her phone back and grabbed mine off the charger. I took my time reading each comment I was tagged in. The comment I was currently stuck on had over three hundred comments and was from this messy ass bitch from the projects, Kayla.

kayla_is_a1 *I thought that was Gucci's man.*

TheColdestWynter @kayla_is_a1 *Imagine that.*

I was over Instagram, Sosa, and that bitch, Wynter. Once I got myself together, I was gonna turn the fuck up. That nigga had me fucked up if he thought I was gonna play the background to any of these bitches. Nigga better ask about me.

This was the main reason I didn't fuck with local niggas. Everyone felt like they had an input on your love life. These desperate hoes were big mad when they found out I was fucking Sosa, and now this Wynter bitch gave them something to talk about with this picture. A part of me wanted to call his ass, but at this point, I ain't even have the energy.

A tear fell from the corner of my eye. I wasn't hurt by the news. He wasn't my man, but the way he was talking, I thought what we had was special. Mad niggas tried to fuck with me on the regular, and I was turning them down because I thought we were building something.

"I know you not crying over Sosa's hoe ass? Girl, fuck him.

He's a dog ass nigga. Use him for what he's good for. A nut and some bread and keep it pushing. When was the last time you got a period? Cause you ain't been complaining about cramps like you normally do, and you mad emotional. You might want to go get you a test." Fendi said in between bites of her food.

"I'm not pregnant. Stop saying that stupid shit before Ma hears you."

Kash walked into the room. I hadn't seen much of her since we had been in the clubs. She had her natural hair out today, and it was pulled up in a long genie ponytail that hung to her shoulders. I was assuming she just came from working out because she was dressed casually in a Nike sports bra with the matching leggings, and she was holding one of those clear milk containers filled with water.

"What y'all doing today? I was thinking we could go down to South Carolina and stay for a couple of days. This club promoter hit me up earlier, and I have a couple of niggas who get work from me down there." Kash sat down on the foot of the bed, pulled up the club's page, and passed the phone to Fendi.

"I'm down. I heard South Carolina's clubs be hitting." Fendi passed Dior the phone, and she nodded.

I was too busy going through Wynter's page looking for clues. Her page was filled with pictures of her in various locations. She was slim-thick, and I assumed the pictures were pre pregnancy.

"Gucci, get off that girls page and look at the club!" Dior shook my leg, and I accidentally liked one of Wynter's pictures.

"Damn, Dior. Chill. You made me like one of her pictures," I snapped. My finger quickly tapped the unlike button, and I placed my phone down next to me. The last thing I wanted was this bitch Wynter to know I was pressed about her little announcement.

"Whose picture?" Kash was lost about what was going on, and I didn't feel like discussing the situation. Of course, Fendi had to go into detail about Wynter and Sosa like she was reporting for the evening news.

Kash's eyebrows twisted, and she sucked her teeth when she looked at the picture on Fendi's phone. I was lost on why she gave a fuck about what Sosa was doing with his dick.

"I don't believe that shit. She's not his type." Kash rolled her eyes and passed Fendi the phone back.

"Girl, bye. That girl is beautiful, and from what I heard, she's the plug when it comes to scamming, and I think she sells x." Fendi was very much on her groupie behavior. Yeah, Wynter was cute, but she wasn't all what Fendi was trying to make her out to be. Wynter was the typical light skinned big bootie hoe that rocked designer clothes. It was 2021. Everyone wore designer, so that ain't about shit.

As they continued to talk, my mind was filled with feelings of betrayal. Sosa was my ticket out of my fucked-up situation. I never took the time to think about him fucking with other bitches. My stomach rumbled, and the urge to throw up came over me again. I ran to the bathroom and barely made it to the toilet when everything in my stomach came up again. Tears ran down my face as I clutched the side of the toilet. The sound of footsteps racing toward me did nothing but add to my embarrassment.

Dior grabbed my ponytail, and Fendi patted my back softly while Kash stood back and watched. My eyes locked with Kash, and she quickly looked away before she walked out the bathroom and slammed the door. I felt like the world was swallowing me. A few months ago, I would have never questioned if I was good enough for Sosa. The room spun as I heaved into the toilet.

Great Kash went and told Ma. Ma stood at the bathroom door watching me for a second before she spoke. "When is the last time you had your period? Please don't think I'm helping you raise no baby." Ma said. This is why I didn't want her in my business. My stomach calmed down. I got up from the toilet and looked over at Ma, not bothering to answer her question. "Nah, we ain't about to do that. You wanna run around acting like you're grown, but you gonna answer my question."

She followed me back into the bedroom and crossed her arms. Kash walked back into the bedroom, and I shot her an evil glare. If she would have minded her business, I wouldn't be in this situation. Everyone was standing around looking at me, and I didn't miss the looks of disappointment.

"Shit, I don't know. I think before we went to Vegas. I really can't remember," I snapped.

"Little girl, that was over two months ago. How the hell you not gonna remember some shit like that? You better hope you not pregnant. Ain't no babies coming up in here, and you are you pushing the abortion cut off. Kash, come with me so we can run to Walmart and get this girl a damn test."

Kash and Ma walked out the room. They were most likely gonna be talking shit about me, but I didn't give a fuck. Can't nobody say they'd gone through half of what I'd been through the past few months. Yeah, I should have gotten a Plan B, but that shit slipped my mind. If I was pregnant, I would deal with it by myself like I did everything else.

Fendi and Dior sat next to me. I laid my head in Fendi's lap like I used to do when I was a little girl. She softly scratched my scalp while Dior hugged me from the back.

"Gucci, I can't say shit because my ass done slipped up multiple times. Don't listen to Ma. If you are pregnant and want to keep your baby, then do that. We gonna support you like we always have, with or without Sosa. The only advice I can give you is don't feel no pressure to get rid of it unless you want to. Abortions are nothing to play with."

'I'm not having no baby." I shut that shit down real quick. To be honest, it didn't matter if I was pregnant. I wasn't having this baby. Sosa had Wynter pregnant, and I wasn't about to fuck up my body when it was the way I made my money. A bitch had goals, and Greensboro wasn't my long-term goal. I wanted to move to a bigger city and snatch me a nigga getting that eight-figure paper.

"Bitch, if you not planning on telling Sosa, I would advise you going to get the abortion out of town," Fendi said. The door slammed, and I knew Ma and Kash were back.

Kash came upstairs and placed the plastic Walmart bag that was filled with various pregnancy tests on the bed.

Fendi's phone vibrated on the bed, and her mouth twisted into a smile.

"Oh, shit. Hold on. This is Sincere. He does hair at Bratz,

that new Salon of Randleman Road. If anyone got the tea on Sosa and this Wynter bitch, he's the one."

Fendi answered the phone and placed it on speaker.

"Girl!" he said in a high-pitched voice. The phone was on FaceTime, so I was able to see his face. He had a full beard and a low cut. I could tell he was gay by the way he carried himself and spoke.

"Don't start with yo shit, Sincere, you already know what it is." Fendi giggled and reached for the blunt she had rolled and lit it.

"Girl, bye. You only hit me when yo ass wants Tea. I've been trying to get all you yellow hoes in my shop for the longest." He raised his eyebrows and looked at each of us.

"Sincere, ain't no one about to come slave up in your shop," Fendi said, waving her hand.

"Girl, bye. We don't slave at Bratz. If you took the time to come check it out, you would know that. All my girls have private rooms they rent out. We don't do walk-ins, and as long as you have my room rent, you can come and go as you need. Y'all need to stop playing. There ain't never enough money. Fendi, you letting that nail license go to waste, boo."

Sincere ran his shop down, and I couldn't front, the concept sounded dope as fuck.

"Let me think about it, Sincere." Fendi shook him off, and I knew she wasn't about to go work at his shop.

"MmmHmm, well, don't wait too long because, baby, we are booked and busy. I only have a few rooms left. All I'm saying is shit done changed for you, and this would be a good look. Now, what did you want earlier girl? I know you ain't hit me to talk about nails."

"You know Wynter the girl who is on the tea page and is supposedly pregnant by Sosa?"

I was acting like I wasn't pressed, but I was on the edge of my seat waiting for him to answer.

Sincere stood up and closed his office door and walked back to his pink and white cow print seat. He was being extra as fuck, and I wanted to scream get to the point, but I chilled and waited for him to get situated.

"This tea is hot as fuck now. I would say it's cap, but honey, I have the insider scope. Y'all ain't hear this shit for me. You know Sosa is crazy, and I don't need his ass shooting my shit up." He paused before continuing, "So, I was doing Wynter's cousin's hair, Moe, and she was on FaceTime with Wynter for damn near half of her appointment. Now, this nigga was denying the baby at first. Made her go out of town to Raleigh and do the DNA test."

"How she do a test? She's barely showing," I interjected, not feeling the direction the conversation was going.

"Chile it's 2021. Anything is possible. You know they can test the baby before it's born now, and with the type of money Sosa has, you know he paid for that shit. I can confirm it's Sosa baby. The bitch was waving the DNA test results and bragging on how he got her staying at his crib. Fendi my phone dying let me charge it and I'll call you right back." Sincere said disconnecting the call.

That nigga and that bitch was gonna feel me if she kept subbing me in her post. One thing I didn't tolerate was disrespect. All that internet shit was for the birds. If bitch wanted to act like she wasn't pregnant then I was gonna treat her like any regular bitch in the streets. Let her keep on tagging me like shit was sweet. She was gonna lose that baby for real.

Sosa had me so hot, I was ready to take the test. Like I said, I was done fucking with him. The thing I was mad about was him allowing this bitch to involve me in what they had going on. Greensboro ain't but so big. There was no way he didn't know about what was going on.

"Pass me one of those tests. The quicker I get this out the way, the sooner I can start with my day. Text Kash, and tell her I'm down for South Carolina. Ain't nothing about to stop me from getting to the bag."

Fendi passed me the bag, and I grabbed three tests and went to the bathroom. This was my first time using a pregnancy test. I read the directions and placed everything I would need on the sink. It took me a few seconds to get the urge to pee. By the time I was finished, I had more than enough to dip all three tests. I washed and dried my hands, set a timer on my phone, and went back into the room to wait for the results.

Kash was now back in the room, and I hoped she kept her weird energy to herself. I had enough on my mind than to worry about what her issue was with me.

"You not ready for no baby. If you're pregnant, I hope you're not keeping it." Kash gave her opinion like I asked for it.

"Nope!" I kept my answer short. There was no point in pretending I was when I wasn't. All the other shit Kash said went in one ear and out the other. She was trying to be funny when she said I wasn't ready for a baby. What she failed to realize was I knew myself, and I would never think of having a baby. No matter how rich the father was.

"Well, damn, bitch. You cold. You said that with no thought," Kash mumbled under her breath.

"Why do you care what I do, anyway? You've been moving real funny since I came back from Vegas. I wasn't gonna address it, but since you in the mood to talk, what's up?" I was done playing around with Kash. She'd been real dry when it came to me, and I had no idea what her issue was. The way she looked me up and down let me know she had some type of problem with me.

Kash narrowed her eyes and tapped her foot on the floor. "You talking reckless. We got enough shit going on, and now you trying to add a baby to the equation. I'm still trying to figure out how you thought it was okay to go to Vegas, and we over here trying to survive."

I had to laugh. When Kash and Fendi used to fight in the past, I would always take Kash's side. Now, I was seeing her for who she was. She was a jealous bitch. As long as she was shining, everything was okay.

The timer went off on my phone, and everyone's eyes went to the bathroom. Yeah, I was putting on a front like I was unfazed, but deep down inside, my stomach was tossing.

"Girl, get up and go check the test. You killing me with the suspense." Dior laughed, pushing me slightly.

I made no effort in moving. I didn't care enough to get up and check the results. To be honest, a part of me knew I was pregnant and wanted to prolong it as long as possible.

"Shit, I'll go check them since you bullshitting!" Fendi said, getting up off the bed.

"What it say, Fendi?" Dior yelled toward the bathroom. Kash was standing against the wall with a blank look on her face.

"Looks like Sosa got two babies on the way." Fendi walked back into the room with the tests wrapped in tissue.

"Nah, them shits broke," I said, still unwilling to face the truth.

"Girl all three positive!" Fendi walked up to me and held them in my face.

"Let me see them! I'm about to tell this nigga he going half on this abortion." I snatched the test out of her hand, snapped a picture, and shot Sosa a text."

I had money to pay for the abortion, but I refused to pay for the whole thing.

Chapter Seventeen
SOSA

I was standing in front of the stove. It'd been a minute since a nigga had to cook up. Between me firing Elle and my normal workers going home for Spring Break, a nigga was back in the kitchen. My eyes were on the Pyrex that was placed inside the pot of boiling water. This shit came second nature to me. I had been cooking work since I was thirteen or fourteen. When the coke started to bubble, I bent down over the pot and blew a cloud of my black in mild smoke toward it. This shit was mathematics, and I had my recipe down to a science. I still had a few more zips to cook before I was done. Not all my workers knew the art of cooking up, so I had to make sure the ones who were not skilled were supplied before I took it down for the night. After a few more seconds of wiping, it started to lock up.

My phone vibrated on the counter. Out the corner of my eye I saw it was Gucci texting. Not bothering to pick it up, I concentrated on getting my shit to rock up. Once it did, I turned the stove off I carefully placed the perfect rocks next to the ones I already had drying. I repeated the process until I was finished. By the time I was finished, a couple of hours had passed, and a nigga was tired as fuck. I had been in the kitchen cooking all day. We had two stoves that helped speed up the process. The kitchen was flooded with a chemical smell that was killing me. I raised the windows, turned the fans on, and lit some candles to mask the odor.

Once I washed my hands, I grabbed a beer out of the fridge and went into the living room to relax for a minute. It felt good to have a second to relax. I popped the top off my Corona and scrolled through my messages until my eyes landed on Gucci's text.

I need you to go half on this abortion. Don't flatter yourself into thinking I'm keeping it because I'm not!

She attached multiple pictures of different brands of pregnancy tests that all had positive results on them.

My mind went back to the numerous times I asked her stupid ass did she take the Plan B. I was not putting all the blame on her because I was fucking her raw and didn't pull out. What had me hot was her coming of like I was the one in the wrong about this situation. The timing was crazy because I had one baby on the way in less than four months. Wynter had decided last minute she wanted to wait to find out the baby's gender.

I hit the FaceTime button and waited for her to answer. She declined the call three times before I shot her a text. Answer yo phone before I come shoot yo shit up. I was lying about shooting her shit up, but she didn't know that. Seconds later my phone started to ring. *Like I thought.*

"What, Sosa?" Gucci snapped. The dark lights and the pasties she had over her nipples let me know she was in the club. Gucci rolled her eyes like I was bothering her and took a sip of the drink she was holding.

"Why the fuck are you drinking and you pregnant?" I barked, gripping the phone tightly. If she was near me, I would have choked her stupid ass out. This bird brain-behavior I would have expected from Wynter. I was starting to see I gave Gucci too much credit based on who her people were.

"Did you not read my message? I clearly said I'm not keeping it, so why would I stop drinking?"

I bit my bottom lip so hard I busted it. This wasn't the girl I spent all this time with. The one who I would sit on the phone with for hours when my day was going crazy. Nah, this bitch was acting like one of the hoodrats I would link with late night after the club. She wasn't trying to hide who she was. Maybe I was blinded by her beauty or the fact that I thought she wasn't in it for the paper.

"Stop playing with me, Gucci!" I light my black and lowered my eyes.

"Um, yeah. I aint playing!" She said dryly.

"How you gonna make this type of decision and not discuss it with me?"

She busted out laughing like a nigga was a joke. Like I ain't have feelings. Gucci walked back into the dressing room.

"The only reason I'm entertaining this conversation is because the club is slow right now. You think I'm about to put my life on hold and have a baby by a nigga who has another one on the way?" She turned the camera off on the phone, and I heard a familiar tapping.

I had to be tripping. She wasn't doing what I was thinking.

"Fuck that. Turn your camera back on." She kept that shit paused for about three minutes, and I damn near lost it when I heard a sniff. When she turned the camera back on, I took a long hard look at her. That shit was sad to see. Her eyes were glassy, and her mouth was twisted.

"What? I'm trying to get ready for work."

"You know what? Fuck it! And bitch, wipe your nose!" I hung up the phone and shook my head.

Damn. had I been slipping that much I ain't realize her ass was sniffing coke. If I wasn't so mad, I would have called her back and tried to talk some sense into her. She could use Wynter being pregnant as an excuse if she wanted to. If I wanted the baby before, I ain't want it now. Since I found out Wynter was pregnant, I had been doing my research on fetal development. If I had to guess Gucci was around two months pregnant. Ain't no telling when she started sniffing coke. I wasn't about to chance having a baby with no birth defects, so I went to Cash App and sent her two thousand and then blocked her. Whatever shorty had coming her way, I wanted no parts. She killed that shit herself.

In a couple of hours, I was taking Wynter to meet my mama, and I still needed to bag this work and run home to take shower. Hopefully this introduction went smoothly and Wynter wasn't on her usual ratchet shit.

Chapter Eighteen
GUCCI

A s I walked through the mall with Dior, my mind was all over the place. Sosa had cut me off, my cousin Kash wasn't speaking to me, and my father's case wasn't looking too good. On top of all that, I still hadn't scheduled an appointment for my abortion. Sosa sent me the money for the abortion, and I was not gonna lie, I blew that shit shopping the same day. I was high as hell and in my feelings, but it was nothing. I had some money in the stash to handle it.

"How none of these stores have the new Jays? If Footlocker doesn't have them then we can leave," Dior complained.

I was over shopping at this point. We had been out all morning, and my feet were hurting in my Prada Lug Sole Combat boots. I fucked around and got the wrong size rushing. I wasn't about to drive back to Charlotte and exchange them, so I decided to deal with the discomfort. Dior continued to run her mouth as we entered Kids Footlocker. The store was packed with people, and we could barely move due to the crowd. It was just my luck that I ran into Wynter. Her back was turned, but I had stalked her page so much I easily recognized her.

This was the first time I had seen her in person, and I couldn't help to laugh. The bitch was funny looking with her wide-set eyes. She had an okay shape, but she was nowhere as thick as me. The pink and white checkered shirt she wore was unbuttoned, and she had a white tube dress on that displayed her stomach. Sosa must have been cashing out on her because I doubted she could afford the Pink and White Rick Owens sneakers she was wearing.

Dior was talking to a sales rep, and I decided to sit down on one of the wooden benches. Everything about Wynter pissed me off. The way she was laughing and smiling excitedly about the baby she was having. Here I was pregnant by the same nigga, and I was miserable. I shook the feelings of self-doubt out of my head and started searching for abortion clinics. The faster I got Sosa's demon child out of me would be the quicker I could move on from him and this little love triangle.

"The girl is going to the back to check if she has our sizes now. Why you looking all crazy?" Dior asked as she raised her eyebrow and sat down next to me.

"Look over by the infant's section. That's the girl who's supposedly pregnant by Sosa."

Dior turned her head, and when she did, Wynter happened to look up.

My eyes locked with Wynter's. She scrunched her lips and looked me up and down then whispered something to the tall girl standing next to her. If she thought she was about to start some bullshit, I was with the shits today. When I saw my name come out of her mouth, I hopped up and walked toward the baby section with Dior on my heels.

"Please don't start no bullshit before we get our sneakers," she whispered from behind me. I wasn't paying Dior any attention. I was about to set this bitch straight. It was whatever, and if her homegirl chose to get involved, she could get dealt with, too.

"You got something you wanna get off your chest?" I walked up to her. I was so close I could smell the cheap ass Bath and Bodyworks spray she was wearing. Sosa's funny as fuck for real. He played me for this basic bitch. It didn't matter how much money he dropped on her, she was still a basic ass bitch compared to me.

"Excuse me? I don't know what you think you heard, but this ain't what you want. All it takes is one phone call to my baby's father, and it's a wrap for you."

She said that shit proudly. Her chest was puffed out like she was doing something, and her scary ass held her phone out. This bitch was talking all that shit on the Gram but was a pussy in person. I wasn't surprised the hoe had Sosa on speed dial, but I was about to pop the perfect ass bubble she was living in.

I laughed hard as hell. The entire situation was comical.

"What, is that supposed to scare me? That's my baby father, too. So what? That nigga's for everybody, sis. Now, like I said, what's up? You got a lot to say on the Gram. I'm here now. Talk that fly shit and watch me drag your funny looking ass through this mall."

Wynter's mouth dropped. I guess she didn't get the memo that she wasn't the only one expecting that niggas baby. The people in the store started talking shit, and a few of them were recording us, but I didn't care. Wynter looked over at her homegirl and burst out laughing. "Girl, bye. The baby you should have already aborted with the two bands he sent you. Boo, you a coke head, and like I said, back the fuck up before I call my baby daddy up here."

She turned to look at her homegirl. That was her second mistake, taking her eyes off me. The first was her blasting my business.

"That's why I hate these young bi—"

That was the last word she got out because I was done talking. I balled my fist up and slammed it into her face. With one swift motion, I grabbed her hair and started raining blows, not giving a fuck where I hit. "Talk that shit, hoe. Didn't I tell you not to fuck with me?"

The weak-ass punches Wynter was throwing weren't connecting, and I was on one today. That bitch was balled up trying to protect her stomach. The difference between us was I didn't give a fuck about the baby in mines. Her homegirl kicked me in the back, causing me to release Wynter and fall backward. That little move gave Wynter a slight advantage because she was now on top of me. I refused to allow this bitch to get the best of me. With all my strength, I dug my long stiletto nails in her eyes. I didn't let go until she was off me, and I hopped back up. Mall security was now inside the store. Two of them were trying to pull Dior off Wynter's homegirl while I was trying to break free of the one who was holding me.

"Y'all, chill out. They calling the police. On the strength of your family, I'm a let you dip," the young guard whispered in ny ear. I nodded my head and walked over and snatched Dior up

"We got to go now," I hissed in her ear. I wasn't about to get locked up, and if Wynter lost the baby, that was an automatic charge. We grabbed our bags off the floor and quickly dipped out of the store.

Later on that Evening

Hours had passed since the fight at the mall. It was all over social media. Some people were on my side, while others were saying it was fucked up what I did to Wynter. I wasn't stunting none of their opinions. Wynter should have thought about her baby before she hopped on the internet talking crazy. I was still pissed off about that shit. I had three broken nails, and one of them was so bad I had to go to the hospital because it ripped my nail bed.

Sosa hadn't reached out to me, and that was fine with me. I was good on him. He wasn't my nigga, and he was causing me too much trouble. Fuck that nigga. I had mad niggas beating my door down dying for a chance to fuck with me. Them other bitches might not be able to pull another get money nigga, but I didn't have those types of problems.

I looked over at the clock on my dresser. I had enough time to do a couple of lines before we left. Thankfully, everyone was downstairs, so I had some privacy. My birthday was a couple of days away, and I couldn't wait to be able to get my own crib. Living with Ma was alright, but a bitch needed her space. I carefully made two lines, tied my baggie up, and placed it inside my bra. As I inhaled them, all I could think about how much money I was gonna make tonight. After I finished, I checked my nose and makeup and then walked over to the full-length mirror. My outfit was giving today. The black Bodysuit hugged my curves. The crop fur coat matched my black and white Richard Owens sneakers, and I finished my look with a pair of black oversized shades with Dolce & Gabbana written across them. I had a fresh thirty-inch jet black frontal sew-in that Dior had installed after I got back from the hospital. I made more money when I did a natural beat. These niggas were perverted and loved the fresh innocent look.

Once I was satisfied with my appearance, I sprayed my Baccarat Rouge perfume, grabbed my purse, and cut the lights off.

When I got downstairs, Ma had a few customers sitting around chilling. I walked over to the bar and pulled out a crisp hundred. I needed a big strong drink to last the car ride. Her ass be taxing. I was mad as hell I missed the ABC store. I could have brought a bottle for what she was about to charge me.

"Don't you look cute." Ma snatched the money, placed it in her bra, and looked me up and down.

"Thank you. Where's Dior and Fendi at?" I purposely left Kash out because we still weren't speaking.

"They rode with Kash to get some work from Sosa. What you drinking?" Ma asked, grabbing a cup.

"Give me some Patron and Pineapple Juice, and they did

what?" I had to have her repeat herself. There wasn't no way they would go see that nigga with all we had going on and not tell me.

"Hmm, chile, I ain't trying to get in the middle of you and Kash's bullshit." Ma poured the drink and handed it to me. She pulled out her pack of cigarettes and handed me one after she lit her cigarette.

"Ain't no getting in the middle of nothing they already know what it is with me and Sosa. At the end of the day, all three of them are moving funny as hell." I grabbed the drink and took a sip.

"How you know you had him first? That would only apply if he was yours first. Now, I'm not saying Kash fucked around with the boy, but did you ever ask yourself that question?"

"Kash and Sosa? Yeah, aight, Ma. She might have a little crush on him, but they not fucking." I refused to believe that Sosa would fuck Kash. I know we aren't speaking but I know she wouldn't do no grimy shit like that to me.

"If you say so." Ma poured me another drink and walked back toward her customers. After I finished both of my drinks, I decided to hit Star up to see if she wanted to ride out of town with me. She was a dancer I had met a minute ago. She stayed in Greensboro and was a get-money bitch.

Hey girl wyd?

While I waited for her to respond, I motioned for Ma to pour me another drink.

The little bubbles appeared in the message field before her response came through.

Star: *Nothing trying to figure out what the move is for tonight. I worked in Winston last night, and they shot the club up, so a bitch needs to make double tonight.*

Me: Girl, I'm not surprised. They ratchet as fuck down there. Wherever you rolling, I'm down with whatever.

Star: Ma don't got nothing popping off tonight? And if we go, you know I don't fuck with yo peoples like that. You not rolling with Fendi and Dior?

Star and Fendi had a little silent beef going on over Bag, but that ain't have shit to do with me. Fendi was tight because Bag had blown a bag on Star one night at Ma's. Like I told Fendi, she was in the wrong. Wasn't no bitch gonna stop their bag because she was tight.

Me: Girrrllll they weren't invited no way

Star: *Say less. Come to my house, and we can figure out where we working*

Star shot me her address, and I quickly gathered my stuff. I paid Ma for what was left in the bottle and slid it into my dance bag. It didn't take me any time to get to the apartment complex Star lived in. When I pulled up, a group of niggas was in front of her building trapping. All eyes were on me as I parked my car, making sure I didn't hit any of the little kids who were running around. No adults were watching them, just some kids who were a few years older than they appeared to be. Yeah, this would never be my situation. Sosa was playing too many games, and I refused to be like these other bitches stuck in the hood looking for a way out. I pulled out my phone and let Star know I was outside.

The sound of a knock on my window made me look up. I was about to go off on the nigga until I realized who it was.

Bird looked into the car window with his signature sexy smirk. Me and Bird were around the same age, but he lived a much crazier lifestyle than me. In our sophomore year of high school, he got snatched up for attempted murder. I quickly rolled my window down, and the smell of his Creed cologne invaded my nose.

"Why are you knocking on my window like you crazy?" I said when I stepped out my car. I had to take a second to appreciate the fineness in front of me. Bird was always a little cutie back in the day. He was just bad as hell. He had to be around six-two, and he had a nice build to him. Not too skinny or buff like them niggas who worked out. He still had that pretty ass black silky hair. His shit was shoulder-length the last time I saw him. Now, it was damn near touching his lower chest.

"Damn, girl. You smell good as fuck!" Bird lifted me in his big arms and spun me around. Bird was always tall and a little on the chubby side, but the years in Prison did his body good.

"Fuck you doing out here?" He looked me up and down.

"My homegirl lives out here." Before I could stop him, he pressed his full lips onto mine and started tonging me down. I was shocked but I wasn't surprised. I smelled a faint scent of Hennessy on his breath, combined with peppermint, so I knew he was lit.

"I appreciate those letters you used to write me," he whispered into my ear. His beard tickled my neck.

He put me down and looked me up and down hard as hell.

"Fuck is this I'm hearing that you stripping?" He wasn't loud, but his voice was cold, and I knew he was no longer playing.

"If you heard all that then I'm sure you are aware of my financial situation."

Bird looked down at me with gentle eyes, and he pulled me in for a tight hug.

"You ain't built for that life, ma. What happened to your people's, I can't change that." Bird pulled back and kissed me on my forehead. "I'm home. All that shit you was doing you ain't got to do that no more. Let a nigga boss you up. I don't want much but your love, loyalty, keep my dick wet, and my stomach full. I don't expect an answer right away. I know a lot of shit has changed, but you know how I'm coming when it comes to you. Tell your homegirl you ain't working tonight. Go ahead and chill for a minute while I handle my business." He reached inside his Amiri joggers and pulled out a knot of crisp hundreds. He separated it in half and dropped it inside my purse and put the rest back in his pocket.

I tried to blink back my tears, but Bird wiped each one that dropped. He was a young nigga, but he came at me with grown man vibes. Yeah, I was feeling Sosa hard. I might go so hard to say I loved him, but me and Bird had history, and right now, I had to do what was best for me.

Chapter Nineteen
SOSA

A nigga couldn't focus for shit. I was just up in the dice game, but I had lost the last three games. After Gucci and Wynter fought, she had to spend the night in the hospital. Thankfully, my baby girl was straight. Yeah, we found out what she was having at the ER. I hadn't spoken to Gucci in a couple of weeks because I ain't want to put myself in a position where I might harm her stupid ass. My phone vibrated, and a text message came through.

Kash: *Same spot*

Me: *Yeah, give me thirty*

I dropped my money on the ground and dapped my niggas up.

"Y'all niggas stay focused after that bull shit that happened last night. We can't take no L's." I looked each of my nigga in the eyes. I wasn't trying to take no additional losses on my end. My trap houses were destroyed last night. Instead of taking my product, they burned down my spot. I was furious when I saw that three of my houses were on fire.

"We good, nigga. You already know how I'm coming." Bag dapped me up and pulled me in for a hug.

I hopped in my Benz, turned my music up, and sped toward the location I was meeting Kash at. I could have sent one of my workers to meet her, but I needed to speak with her about some shit I had been hearing in the streets. Kash ran in a different circle than me, and a lot of niggas fucked with her. There had been rumors that Gucci was hanging out with a well-known Stickup kid from the North Side. I knew how the streets lied, so a part of me was hoping the shit wasn't true.

When I pulled up to my spot, Kash's car was already parked in the driveway. I walked up to her and knocked on the window. Kash hopped out of the car, and automatically, my eyes dropped down to the little ass shorts she had on.

"Here, let me get my shit so I can get back to what I got to do." Kash threw the money on the table. Her voice was laced with venom,

"Fuck is wrong with you?" I walked up on her little ass. She could act like she was mad if she wanted to, but her body was saying otherwise. I traced my hands down her smooth legs. It was something about her dark brown skin that drove me crazy. Her nipples hardened underneath the wife-beater she had on. When she swung her hair, the smell of lavender and honey moved with her. I leaned in and softly bit her neck. Kash moaned and spread her legs slightly. We locked eyes, and I leaned in and kissed her roughly. My hands went to the button on her little ass jean shorts, and I unzipped them. She ain't have on no panties, and her shit was dripping.

"She doesn't deserve you," Kash whimpered while I slowly played inside her warm walls. At this moment, I ain't want to think about Gucci or none of the bullshit we had going on. I pulled Kash's jeans down and dropped my joggers. My shit was so hard, it bounced out of my Versace boxers. I paused to grab a Magnum out my wallet. A nigga wasn't trying to risk having any more kids.

Kash propped her legs up and slowly stroked my dick. There was no turning back. My dick found its way inside her, and I had to bite my lip to stop myself from crying out like a bitch. Kash was slowly riding my shit with her mouth open slightly.

"Sosa, please don't stop," she whimpered underneath me.

The way her pussy was gripping my shit, that wasn't a possibility. I looked into her eyes and pulled her ponytail out. Her bouncy curls came to life as I drilled her shit.

"Stop running, ma. This what you wanted, right?" I was in a zone as I went in and out of Kash.

Shorty had to fuck shit up. "You Know she's fucking, Bird, right? I didn't respond. I was too focused on busting my nut. Kash had the devil pussy, just like her fucking cousin. Seconds later, her shit started flooding and sucking me deeper inside her. She looked up at me with them pretty ass hazel eyes, and I struggled to pull out of her.

The pussy was good, but it wasn't that good to risk busting in her. Once I got my breathing together, I looked over at Kash, who was walking toward the table where her cell phone was laying.

"Repeat what you just told me?"

"I've been trying to figure out for the longest why Uncle Dro would switch up on us. No one can find him, and if he was behind this shit, he would have been popped up."

"Get to the point, Kash."

"I think Gucci was behind everything. I found something I think you should read." Kash reached into her purse and pulled out a stack of letters. I snatched them up and began reading them immediately. The more I read, the more furious I became. I sat down on the couch and focused my attention on what was in front of me. *Bae everything will be ours all you have to do is stick to the plan. I got some niggas from out of town who can get that shit done. Bird.* I tried to come up with a reason to explain the words, but my mind went blank.

My phone started ringing off the hook. That shit could wait. When my other two business lines started ringing, that was when I looked down and snatched them up.

Ma: Where the hell are you? Your sisters been shot call were on the way to Cone Hospital.

Bag: Nigga answer the phone all our spots been hit.

Unknown: Checkmate

Another message came through that made my blood freeze. I hit replay on the surveillance video. That nigga Bird and about fifty niggas was running through my shit. The nigga wasn't masked up. The crazy shit was, when they hopped in the black SUVs, Gucci's Grimy ass was behind the driver's seat.

I tried to process the messages I received. My business

would have to wait right now I needed to get to the hospital and check on my sister's condition. I hopped up off the couch with murder on my mind.

"Next time you talk to Snow. Tell him I give him my condo-ences." I grabbed my phones, keyshi, and headed towards the door.

"Sosa what's wrong?" Kash ran up behind me, but I didn't have time to explain shit to her. I said what the fuck I said.

To Be Continued

Coming Soon

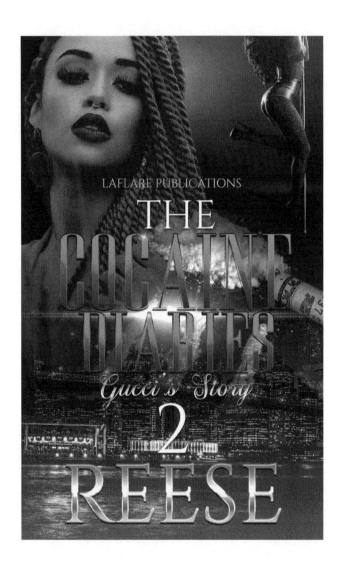

Made in the USA
Coppell, TX
14 January 2022

71576032R00159